ADVANCE PRAISE FOR
MOVING IN STEREO

"Tom Trondson uses his considerable first-hand knowledge of professional tennis—its history, psychology, mores, and endorsement deals—for this seriocomic bildungsroman. His protagonist, Richard Blanco, is an erratic also-ran of the pro circuit: capable of winning on Centre Court but more likely to flame out spectacularly. Trondson has given us a persuasive, compelling bad boy: a caddish libertine and a haunted searcher who might be careening towards some sort of enlightenment. A crosscourt winner."

Dylan Hicks, author of *Amateurs and Boarded Windows*

"Having been a tennis coach for over 60 years, I've had my share of difficult students who've struggled to overcome their personal challenges. Tom Trondson's deep knowledge of professional tennis brings to life the story of a talented but dangerously troubled bad boy, who desperately needs to mature."

Nick Bollettieri, Internationally renowned American tennis coach and developer of the world's first tennis academy.

MOVING IN STEREO

TOM TRONDSON

CALUMET EDITIONS

Minneapolis

**CALUMET
EDITIONS**

Minneapolis

FIRST EDITION DECEMBER 2020

Moving in Stereo, Copyright © 2020 by Tom Trondson.
All rights reserved.

Printed in the United States of America.
10 9 8 7 6 5 4 3 2 1

Cover by High Touch
Cover photograph by Karl Herber
Interior design by Gary Lindberg

ISBN: 978-1-950743-37-7

To Steve,
Anp fellow author,
Looking Forward to more
talks!

MOVING IN STEREO

To Susan

PART ONE

Today's ticket is no good tomorrow. Most patrons don't know that. They think a ticket means guaranteed action. What a ticket will get you is admission to the grounds. And if it rains? I don't want to think about that.

In case you're just tuning in, World's #4 and I sit on a changeover. We're three hours and four sets in. Chasing, after that many hours, would do most in. Not us. We're fit as gods. We are the new gods. I'm winning two sets to one and five serving six in the fourth. This may come as a surprise. The guy with strawberry-blonde hair and comput-er-blue eyes seated opposite has won the Championship three times. He's a former #1. He's got endorsements up the wazoo.

I'm forty-three digits back. I've been ranked as high as #21. The year Dad died, my ranking plummeted two hundred places. I'm damn good, but a bit spotty. I guess what I'm saying is I'm hugely capable of blowing this lead. Anything could happen. It could rain. Scratch that. It will rain. The question is—will I put World's #4 away before the deluge hits? By the way, I've never beaten him, not in seventeen tries. I've come close. Last year, in Stuttgart, I pulled a volley wide on match point. I guess the losing streak is the most ever, that is, if sports records are your thing. Me? I think stats are overblown. But do I think I can win? Good question.

How can you think that, Blank? Hear that? That's a voice inside my head. I sometimes see things, too. I guess they call them visions. Dad sometimes. Or Luke Scream, front man for the punk band The Fangs, in the motorcycle jacket he bequeathed me in his suicide note.

"Two minutes," the Chair Umpire says into his microphone.

I look above Centre Court's sage roof, above the hordes, most bustling with excitement, at a sky that wants to drop its charge. Don't rain. Jesus, rain in an hour. I don't ask much. After Dad got sick, I prayed he'd go quickly and without pain. But God—please, if you exist, if you believe in fair play, if you think the bullies of the world should get their comeuppance, *if you believe in me*, then cork the rain for now. I think it's better if I win this one time. *He means for World #4's character development.* Luke interrupting again, sorry. The first time I saw him, he'd been dead a week. And his voice was so real, so alive, it was like he was in the room. I was at Fred Segal buying an Armani suit for the funeral. The tailor was measuring my inseam when Luke appeared. Seeing him in the trifold mirror, cut into thousands of slices ad infinitum, was the most terrifying moment of my life. Over the next few months, Luke kept popping up, sometimes he said things, sometimes he was like an annoying friend I couldn't shake. My sports psychologist referred me to a psychiatrist in Sarasota. Dr. Goldberg and his gnarly breath. Every therapist has office rules, office practices. With him, we sat opposite in teak chairs with leather seat cushions. Which brings us back to his halitosis. Dr. Goldberg's dead animal breath stunk up the room. The smell clung to clothes and hair. It caused eyes to well with tears (mine, at least). When Dr. Goldberg heard about my voices, he prescribed antipsychotics. Look, I'm a professional tennis player. I interpret trunk rotation, ball velocity, body position, the sound the ball makes at impact—all in nanoseconds. Clarity is king. I don't have time for meds.

"Time."

World's #4 and I move toward our respective corners. The buzz inside Centre Court turns clamorous. Then, World's #4 slips a ball into his short's pocket, that familiar hush comes over the crowd, and the bit actors, the Chair Umpire, lines-people and ball-kids, lean in. I sway back and forth on my crouched line.

"I love you, Richard!" a woman cries out.

"He's mine!"

"No, mine, luv!"

World's #4 backs off the line.

"Quiet, please," the Chair says. "Thank you."

Once things settle down, World's #4 tosses up a serve that lands long. The second is a kicker that lacks the mean-spirited spin I've battled all day. I get absolutely all ball, as pure a strike as you could wish for with the tension the way it is. My return has World's #4 backpedaling something mad. He misses in the net. Then his eyes go straight for the Player's Box. His camp—the wife, the coach, the nutritionist, the trainer, the masseuse, even George Harrison—rise and cheer their bloke on. World's #4 follows with a cold, calculating slider up the center vein that makes a slap sound whacking the backdrop. I trudge to the deuce court, no worse for wear. At 15–all, I get a bead on his fired laser and chunk a fatty low. My return isn't pretty but shakes or fatigue has World's #4 stubbing his volley in the net.

"15–30," the Chair says.

Two to go, I think. And it's misting. Great, just great. If you're still tuned in, you know what's happening next. The freaking rain, that's what.

World's #4 serves his way out of trouble again. This tends to be the pattern. I figure I got two options. I can either let World's #4 dictate play or go down swinging. So, at 30–30, I charge in off his serve like a madman waving a machete and knife a backhand that's darting and nasty, corner bound. World's #4, approaching the net, has to lunge like a wild cat. He stabs at the ball, praying it flies the mesh. I place the volley into open court.

"30–40."

Match point? You mean this is it? The streak's over? Wimbledon semifinals here I come? I suddenly feel this heaviness in the thighs. My breathing's gone thick. *You're not going to choke, are you, Blank?* Hey, Luke? Fuck off.

"Pete Townsend!" someone screams.

"Show us your stuff, Blank!" The fan means my guitar imitations. Hey, why not, maybe it will calm the nerves. I flick my racquet in the air—think military rifle salute—and catch the head in my right palm. There's a surge of noise. I let loose the swinging Ferris-wheel power chord made famous in epics like "Won't Get Fooled Again." Once, twice, three times. I do it for the losing streak. I do it for my ex-fiancé, the Russian. And I do it for Dad, may he rest in peace.

Blank. That's what people sometimes call me. They've even named a shot after me. You ready for this? The Blank shot. It encompasses any attempt considered illogical, low percentage or plain odd, which might explain why I've never made a Grand Slam quarterfinal until today.

With the match riding on the next point, World's #4 sends one toward the seats. My foot slips, chasing the scorcher wide. Then, as I swing my stick around center, a feeling like a clenched fist blooms in my core. Call it a cramp of conviction. Contact is splintered and high, a bloody mishit. The ball comes off my strings like a bottle rocket.

My shot clears, barely.

World's #4 closes the gap between my squirrelly ball and the net with a fluid efficiency. He drops his racquet as his body lifts and finger-rolls this delicate half-volley a few feet over the net.

Sprinting in, I calculate the distance between World's #4 and a possible interception versus me flicking a roller over the net's zenith. This happens in the blink of an eye. Yet I know I have him. World's #4 can't cover the ground fast enough. At the last conceivable moment—a stroke of brilliance, really—I change the ball's direction. The opening crosscourt is narrow and closing fast, a Blank shot like no other. And what a way to go—match point, Centre Court, against my sworn enemy, London, England, Dad.

It's when I'm skidding to a stop so not to touch the net that World's #4 flings his stick with frustration. His racquet gets tangled in the net. And my attempt? It isn't exactly spectacular. In reality, the ball is dangerously close to clipping the net tape. This can't be.

No. No. No. No. No.

"The score is deuce."

London cheers. They gave me a rowdy ovation walking out this afternoon—Dad grew up near here, in Barnes—but now they're hoping for more tennis. Even Luke claps slow and sardonically in my ear. What was I thinking? A Blank shot on match point? I look toward the Player's Box. This is what we athletes sometimes do. It can be lonely playing big-time tennis. One's box—the row or two awarded coaches, family and friends—can be the difference between feeling like the only living person in the world or part of something bigger. Coach Destafano, the old geezer, holds his hands up, a symbol of calm and forbearance. My corpulent agent David Ostrahoff looks completely spent. Then my eyes focus on the empty seat. Mom's second husband, Brody Simmons, has stage IV melanoma. I pulled him a pass anyway. Poor old Brody.

Back on Centre Court, World's #4 is all smiling eyes and jerk-off smirks. God, I hate him. I want a retry, a do-the-fuck-over.

The Belgian Jan Sverdes umpiring today's match peers over his readers. "Deuce."

"He tossed his racquet," I say. "That's a rule violation. Look, I'm trying to be reasonable."

"I appreciate that, Mr. Blanco."

"If he doesn't toss his stick, the net doesn't move. If the net doesn't move, my shot doesn't hit the tape." Still, nothing. "But he violated the rules."

We both steer our gazes at maybe the most recognizable tennis player on the planet. Curious blue peepers. Sandy-red shock of hair. Tree trunk thighs. Boom-boom Becker, the Deutsche *wunderkind*, the youngest lad to win Wimbledon, age seventeen, seven months, fifteen days.

"Let's keep our racquet in our hands, Mr. Becker. The score is deuce."

No one treats me like that. If the shoe were on the other foot—mine, I mean—and I let slip my stick on a pivotal point, they'd cut off my non-dominant arm and say, "Play on, sucker." The truth is Boris Becker sells tickets and TV sponsorships and merchandise. He makes the bloody tennis world sing.

I waggle my hand in my face—standard protocol when a player wants to wipe down. This teenager runs up, towel in hand. I was his age the first time Dad and I visited Wimbledon. I wipe my brow, then toss him the terrycloth. "Beat it, kid."

That's what Becker does on the next serve. He fucking beats it. I see the ball. Then it's gone. The Kraut encourages the crowd to pump up the volume. He thinks he has me, that it's only a matter of time before I self-destruct.

"Not today," I growl over the groundswell. "NOT. TO. DAY."

The fucker gets under my skin.

The mist is now a drizzle. My gut tells me Becker will spill one into the first row again. He's a creature of habit. All tennis players are. We're a superstitious lot. Me, on a winning streak, I'll wear the same underwear, set after sweaty set. I won't launder the crusty rag, either. Once, I had undies that went ten sets without a cleaning. Talk about airing out the room every night. Becker's cut from the same mold. He rents the same house every fortnight. His post-match meal is always spaghetti. Yes, Becker does exactly as I expect and pounds one in the corner. But I'm Michael Jordan flying high over the paint. I'm an apparition, a fleeting ghost. My ball ricochets past Becker, a clean winner.

"Deuce."

Becker approaches the Chair.

"These conditions, they are too slippery," he says in his thick accent.

"He wouldn't be complaining if he was winning," I tell the crowd.

The Chair climbs down the ladder to whistles and jeers. Becker watches with a keen eye. I know how the man thinks. I once saw him and a buddy at a nightclub chatting up two models, both cut like Giacometti sculptures. When Becker and his boy visited the Ladies Room, I approached the lovelies. They split with me. Boy, was he livid when they showed up in my box the next round.

The Umpire swipes his fingers through the damp grass, then scurries back to his crow's nest. "Play will continue."

"What if I roll ankle, Jan? Who will play Krajicek?"

"*Jan*? You two are on a first-name basis?"

"See, Jan? This is what I mean. Blanco is always manipulating situation."

"Gentlemen, please. Shall we continue?"

Why do I let the guy get to me? If I hadn't tried a Blank shot, I'd be chewing the fat right now with Bud Collins in the exit interview. I happen to skim the mostly wan faces above the photographer's dugout. My eyes latch onto this beauty wearing Jackie O sunglasses when the forecast is a landing pad of wet, hoary weather. Next to her sits the American, Trevor Hamasaki, the man my agent is attempting to woo. Hamasaki owns Saiko Investments, a hedge firm based in Tokyo. So, this woman is his wife? Soon Becker is rocking that momentous serve of his. I'm thinking about the Joan Chen doppelgånger when the ball throbs past. Advantage Germany. The ball-boy scurries over. I ask him where he'd go if he was nimrod over there.

"Don't know, sir. Out wide?"

I'm having fun with him. The tennis world knows me as the tour's *enfant terrible*. They recognize the shanks of honey-brown hair, the deeply tanned face, my 8 percent body fat. They've seen the highlight reels. Bad boy Blanco, that's me.

Funny, Becker does exactly what the kid says. I pick off his serve like I'm fielding a routine grounder.

"Deuce."

"Same place again?" I ask the boy when he runs up. He's all of fourteen with knobby knees and a mess of dark curls under his cap. He shrugs then trots off. Mom and Dad separated in my early teens. I won't mince words—the divorce fucked me up. The truth is, I'm still fucked up. Dissect anything you want, my career, my promiscuity, my mental proclivities—I struggle.

While I'm grumbling to myself, a Slazenger burns past my ear.

"Advantage, Mr. Becker."

The ball-boy comes back around. I sling an arm around his bony shoulder. Everyone laps up this exchange—even the woman with Trevor Hamasaki.

"You tell him there, lad!" a woman shouts.

"Cute as peaches, that kid!"

I eye the boy. "You think you're pretty smart, huh?"

"No, sir."

"Where to this time?" The boy says it's a tossup. My grip around him stiffens. "You see his serve? It's always a tossup. Don't you play the game?"

He runs off like a dog with its tail between his legs. I've hurt his feelings. The boy is becoming the great disappointment of my life. Luke's in my ear, too, like a chatty squirrel. *Seventeen consecutive losses? How many more chances do you get? Your old man got one. At least he ran with it. Think stacking cubes, Blank, one block after the other. Be here now. Isn't that a George Harrison song?*

Jesus, Luke. Stop already.

Call it payback from the tennis gods because I butcher the next return.

"Game to Mr. Becker. The twelve-point tiebreaker will decide set four. Mr. Blanco to serve."

The balls change ends.

I stroll over to where Trevor Hamasaki sits. "Why not let your lady friend try. I'm serious. I've had enough of that guy over there." I hand my stick to a photographer with three cameras strapped around his neck. He sends my Head Prestige 600 up the rows while snapping my mug like David Hemmings does willowy models in *Blowup*.

Thinking the woman is someone famous, the photographers turn their viewfinders on her. Like everyone else, I take her in with a wild splash of the eyes. She wears a carefully wrapped kimono. Her lacquer-black hair is draped over a shoulder like a pet lemur. Some of you watching are probably scratching your heads. Trying to score with a gorgeous woman and the tournament on the line? Hey, this is how I roll. Here's what you need to know about me. I grew up in Los Angeles. I'm a fifteen-year circuit veteran. I've made five million dollars in endorsement and prize money over my career. I've got homes on both coasts. Things come naturally to me. I surf. I can heave a football seventy-five yards. I'm a sexual dynamo.

"Time, Mr. Blanco," the Chair says with a trace of irritation.

"Give me a second, luv."

The spectators laugh. I've got them eating out of my hand. Well, minus one German. For he stomps toward Chair Sverdes. "Do we play tennis? Or is this dating service?"

"Mommy," I say in a child's voice. "Richard's not playing fair."

"Warn him, Jan."

"Can't you see I'm waiting for my racquet?"

"Warning. Code violation, Mr. Blanco."

"Seriously?"

Tiebreakers are strange beasts. First to seven by two, players alternating serves. Breakers are like the lottery, games of chance. They favor the big striker. The beef on me isn't my game (it's big enough). It's my inconsistencies, *my instabilities*. Dad would have me control my mental processes with ritual. He was old school. He read the classics. He dressed fashionably conservative—things like worsted wool sweaters and pleated linen slacks.

And hey, I like my prospects even after Becker rolls off three points in a row. I fight hard, digging in. We play the point of the match, fifteen, twenty strokes, throwing our bodies around like on a wrestling mat, sweat inking off us, the breath stiff. Becker's last forehand stings the tape. I go straight to my strings. I hear my name called out. I sense the spirit of these good people pressing in. But I am merely a man and his rituals—breathing through nostrils, straightening string patterns, controlling where the eyes roam. Then a little luck—Becker muscles a backhand long. I'm down a minibreak but getting my fingers into the meat of the tiebreaker now. Sinister clouds stall over Centre Court. Like the threat of rain, the ball-boy is just there. At 2–3, we rap a few forehands before I snap-hook one up the far post. The ball lands on the confluence of both lines. Becker stops dead in his tracks. He looks at me, like wow. I can hardly believe it, either. Fucking incredible, that was.

"3–3, change ends."

We're at that critical stage where one missed opportunity is the difference between winning or playing a fifth and final set. We throttle groundstrokes when one gets away from me. 4–3, the German. The ball-boy is now a ball-girl with braided hair. I'd forgotten he didn't follow me around. This throws me but only for a beat or two. Then I'm tossing her the towel and slowing everything down—my thoughts, my beating heart, time.

My first serve sails long. A glance at my team has the chest tightening up. The moment is suddenly too big. I'm having a hard go at it. I feel out of time in a bad way. Then, stupid me. I bounce the ball off my toe, a bad omen for sure. Of course, I send the second long.

"5–3, Mr. Becker."

Rain falls, a quick burst, loud, thumping, centralized. "Oh, so now it rains."

At 5–3, the *haut monde* rise from their seats. They cheer the score. They cheer Becker's persistence. They even cheer poor old me. No, the signs aren't good. At least I get my serve in. Becker plays the safe return, an edged backhand that skims the net like a great winged bird over glassy water. We clock backhands, four, five, six times. Miss it, I think. *Noonan!* Luke screams. Then Becker tap-danc-es around the ball and whacks a silly hard forehand in the absolute corner. Chalk flies up.

"FUCK ME."

Oops, I've done it now.

"Point penalty, Mr. Blanco, for unsportsmanlike conduct. Tie-breaker and set to Mr. Becker, 7–6."

* * *

For ticketholders, the interim between sets four and five means stretch-ing the lumbar, bolting for the champagne bar, or opining on the South-ern Californian's dwindling chances. I've marched up to the Chair.

"Jan? I'm going potty."

He sends along his messenger boy, this bookish young man wear-ing a Wimbledon rain slicker. I feel nothing walking into the locker room. Somewhere inside me—the spleen maybe—is this engrossed lit-tle man plodding away. He's forecasting rain. He's soldiering forward. He's whipping Mr. Willpower off his haunches for one last run. Out beyond the little guy's tinny voice, though, is nothing. I'm flat. I'm indifferent. I'm not there.

While I empty the vessel, the young man leans against the wash-basin cleaning his wire-rimmed glasses. Everything about the Champi-onships is by the book. No coaching during breaks of play. No injecting suspicious-looking substances behind stall doors. No going anywhere without the messenger boy and his walkie-talkie.

"Do you think the world conspires against us?" I have to crank my neck since the urinal faces the wall opposite. Like so many young men these days, the messenger guy shrugs as if a great weight rests on his slim shoulders.

"Perhaps, sir."

"Can I call my girlfriend? I know it's against the rules, but she doesn't play the game, if that's what you're worried about. She's an exotic dancer, and she's gorgeous, long blonde hair, perfect tits, and they're real, man. No saline implants in my Heather."

He stands a bit taller. "Is that so, sir?"

"You wanna know why she's not here? She doesn't embarrass me, if that's what you're thinking." The bladder empty, I walk to the sink. The guy gives me plenty of space. I lather up my hands with soap. We make eye contact through the mirror. "My girlfriend is the nicest person in the world. I was lucky finding her. But she doesn't travel with me." He hands me a towel. "You're not curious why?"

"No, sir."

"Why are you upper-crusts so courteous? Don't you ever let your hair down?"

"Sometimes, sir," he says. "On holiday."

"Hey, was that a joke?"

"We should be getting back, sir."

I don't say another word until we've reached the Player's Entrance. "You're okay."

"I try my best." He looks me straight on. "Good luck. I mean that, sir."

The reason Heather's not here is the Russian. You see, I'm not quite over her. We were a good team. But she left me for that idiot actor whose face is plastered all over kiosks from Chelsea to Regent's Park. CHRISTIAN BROTHERS IS TRACE RIDGE IN *ESCAPE VELOCITY 2*. What's worse, the Russian's pregnant. That kills me.

I also fibbed a little. Heather *used to* dance at the Golden Banana. Her official title these days is Personnel Executive. She gets a salary and benefits. There's even a Golden Banana 401K plan she contributes toward. Heather is in charge of scheduling. She mentors new recruits. She sits in on the girls' physicals. They trust her. They talk to her if they're weirded out by male staff or sicko customers. Management considers Heather the eyes and ears of the operation.

* * *

The cloud mass hasn't moved.

"We're about to be dumped on," I tell the Umpire. "It makes sense stopping now."

"He's stalling, Jan."

"Stalling? Like you did in the fourth set?"

Becker rises from his chair with his racquet in his hand. "Blanco is doing his tricks."

"Maybe with your wife. She's always fancied me, you know."

Becker cocks an eyebrow like he's not sure he heard me correctly. What gets his venom up is the grin I let drip from my mouth. We do that dance men do, puffing our chests out like colorful birds, slinging *fuck you* and *no, fuck you* back and forth. Then my eyes go blank. No color, no images, nada. When I snap to, it's like waking from a dream. And Becker headbutts me. I don't think it's intentional. It might even be my fault.

The collision knocks me off balance. In trying to catch myself, I snag a heel on my gear bag.

And then I go flying.

I land on the grass. Becker rushes forward, hand extended. I hear the Chair ordering us to stand down. Ticketholders, all fourteen thousand, are up from their seats, the clamor loud.

"Sorry, Blanco. You okay?"

I'm up fast. "That's easy for you to say. You weren't just laid out on your ass."

"Gentlemen, please."

I want to punch Becker so bad. You know what stops me? The ballboy. He stands there all pink-complected and embarrassed. That just does me in. I do the only thing I can think of—I pretend I'm injured. "First he tosses his stick on match point." I pause as if overcome with horrible pain. "Sorry. Where was I? Oh, yes. Then Becker headbutts me. He should be thrown in jail." I hunch over, wincing. "Well? Call the goddamn trainer, Sverdes. I think I broke a rib." While the Chair fumbles with the microphone, I glance at the sky. Will it ever rain?

What would you suggest I do, dear viewer? Run away? And where to? We're nearing the century's end. I may not be OJ Simpson blazing down the 405 in a white Bronco, but I'm famous enough. I've been photographed shirtless by Helmut Newton. I've graced the cover of *GQ* in only a bowtie and a woman's hand over my privates, holding three strategically placed tennis balls. Dad didn't shirk after he got AIDS. He held a news conference. He told the world it was time they woke up. If Dad faced AIDS with dignity, I can finish a silly set.

A few minutes later, the trainer walks onto Centre Court. Becker's not a happy camper. He spouts off about dubious players like myself giving the game a bad name. I make a bird with my middle finger and pretend to scratch my face. The problem with Becker is he lacks the necessary observational skills to notice.

Meantime, the trainer has me lift my shirt. This, of course, creates girlie shrieks among the female ranks. "Can Richard play with his shirt off," a woman calls out. "PLEASE."

The trainer digs his fingers into my flesh. I grimace, looking across the court. The Asian woman has slipped on Trevor's blazer. She is like a black-eyed Susan in a thicket of desiccated weeds. Over in my corner, Coach and David look grim. Above them, in enemy camp, George Harrison sets his beady eyes on me. Then he does something startling. He runs his fingers under his chin, flicks his scruffy beard, the Italian brush off, the Mafioso fuck you. What's wrong with George? Is he pissed because I've never impersonated his playing style? There's a reason for that. As guitar players go, George is sensitive, even lyrical, but where's the show, man? Give me something I can work with, a snarl, some *Headbangers Ball* bobbing hair thing, smash your Gibson into smithereens. *Something.*

I've finally had enough. "You got a problem, Harrison?"

The stadium goes quiet. Then someone yells out, "Sing us a song, George!"

"*The Long and Winding Road*?"

"*Norwegian Wood*?"

"*Here Comes The Sun*?"

"Good luck with that one!"

Fans break into song. At first, it's only a few brave souls. Soon, thousands sway back and forth. "Little darling, it's been a long cold lonely winter, Little darling, it feels like years since it's been here."

I tune them out. I tune everything out. Except the blacking out part. Last time that happened, the Russian was making *An Errant Husband* with Christian Brothers. Sick Puppy here had followed her to New York. I found them in Central Park. They stood under a stone-arch bridge, waiting out a summer shower. It was the way Christian Brothers held the Russian. It was the way she looked into his eyes. I boarded a plane for Los Angeles. The episode happened at 34,000 feet. The pilot made an emergency landing in Denver. That was two years ago.

"One minute."

The trainer manipulates my arm obliquely over my head. "Tell me when you feel pain."

"Pain? Don't get me started."

Dad would not be impressed. If he saw what I was doing—manipulating the rules all in hopes for a downpour—he'd pinch my ear and march me off the grounds. Not Coach D. With him, it's win at all costs. He believes in realistic endings, final scores, the tangible stuff, the black and white of life. Results count. Dad was more of an artist. He painted portraits. He was an avid reader. He inherited his passions from Grandpa Gerald, a dreamer in his own right. My grandpa was an inventor. He concocted products to transform society—chalkless billiard chalk, a bicycle tire that didn't need air. By the time Dad finished university, Grandpa had lost everything—the family savings and the house in south London. Dad was twenty-four and helping coach the Junior Davis Cup squad. He met Mom at West Side Tennis Club, Forest Hills, when the team flew over for a rubber match. They married within the year and settled in Greenwich Village in a building that Mom's family owned.

Dad loved the Village. Even after he and Mom divorced (he got the apartment building as part of the settlement), Bleecker Street and its lively environs was home. He cut quite a figure. Dad had fantastic energy. I could see why Mom fell for him. She was a looker herself. As a teenager, she modeled for Dayton Hudson, a department store in Minneapolis. We moved to Los Angeles when I was six for Mom's acting career. One day Coach Destafano walked into the club where Dad taught tennis. He was opening a tennis academy in Florida for top-flight juniors. The school ran nine months a year. So, in 1977, with Mom's consent, Dad and I moved to Bradenton. At the time, I was the #7 twelve-year-old in the country.

"Time."

The trainer digs one last item from his bag, ibuprofen.

"I was hoping for something stronger."

Like morphine, Blank?

A quick swig from my water, and I'm up.

You're probably curious about what Luke looks like. Try the punk version of Ichabod Crane. Think hellishly skinny, pale as the moon, coarse black hair growing out his head like prehistoric roots.

Becker already prowls the baseline. The crowd attempts the ridiculous wave. I happen on the ball-boy.

"Did I blow it?"

"Sir?"

"Are you rooting for him now?"

"Who, sir?"

"You know what I mean."

"Mr. Becker, sir?"

"Oh, forget it." I throw my towel over the boy's head. He takes this without fuss. As if being humiliated by moronic tennis professionals is part of his job description. The crowd turns on me then. They hew, they haw. They make ugly faces. Even Becker gets in on the Blanco bashing. Yes, he comes out throwing mean darts. And I can't find the cork.

"Becker leads 1–0. Change ends."

The fifth set is a race to the finish that moves in a matter of degrees. It's about containment. Starting strong is critical. This sets the tone. You mean business. You won't be pushed around. I think about what this first point means. I even think about Dad tossing the ball into the charcoal sky. Then I chase it like a dog does a stick. Becker hardly moves. His backhand—a stiff, muffled reply—dies at my feet like he pried open my skull to see what I was throwing. So much for winning the first point. I feel that pressure again. I curse the sky. I curse my luck. Coach D would speak to seizing what is mine. Dad was never so melodramatic. The modern game left him cold. He loved tennis etiquette, the gentlemanly rules, competition for competition's sake. He used to say the day tennis went professional was the day something went missing.

I sling a serve up the T. And goddamn it if Becker isn't there. And goddamn it if he doesn't skull it off the frame for a clean winner. "Love-thirty."

The noose tightens.

High above Centre Court is a ripple of thunder. I'm not far from the fetching kimono woman. I attempt a smile. "I need a rainmaker, and I need him fast."

This is why I never beat Becker. This is why they call me Blank. Because I meddle. Because I tinker where I don't belong. It's a voodoo box. The gods like seeing me suffer. I know all about the gods—Zeus and all his complexes, Poseidon's ever-changing moods. It was the gods who kidnapped this match. They took Dad. They've got Luke sniffing around in my head. Well, fuck the gods. "Take this, Zeus!" I stick my racquet between my legs and do a couple energetic porno thrusts at the sky. Of course Becker beseeches the Chair to do something. So I turn my phallic tirade on him.

"How's that strike you, number four? When I'm through with you, they'll be calling you number eight."

I'm not proud of what I just did. Sometimes I can't help myself. Maybe I'm what Damian Hirst is to the British art scene. Yesterday, after practice, I took the Tube to Saatchi Gallery, where Hirst's *The Physical Impossibility Of Death In The Mind Of Someone Living* is housed. As I stood gaping into the embalmed shark's cavernous mouth, this revelation passed through me. For what being—other than a crafty, villainess god—imagines a mouth like that. Those clusters of sinister honed teeth, that black hole of a mouth.

I miss both serves. Neither is even close.

"Love-forty."

The sky finally opens up. Rain falls like pigeon dung, buckets and buckets of gray shit. I'm hustling off with my bag when I spy the ball-boy getting drenched. I toss him a souvenir, a prized Wimbledon towel. "Sorry about all that." I could be talking to the ticketholders. I could be talking to Dad. I could be talking to me.

Then I rush for shelter, soaked to the bone.

THIRTY-SIX MINUTES LATER

UNSEEDED MEN'S LOCKER ROOM

"I should have punched his lights out, Coach."

"That would have showed him." Destafano Tennis Academy founder, Anthony Destafano, plops down on a wooden bench with his veiny hands and rickety knees. He wears the white Adidas warmup with blue stripes and the blue Adidas tennis shoes with white stripes. Sponsor contract rules. His tag along, the peppy, full-figured Valerie, walks behind him and starts massaging his shoulders. It being late in week two, we practically got the locker room all to ourselves. "I liked the restraint you used."

"He's an asshole."

"Richard?" Coach jerks a thumb toward his girlfriend. "Can you watch your language?"

"I'm the laughing-stock of the entire world."

"I wouldn't argue with you there, son."

"How is this helping me?"

"I think you're overreacting."

"I had my ass handed to me on live television, but I'm overreacting? I'm finished. Reebok? Good as gone. That Adidas contract David was working on? I can kiss that goodbye, too."

"Let's focus on what we have control of."

"I'll let you in on a secret, Coach. We have no control. Free will is bullshit."

"Then why fucking try?"

"Language, Coach."

He gives Valerie a sheepish glance. "Sorry, girl."

"I don't think I can beat him."

Coach leans forward with his neck jutted out. He looks like he's either going to bop me or hug me and never let go. "I'm speechless, son."

Valerie shoots me a reproachful glare while digging into Coach's flesh like she's kneading dough. "Stay calm, Anthony. Remember what the doctor said."

I lean against the opposite locker in only my sporty underwear—micro-fiber briefs tight in the buttocks and crotch—when I shove a hand down the front and give Johnson a scratch.

"Who invited her in here? Isn't this the *men's* locker room?"

"I'll pretend I didn't hear that," she says.

"Claudia called," Coach says. "She gave me an earful."

Claudia is the Academy's sports psychologist. "I didn't do myself any favors by sticking my racquet between my legs."

Coach sigh-chuckles. Valerie, on the other hand, looks like she'd rather jam my racquet somewhere else. Like down my throat. "What are you teaching young men by doing that disgusting thing?"

"Do I really need to hear this, Coach?"

"You don't have to shout," she says. "I hear perfectly well."

"You think this is shouting? THIS IS SHOUTING."

They met at the golf club. Valerie drove the beer cart and spread the relish Coach liked on his hot dog. On their first date, they saw *Get Shorty* when Coach felt a pull in his chest, what he later described as feeling like his heart being tugged by a fishing line. The cardiologist diagnosed a mild heart attack that could be managed with diet and pills.

I start in on the mess I made. Before showering, I had a little moment flinging shit around. I smashed two sticks and upended my bag. No damage—not to real property. I notice a chipped valium on the floor, a remnant from my more troubled past.

Miles Bennington, club member and all-around good guy, pokes his creased face inside our camp. He wears a dark suit and Wimbledon tie. "Were we sabotaged by hooligans again?"

"Hooligans, my ass," Coach says.

I reach down, pluck the pill off the floor, then clamp it in my fist. "Sort of lost my temper. Sorry, Miles."

Bennington turns down the volume knob on his walkie-talkie. He's lean and battered like a weathered pole. "We're waiting word on the storm. They've slotted the press conference in, just in case. The Saiko Investment people are here. Shall I send them back?"

Coach D wrestles free from Valerie's manicured nails. Everything annoys him. Airport security lines, the kids begging for autographs at the practice courts. And especially the business end of pro tennis.

"We're trying to win a fifth set here."

"David set it up."

"What if the rain stops?"

"Cats and dogs, Coach. All night."

"Now you're a meteorologist?"

"Will you fill him in, Miles?"

We look to our voice of reason. Dad's former doubles partner speaks of cold fronts, failing light and the probability of postponement.

Coach shakes his grizzled jaw. And Valerie and her Carmen Electra rack gives me the evil eye.

"You keep this up, and you'll need your pill," she tells her man.

Coach sets his hands on his knees. "Wimbledon quarters, and you're thinking about money?" He's up with a grunt. "I don't have time for this."

"Don't leave. Come on, Coach. I'm just saying hello."

"In your underwear?"

"I can explain that."

He pulls himself around. "Well?"

"I'm thinking, okay?"

"This is about a woman, Val. It always is. Take me to the hotel."

His girlfriend is digging inside her purse. "What about your pill, honey?"

"Screw the goddamn pill, Valerie."

"It's not what you think." I've set the valium on my locker shelf. "Okay, maybe they join David and me for dinner. Where's the crime in that? Then it's off to bed. It's lights out, Coach."

"Oh, we know all about you and lights out, son."

Miles and I watch Valerie escort Coach out. I give her a little wave. "She's half his age. What'll give him another heart attack is her needy face. What's he see in her?"

Miles thinks on the subject. "She looks the sort who'd be very caring in the sack. Before I forget, your sports therapist called. She's being patched through on the rotary."

"Say, Miles? Was it as bad as I think it was?"

He places a hand on my shoulder then gives me a fatherly squeeze. "It was an accident. You are still very much in this match." Miles moves to the mirror. "I hope I'm not overstepping my bounds when I say you've got the talent, even at the ripe old age of thirty-one, of making a mark out there." He fluffs up the little hair he has left. "Now, don't do something sensible, Richard, and get dressed. Where's the fun in that?" And Miles leaves.

When Dad died, it was Miles who handled the details on this side of the pond—burial plot, arrangements with the cemetery and church. He's the uncle you see on holiday. Coach D tries to fill the same boots.

They forget I'm a seasoned professional. Only a player who's been up and down the rankings like me knows what tomorrow needs. This doesn't mean I don't fear the worst—a career-ending injury or I wake up one morning and realize the young guns have passed me by. That's why my agent is gung-ho on the sponsor deals. I'm on the tail end of a ride that's been a joy, a thorn in my side, and frankly, all I know.

The old phone clangs to life. I begrudgingly pick up. "Hello?"

"Richard? Claudia here. We need to chat."

I stand at the mirror, flexing one pectoral at a time. "I'm kind of busy."

"What you did today, that barroom behavior, putting your racquet between your legs, was very immature."

"Interesting perspective."

"You blew it. You let slip the biggest opportunity of your life."

"You really know how to pump a man up when he's down, Claudia."

"Tomorrow is a chance at redemption, Richard. Most of us never get to rewrite history. I suggest breathing exercises and acute visualization. Would you like to turn down the lights, get on the floor, and do a session now?"

"David's sending an investment group in. You know how it is."

"Any worries? How's the blathering in your head?"

"So far, pretty smooth sailing."

"Be on your best behavior tomorrow. Have positive energy. And whatever you do—"

"Don't think."

"I couldn't have said it better myself."

* * *

My problems began shortly after *60 Minutes* aired the special on Destafano Tennis Academy. This was 1978. Pre-anxiety disorder, I was a normal teenager. My favorite band was Led Zeppelin. I wore my hair shoulder-length and feathered like Shaun Cassidy. And I had designs for one day playing in the Show. Morley Safer had asked the DTA co-founders if tennis academies were a fad like Bermuda shorts or disco. Safer then digressed. He said he'd shot a hundred hours of film. He'd interviewed umpteen students and coaches. He'd sat in on Claudia's "How to Walk Like a Champion" presentation. Safer thought making a world-class tennis player was more complicated.

"What about intangibles?" he'd asked Dad and Coach. "Like grit and drive and character? How does mindlessly hitting tens of thousands of tennis balls make the next Jimmy Connors or Chrissie Evert?"

Dad proffered a finger. He then went on in his mannered English, stroking his mustache for emphasis. He agreed that tennis academies wouldn't be taken seriously until a player from inside the system reached superstar status. He said it was still early in tennis academy development, that he and Coach "were sorting out the kinks as we speak." He told Safer he believed a system where athletes with varying psychological profiles, top-flight coaches, and state-of-the-art facilities could come together under one roof, a balance could be achieved where "a player, or players, rise from the ashes to dominate the sport like the United States hasn't seen since the 1950s."

That's when Safer asked if the DTA had a bona fide star in the making. 1978 hadn't been a banner year. My body was growing faster than my legs could keep up. I missed Mom and my friends in Los Angeles. I felt my game had plateaued. And Dad told Safer and like half the country sitting in their living rooms that Sunday night that I was not only DTA's savior, but that me and me alone would shoulder the nascent tennis academy phenomenon into powerhouse legitimacy.

Dad's boast felt like being pummeled by wave after wave of storm-surge surf. And it wasn't only between the lines. The pressure spilled over into my private life, too. I'd be standing in line at a record store with sweat dripping off my forehead. And thinking? I couldn't shut my mind off. *Jesus, why is this taking so long? Did I really need* Physical Graffiti? *Why is the cashier staring at me? Can he see that I'm freaking out? Can he see that I need help?*

Then came the on-court incident. I was losing badly to Kenji Matsuyama during fall challenge matches. It was my turn to serve. Only I couldn't move. My arm even refused to toss the ball. By the time Dad arrived, I was mumbling things like, "It was said. The world knows. It can't be undone."

My parents thought my breakdown was their fault. They blamed the cross-country move. Claudia referred me to a local psychiatrist. Talking sessions between therapist and patient, me in tears, describing the weight of expectations, my newfound fear of malls and tennis courts. The therapist listened patiently. Then she wrote me an anti-anxiety prescription.

I wasn't the only confused Blanco. Mom's shrink was near the movie studios, perfect after a bad day on set. Then there was Dad. Sure, he came across posh and put together with his eager blue eyes and snappy British accent. But if you were his son, you knew he carried a heavy burden, too. The nights he spent locked away in his room. Those moments on airplanes where I'd catch him staring out the window like he'd jump if he could. Worried, I'd ask Dad if everything was okay. He'd give me the saddest smile in the world. So I asked Claudia how a person went about suggesting a friend seek professional help.

"Do you have someone in mind, Richard?"

"I'd rather not say."

"Why do you think this person would benefit from psychotherapy?"

"Because he seems so lost."

"I'd suggest you tell this person exactly that."

"What if he takes it the wrong way?"

"Speak from the heart, with your best intentions. And hope for the best."

I did as Claudia recommended. And Dad was so intrigued with therapy he waved me off like I was a complete imbecile.

* * *

"The Saiko Investment people are here, Richard."

Miles stops short so the attractive couple can enter. Trevor Hamasaki takes one look at my outfit and smiles so hard I feel his incisors in my gums. "I knew I liked this guy."

I give the slinky thing in the couture dress a fervent gaze. "I was just getting dressed." She steals a peek at my underwear. "Do I make you uncomfortable, Ms. Hamasaki?"

"My sister uncomfortable around men? Hilarious."

"Your sister?"

"I'm Trey. I handle player relations." She's older than I thought, early thirties. "Are we intruding?"

"No, not at all."

"Trey means the Hugo Boss."

"You want me to put some clothes on, is that it?"

I sense adventure in her not-quite-brown eyes, cross-pollinated eyes, eyes of the postmodern world. This can mean only one thing—she digs me.

"That's completely up to you."

"I can. Just say the word."

And we all laugh. Even Miles.

Just then, we hear a distinctly American voice in the corridor, male in gender and quite loud.

"Here comes trouble," I tell the brother/sister team.

In walks David Ostrahoff, my agent of twelve years. He speaks on his brand new Motorola StarTac. "Remarkable staying power for a guy his age," he says, checking out the Hamasaki's. "He's trending upwards in the best possible way. The thing with Becker? That was child's play."

David's a big guy. His head alone must weigh forty pounds. The rest of him settles around his midsection like a sleeping bag wedged into a stuff sack. David prefers designer clothes—tailored shirts, double pleats, suspenders. Suits heavy in the shoulder. Suits that swagger. Today it's sharkskin with a black dress shirt and silver tie.

"He's not over the hill. Richard's twenty-nine."

"I'm thirty-one, David."

"He may be thirty-one, but he's a youthful thirty-one." David extends a hand to Trevor Hamasaki. "You really think that fight, or whatever it was, was tragic? This second, they're showing the highlights on NBC, BBC, ESPN, shit, everyone in Europe is talking about it. You know how many people will be tuning in tomorrow?" David winks while the representative gets a few words in. "I probably shouldn't mention this, but Reebok is faxing over a contract. Why would I make that up? Of course, Adidas is our first choice. Okay, see you tonight. Nine sharp, Richard's flat, 26 Gladstone." David snaps the phone shut. "So, you've found Richard in his, um, his undies."

Ms. Hamasaki has her business card out. Her brother, along with David, pull out their wallets. Even Miles procures a crisp, clean card. Soon they're exchanging phone, page and facsimile numbers, email addresses, office street names, provenances, even sexual predilections.

I give myself a pat-down. "Where's my card?"

"I'd like to see where you stored it in that outfit," Ms. Hamasaki says.

"I'm okay with a strip-search. Honestly."

She smiles. "You'd like that, wouldn't you?"

The men don't notice Ms. Hamasaki and my flirtatious back and forth. They're too enamored by the technology. "Is that the new Motorola?" Trevor Hamasaki asks. "I heard it weighs next to nothing."

"3.1 ounces," David says.

"And you can send a message by tapping the keys?"

"Yep."

"How much did it set you back?"

David looks at me, beams. "It was a gift from my man here."

I give my agent a smile. "This guy is worth every penny."

"Aw shucks, Richard. I blush."

People have long criticized David. They find his weight offensive. They call him a blowhard. They think I could do better with a slick outfit like ProServe. Maybe that's true. There's also something to say about trust and loyalty. Dad taught me that. Hey, I'm not saying money's not important. I'm only saying I value friendship more.

I nudge Ms. Hamasaki toward the room's other end.

"Just what happened here?" she asks, looking over the mess.

"I came back from the showers and found this. Becker's probably behind it."

My phone buzzes from somewhere under all the detritus. "I was wondering where that was." I dig it out from under the bench and dirty clothes. David's calling? I look over my shoulder. He stands some distance from the other men (Miles is explaining All England's extensive membership process), facing away, phone to his ear. "Do you mind?"

"No," Ms. Hamasaki says. "Go right ahead."

I press the Talk button. "Yes?"

"Just act natural," David whispers. "Bengay won't return my calls. I think I've pacified Reebok. But you heard Adidas. They have real concerns. And now you've got a hard-on for this woman? Where does Heather fit into this?"

"Everything's cool."

"You were drooling on Centre Court, Richard."

"Are we done here?"

"Play it any way you want, Mr. Hugo Boss. But you're still in the draw."

"Is that so? I thought we were in London because of the bloody fantastic weather."

"And spinning plates isn't your forte."

"Goodbye."

When I turn around, Ms. Hamasaki is about to light a cigarette. "What? I can't smoke?"

"This is a locker room."

"But no one's here."

"My point is, it stinks. Smokers have nasty breath. The smoke gets in everything, every particle of fabric, every strand of hair. And smokers have weird behaviors."

"This ought to be good."

"Like chewing gum. Like bathing in perfume. Like sneaking behind their boyfriend's back for a stupid habit."

"Are you the boyfriend in this example?"

"If you want to be a slave to an addiction more powerful than heroin, then be my guest, Hamasaki, but do it on your own time."

"Fine. I won't smoke."

I give her a sideways glance, thinking I was rude. "It's nothing personal. My last girlfriend sucked those cancer sticks."

"Marta smoked?"

"She probably doesn't anymore," I say, sighing. "She's pregnant, after all."

"Tell me about your breakdown."

"Why all the questions?"

"Saiko Investments wants to be sure you're a good fit."

"Do you want to sign me or what?"

Ms. Hamasaki studies me like one animal does another, with cool detachment. "I haven't decided."

"*She hasn't decided,*" I say to the room. "And so you know—there was never any breakdown." I've stepped closer. "Are you flirting with me? Or is this your idea of a thorough background check?"

"You're something else."

This urge comes over me. I want to tear open Ms. Hamasaki's kimono and plant my face where it doesn't belong. "Sit in my box tomorrow."

"Your box?"

She smells like jasmine and freshly applied lipstick. Her eyes sort of glow. "Do you have a boyfriend?"

A beautiful color rises in her scored cheeks. "Yes, I do."

"I take it he knows you're here."

"You mean in the men's locker room with a player wearing only his underwear? I don't think he'd guess that. No, definitely not."

"I mean that you've come to sign Richard Blanco to a multimillion-dollar deal."

Ms. Hamasaki smiles like I said the funniest joke ever. "Ooh, I may disappoint you on the money front, Blanco. But my boyfriend's been aware of my profession for some time now. He went to college and everything."

"And he approves?"

"Approves of what?"

"I'm flattered, I really am, Hamasaki. But I have one, too."

"A boyfriend?"

"Funny."

"You think I'm into you?"

Miles, who's been speaking on the walkie-talkie, interrupts us. "They've officially postponed until the morning. Why doesn't everyone follow me so our young athlete can prep for the media."

I watch Ms. Hamasaki move across the room. Her hips in the tight little outfit have a life all their own.

Miles walks over.

"The room is twelve deep. Every journalist from here to Dublin is in the house. So keep your wits, keep things light. Give them the old Crutchley charm."

Crutchley was Dad's surname. It was Mom's idea I take her name. She said Richard Blanco sounded more like a movie star.

Ms. Hamasaki starts to leave.

"Don't be a slave to nicotine," I call out. "Be a slave to love."

"I'll remember that, Bryan Ferry."

The men follow, one after the other, like the Three Stooges. She waves once over her shoulder, a cutesy toodle-oo, not turning around.

And me? What am I doing? Other than thinking with my dick?

I check my messages. Heather called. So did Mom—twice. I hope that doesn't mean... no, Brody's a rock. And yet I dial the international operator. A woman patches me through to the States. I'm connected to Cedar Sinai, Los Angeles. A few minutes later, the phone's ringing in Brody's room.

"Yes?"

"Mom? It's me."

"Well?"

"Rain delay. How's he doing?"

"The doctors are monitoring him closely." Mom's voice catches. "I'm scared, Richard."

"I had knee surgery at Cedar Sinai, remember? Brody's in good hands."

"I don't know this time."

"You think cancer intimidates a guy like Brody Simmons? He'll be running around the court in no time." The second these words escape my mouth, I hear the false assurance, my sunny denial.

"I did hear good news today. I got a call back on Peter's new film."

"That's great news. Who's Peter again?"

"Peter Bogdanovich. He's only Brody's dear friend. He only made the most important film of the 1970s, *The Last Picture Show*."

"Better than *Star Wars*?"

"Oh, Richard." She holds back a sob.

"Tell Brody I'll see him in a couple days. Hang in there. I love you."

"Likewise, *muchacho*."

* * *

It's official. I've put on my Prada suit. And all by myself. The press conference starts any minute now. I'm clasping my Omega Seamaster onto my wrist and the only thought buzzing through my head is how the media is going to ruin me. I was a buffoon today. I should call Heather. Her voice soothes me. She'll put me at ease. Again, I go through the rigamarole of calling overseas. A couple minutes later I'm defending myself to her daughter.

"You got into a fight?"

"It wasn't a fight, Cherokee."

"Then why did you end up on the grass?"

Cherokee is fourteen. She doesn't know who her father is. Her mother works in a strip club. I keep these things in mind whenever she's annoying me.

"Is your mother home?"

"Mom," Cherokee hollers. "It's your *boyfriend*."

Soon a breathless Heather gets on the line. "How do you feel?"

The moment I hear her voice it's like coming home. "Like I blew it."

"Let it go," she says. "You're always telling Cherokee—short memory, next opportunity. Look at the rain like a second chance."

"Did it look as bad as I thought?"

"You tripped. Even the announcers said so."

Should I tell her about blanking out? "I spoke to my mom. It doesn't look good."

Heather lets this news sink in.

"I'm so sorry, honey. I know how much Brody means to you. But you are so in this match. One break is nothing."

"I'm down love-forty, serving. It's not a break, not yet."

"See?" Heather's voice brightens. "You can *so* do this."

* * *

I first played Becker in an ITF-sanctioned junior event in Berlin. He beat me soundly that day. That was the same year Mom pulled me aside at the divorce proceedings.

"He's gay, you know. That's why we're getting divorced."

Two years passed. In the interim, I graduated high school, lost my virginity and took Xanax for my disorder. I even turned pro. And I never once asked Dad if he preferred sex with men. Then came Wimbledon, 1985. I'd lost early, but we stuck around London, visiting relatives. We were staying in the same crummy flat I rent every fortnight. My record that year was an unremarkable 4–22. I had zero sponsors. And Becker was on the TV having won the most prestigious tournament in the world.

"Christ, he's younger than you are, Richard."

It felt claustrophobic seeing Dad so giddy. He'd also never surrendered his secret, something I felt needed prodding. "We talk about stuff, don't we?"

He didn't hear me. He was having a religious experience. "The first time you played him, son, I knew. Becker was special."

"You'd tell me, wouldn't you? If something was bothering you? Are you gay, Dad?"

This time he heard me. A darker mood fell over his features. "Why would you ask that?"

"I was just wondering."

Dad stroked his mustache. "Did you hear something?"

"Mom told me."

Dad sat back and smiled. "Did she now?" On the television, Becker walked Centre Court in his sky-blue Ellesse warmup jacket with the trophy in his arms. "I've been meaning to speak with you. I'm moving to New York. I feel like I've taught you everything I know. A change will be good for both of us. And to answer your question, I think I am gay."

* * *

People always ask me—what's the tour like? Like living in a bubble. You're bored a lot. You read more than usual. You spend time in the hotel lobby because it's important to be near other living, breathing bodies. You see movies. You stay abreast of current events without getting emotionally involved. Everything revolves around game day. Who you play, what time you play, what the court surface is—these thoughts run concurrently with energy levels and the state of your game. You probably don't have a coach, either, it's not in the cards financially, or you're at the stage in your career where you're fine on your own. You hopefully know the venue, have fared well there in the past. Your goal is getting the biorhythms in tune. Lots of sleep and hydration; hit lots of balls. It's about minimizing static. It's about compartmentalizing. It's about putting all your focus and energy into the next match. Nothing else matters, not your money situation, not the girl waiting back home, not your ranking, not a hangnail or if you're running a fever, not if winning means an invitation to play the following week in Buenos Aires or flying home, a loser.

Then there's the flow. The flow is the rhythm on tour. Hopefully, your flow borders on the liquid. Like you're floating inches above reality. Like you're removed from the petty shit most people deal with on a daily basis. When your flow is liquid, everything is crystal-clear. You wake energetic. Practice is an extension of competition, something you can't wait to do. You hunger for victory like it's a drug. If you think about the big guns, it's without awe or envy. They are just a means to an end, the end being the channeling of more flow. How does it feel playing that well? For huge chunks of time having that flow? Honestly, it's best not to think too much about it. Just go with the flow.

* * *

Press conferences are tricky. It's not easy being interesting, articulate, *and funny*, especially when you're being videotaped, recorded, questioned, pondered, poked and later written about by smart people looking for an angle or juicy slant, for you to slip up, spill your guts, say something inappropriate, racist, sexist or plain dumb. Though today feels different. Today feels like being honored for an ESPY, but when you reach the podium, acceptance speech in hand, you realize they actually called another athlete's name.

Soon a Wimbledon press agent escorts me in. Becker's leaving at the same time. In that narrow space between wall and table, there's this moment where we have to navigate past the other. Becker sports a sharp suit, though unlike me, he's elected to wear his collar outside the jacket's lapel. His countenance is serious, tense perhaps. I remember what Miles said about keeping it jokey and bring my fists up, then weave and bob like in my boxing class. Becker smiles, then lifts his hands, and we pretend jab the air. The journalists eat this up. Becker breaks character first. I'm reminded of our shared friction as he exits the room.

I sit, flip back my mane, then sweep my eyes over the crowd.

A hand shoots up in the second row. "Dennis Ginter, *The Sunday Times*. Can we expect more violence in the a.m.?"

I force a grin. "Seriously, gents. I think I'll just try to hold serve. The whole episode was incredibly embarrassing."

"Why all the antics then?"

"Everyone in this country thinks I'm mental. I'm just trying to live up to the hype."

"Have you ever tried playing it straight?"

"You got it all wrong, Dennis. I play it as straight as I can. I fail to close out matches. There's a news flash. I would have won today if I didn't lose my temper."

Janet Stipe, a journalist with the *Los Angeles Times*, raises a #2 pencil. Long ago, Stipe wrote a deferential article on Dad and me, him living with AIDS.

"Should you have been defaulted today?"

"Look, this is Shakespeare, low brow meets high. Becker and I are giving the people what they want. It's a show. I need to be sharp in the morning. I dug myself a little hole. But can I beat him? As long as I don't think too much, yeah. I've got a good team behind me. They're working overtime, getting me ready. If that means putting me in a straitjacket and plopping me in front of *Masterpiece Theatre* tonight, so be it."

"Any comment on Christian Brothers' new film, *Escape Velocity 2*?"

"Nope."

"The latest *Vanity Fair* quotes Mr. Brothers saying he was buying Marta and the baby a castle in Wales. Is that a bitter pill to swallow?"

"Interview over." I push my seat back. The room erupts with more questions, but I'm already moving toward the player's exit.

* * *

I nod off on the ride over to the flat. It's eight p.m., but with the dreary weather, car headlamps flick through my closed lids like lit matchsticks. David's on his phone. We've eaten dinner at our favorite restaurant on Petersham Road. Now we're on our way to negotiations. Our driver, a big guy with a chin like a poppy lemon muffin, listens to the BBC and fallout from the Everest disaster in May that killed eight. I think about Ms. Hamasaki. I see me slowly unwrapping her kimono. I see me brush a finger over her lips like I need complete and utter reverence. Then I see Heather's smoky blues, and immediately there's despondent me flying through the air. There's me tossing a towel over the kid's head.

If only Heather were here with her raspy voice and naughty curves. She'd keep me centered. We met at the tennis academy ten months ago. I'd just stepped off an airplane, still in street clothes, when I saw this striking blonde standing outside the clay courts. She was watching students pick up balls at the end of the day's session. I walked over, set my bag on the walk, and observed along with her.

"Teenagers," I said. "They're just great."

"Which one's yours?"

"Me? Children? God no. I mean, if the right woman came along, definitely maybe someday. But right now? No." I realized how I sounded. "Can I try that again?"

She laughed, which I took for encouragement. I introduced myself. I liked that she didn't recognize my name. The players were coming off the court now. A younger version of her appeared carrying a racquet bag, same sunny-blonde hair, same cheekbones. I joked, said this must be your sister. Heather smiled without showing her teeth like she was used to being hit on by men. Her daughter slowed, seeing us.

"She's at that age where everything I say embarrasses her."

"Funny, my mom says the same thing about me," I replied.

Her daughter stopped ten feet short. "Mom?"

"You're totally right," I said. "She's horrified."

"Mr. Blanco? I want to apologize for whatever my Mom's already said, is about to say, or will say in the near future. She's not a tennis player. She can't even keep score."

Her mom was looking me over with amusement. "What was your name again?"

"Mom!"

"No, it's cool. In fact, outside these walls, I'm not that big a deal." I turned toward her daughter. "And you are?"

She got this goofy grin on her face. "Cherokee Harper."

"Hey, maybe you can help me out, Cherokee. These executives from New York are taking Coach and me out to dinner tonight. I was wondering if you'd help convince your mom to join me. I promise to have her home by curfew."

"I can't believe you, Mom. Richard Blanco asked you on a date, and you said no? I'll never live this down."

* * *

"I see."

David's voice pierces through my consciousness, jarring me awake. We've reached Wimbledon Village. Neon lights bleed through the cab window. "Yes, that's how it went down, but—" There's a long pause. "No, Demetri. Why would I squander an opportunity like that? When you win, I win. You know I think the world of you." Another lull, this less lengthy. "That's not true. Would you have gotten LA Gear without me? Demetri? Hello? Hello?" David closes the phone softly. "You win some, you lose more. Isn't that your stock phrase?"

"You okay?"

"I needed that contract. Madeline's cocksucker lawyers are sucking me dry. What I need to do is diversify."

"Wait a second. Then who'll travel with me?"

"Trevor Hamasaki says there's big money in sumo wrestling."

"Aren't you a little old, David? But if it's important, I'll watch you wrestle, fat man diaper and all." I pat his knee. "I'm sorry your wife is bleeding you dry."

Rain raps the windshield. We pass a bus kiosk with an advertisement for Guess Jeans' new "It" girl, Claudia Schiffer. I think about another famous German then curl up against the door. I shouldn't be in this predicament, down a game and love-forty in the fifth. Why do I make things so hard on myself? What I need is a release. The valium safely stowed in my pocket? Sex with my new investment friend?

Traffic snarls. I see another *Escape Velocity 2* poster. Christian Brothers and his Rick Deckard buzz-cut sits on the ledge of a tall building, holding a blunt handgun, this futuristic city blazing liquid-blue below his combat boots. The caption reads: *It's 2041. Earth is a zero re-*

source planet, a rest-stop between worlds. Can Trace Ridge turn back time? Can he save the galaxy? Can he save himself?

JULY 3, 1996, 9:32PM

26 GLADSTONE, WIMBLEDON VILLAGE, ENGLAND

Picture the Adidas representative in swanky Chuck Taylors. Picture the rep from Bengay with ring around the collar. Picture my agent—all 248 pounds—sweating while opening a Diet Dr. Pepper. The four of us are inside my flat. The owner Mrs. Finch and her three Scottish terriers live downstairs. The apartment, a converted Victorian, is essentially a long, cramped room with outdated furniture, a galley kitchen, the bedrooms and bath in the rear.

"I'm going to say the number bouncing around in my head," David says, pacing the room.

"Candor? From a sports agent? How novel," the man from Adidas retorts.

"1.3."

"As in million?"

"You wanted candor."

I lie recumbent on a worn velvet fainting couch, still wearing the Prada threads from the press conference. The same couch on which I watched Becker hoist his first Wimbledon trophy. I guess it's stupid nostalgia me staying here.

"You think your client is worth 1.3?" Adidas says. "No offense, but he's what—sixty-nine in the world?"

"He's forty-three with a fifteen spot positive gain when the new rankings come out."

"Well, no one forty-three—"

"—twenty-eight or so."

"—is worth that kind of money. That's Sampras' world."

Ostrahoff tosses off his coat. "Look at him," he says, rolling up his shirtsleeves. "Will you look at my client? He's easy on the eyes, don't you think? And his legs—oh god—women go ga-ga over his legs, gentlemen."

Adidas frowns. "I thought we were talking about a shoe contract?"

"Richard is the Gabriela Sabatini of the men's circuit," David says. "Show them your legs, Richard. Don't be shy." Then my agent, in suit pants and suspenders, frontal vein throbbing, descends the floor like an old elephant, one careful leg at a time.

"You're embarrassing me."

David, still on all fours, swats at my ankle. "He shaves them, you know. Like those Tour de France guys. Richard is very chic. He's very clean."

"I guess I should see the product. We are talking about 1.3."

I stand and sigh the way a supremely talented professional athlete does with millions on the line and drop my trousers to the floor. Adidas pores over every inch of me like some sleazy trafficker in the prepubescent slave trade. Even Bengay dons reading glasses for a closer look. This was how it was in the old days. Dad admits an attraction to men, and I scale the rankings like a kid bent on reaching the sun. I beat players supposedly out of my league. My ranking jumped over a hundred places. Product endorsements followed. Orange Crush. Ralph Lauren. Omega watches. It got to where I never thought about money anymore. Dad's fiftieth birthday present? Try a Patek Philippe Perpetual Calendar watch. The 911 Carrera Cabriolet in pearl-white? Sold to the tan guy with his arm around the Bond girl from *A View to a Kill*. Women liked me. They could talk to me. I could open up about Dad in a way that wasn't awkward. Dad found himself, too. When I'd visit the Greenwich Village apartment another man might answer the door. Dad would pop his head out the bathroom with shaving cream on his face.

"Say hello to Jack," he'd say. "He was just leaving."

* * *

There's a knock at the door. Ms. Hamasaki comes in, unannounced, holding an umbrella. She wears the stylish mackintosh I saw in the window display at JOSEPH on High Street.

"Every time I see you, you're parading around in your underwear, Richard."

"I thought you might think that."

The captivating Ms. Hamasaki has Adidas and Bengay advancing for the door so fast you'd think the Queen had entered our little party on the hill. I pull up my pants then help the big man off the floor. I'm charged she's here. I'm at my best, fully engaged. It's like playing in the pink tutu after Dad died. Competing for something outside miserable, messed up old me, be it AIDS funding or Ms. Hamasaki—even that ball-boy this afternoon—gives me an edge.

Spinning plates, my man, spinning plates.

David and Adidas have retreated to the bay window. I'm walking toward Trey, whose been cornered by Bengay.

"May I get you a Perrier?" he asks.

"That would be wonderful."

We watch him go. "Where's Trevor?" I ask. "Parking the car?"

"He's out with an old college buddy."

"Is that so?" We have a moment, staring each other down. I feel that urge I felt this afternoon.

I hear Adidas say, "What if your client wore a hat with the Adidas logo?"

"Um, David?" I yell across the room. "Hats bug me when I serve."

My agent silences me with a glazed smile. "What if he wore the hat when he received serve?"

"What if he forgot?" Bengay offers up from the kitchen.

"I'm sorry." David gives the sports rep a stern look. "But didn't we work out an agreement with you twenty minutes ago?"

Bengay slams the icebox closed. "No need to get huffy."

Over at the bay window, Adidas bends down as if to tie his sneaker. Instead, he licks his finger and removes a smudge from his Converse All-stars. "He makes a valid point. Say your client forgot? Or he refused to put the hat on? Would that void the contract?"

"We can write the contract up any way you like."

"Except I don't wear hats."

"Richard—a word in my office."

"You go," Trey says. "I can manage here on my own."

I give my new friend a wink then follow David into his office—a half-bath with a sloped ceiling. He shuts the door behind us then pulls the toilet chain. The water drops from the tank with a noise like an old geezer blasting snot through a clogged schnoz. "I think our man Adidas is ready to throw down some serious *dinero*."

"It looks that way."

"He wants the hat."

"I'm trying to reach the semis at Wimbledon, not please a potential sponsor."

The rain is sporadic, a loud clatter, then nothing, then loud clatter again.

"Might be worth an extra 300K. To wear a hat, Richard. For thirty minutes, tops. It's not like he's asking you to wiggle your one-eyed monster at the Royal Box."

"Now that I might do."

"It's one set for crying out loud."

"What do you think of her?"

"The ninja in tight jeans?"

"I think she digs me."

David uses his tie to mop his perspiring hairline. "Last year, you wore a hat at the Australian."

"I need more, David."

"You were playing a lefty, dangerous serve."

"Tarango?"

"He was from south of the border. Good looking kid. Tall."

"Gomez? Look, I lost to Medvedev, but he's right-handed."

"My point is you wore a hat," David exclaims. "How about on returns? Let's do this."

My mind is elsewhere. "You think I'm being stupid?"

"Heather's awesome." David turns on the cold tap then splashes water on his face. "But you know that."

You're being obstinate, son. It's a bloody hat.

This voice is Dad's, which is strange. Very strange. I swallow hard, then stare at my agent, wondering if heard what I heard. His face is void of suspicion.

"Fine. I'll wear the hat. Now get out. I need to take a leak."

I'm pissing in the bowl when the apparition appears. I should explain what that means. Dad's ghostlike when I see him, granular and semi-transparent. He trembles like frail old hands. Today he wears linen slacks and a cable-knit sweater. Hey, I know it's a psychological phenomenon. But if you saw what I saw, if you interacted with ghosts on a visceral level like I do, it would freak you out, too. And when that motherfucker Luke Scream shows up in the flesh, so to speak, I'm in real trouble.

I reenter the apartment. No one notices my agitated state, not even David. I hear him say the hat is on the table. Numbers are tossed out so fast they seem arbitrary. There's a counteroffer, a retort, and then another counterattack. "What if the contract ran through 1998?"

David whirls around, his eyes conveying an excitement his face fights. "That could work."

Trey walks over. "You seem spooked."

I force my mouth into a softer line. "No offense, but you people make me sick."

She leans a shoulder into me. "It's rough being Richard Blanco, huh?"

A deal is reached. I'm not exactly ecstatic. Don't misunderstand me. I know how important this deal is. I'm just shaken up a bit. The last time a vision felt that real was after the Russian broke off our engagement.

The flat phone rings. Meanwhile, a contract's been laid out. David flips through the pages, oblivious to the chiming. He has me sign here, initial there.

"Do you want me to get that?" Bengay says. "Because I will. Just say so."

"We spoke to the press this afternoon," David says, glancing at me.

I get that awful feeling you get when a phone rings in the dead of night. "Maybe we should answer it."

"Allow me." Trey walks over and picks up the phone. "Richard Blanco's room. Hello, Mrs. Blanco. My name? Trey Hamasaki. I'm in Richard's room at this late hour to discuss a business deal." She smiles into the phone. "Not that sort of deal, Mrs. Blanco. I represent a company called Saiko Investments. We're interested in signing Richard. Yes, I'll put him on."

Walking across the room, I know the news isn't good. "Hello?"

"I went outdoors for some fresh air. When I got back to the room the nurses said there was nothing they could do."

"Hold on a second, Mom." I cup my hand over the receiver. "Hey, David? Can you wrap this up somewhere else?"

For a split-second, David's face clouds over. "Shall we head to the pub, fellas? Will you join us, Ms. Hamasaki?"

I suddenly don't want to be alone tonight. "I was going to walk Trey to her hotel. If that's okay with her."

She walks over and picks up her umbrella and coat. "How about we talk tomorrow, David. Meet you downstairs, Richard."

I wait until everyone gathers up their things and leave.

"Mom?"

"I thought we'd have more time. I never thought it would end now. When your father died—it was that awful disease—there was no stopping that, not then. But Brody? He played tennis on Wednesday. He seemed fine. What am I going to do without him?"

"I'll book a flight in the morning."

Mom blows her nose. "You will certainly not. You will finish your game."

"It's tennis, Mom."

"You know what Brody would say? He'd say, 'Bust a move, Richard. Bust a move.'"

You think a phone call can stop your world? Try bringing an insidious ghost into the mix. One minute you're flushed in plastic, in the make-believe world of dollar bills, dolls made up like cinema stars, sex, stardom, men like Adidas throwing around serious coin—and wham—life kicks you in the solar plexus. I can barely keep it level. I need to remember why I'm in this godforsaken pad—Adidas, Bengay, Saiko Investments. Money makes the world go round. Money helps the pain go away. How to disappear completely? I'll tell you. You give yourself over to the breathtaking Trey Hamasaki. You sink into her like a warm bath. The fifth set? It is what it is, now.

I walk to the dresser and pocket my wallet. Dad would tell David the truth. They'd hash everything out, the emotional toll, the strategy going into tomorrow, now that Brody's gone. Dad might even call

Heather. Me, I'm locking the door to the flat. I'm heading into the dark unknown. A few years back, during my *idioteque* days, I caroused bars for sex. I thought the Russian cleansed me of that sordid shit. Trey is what I need tonight. Without her, I'm finished. The losing streak lives on. The chatter in my head escalates. And I go to that bad, bad place.

The hall is clammy like my therapist's handshake. I know what Claudia would say. *Let's talk about your feelings, Richard. How does Brody's death make you feel?* I think about his sons. You're never prepared for death, no matter what you pretend. When Dad died, I was numb all over. But that didn't mean I didn't hurt. I just pushed those emotions down. Certainly, when I competed, I felt slightly off, slightly not there. Since then, it's been like balancing on a tight rope over a bone-chilling abyss. Lean the wrong way and you're somersaulting into oblivion.

Let me tell you—*I'm on edge.*

Then, on the stairs, another bad omen. Smoke from a clove cigarette hangs in the air. Luke's nearby. I can feel him. Any moment now, he'll sink his teeth into my neck.

Feeling in limbo, I halt at the landing. Down below, Trey leans against the entrance, arms crossed over her chest, smoking. She looks up and sees me. "Everything okay?"

Her voice wakes the optimistic little creatures in the downstairs flat. I start down the remaining steps. We hear the old lady scold her terriers. Then the door's closing behind us, and we're walking toward the village shops, the umbrella like a protective shell.

There's a run-down house across the way with a wild hedgerow, shutters hanging precariously by the nails and weeds sprouting on the roof. I don't look its way for fear it will swallow us whole. Then I think I see Luke crouched in Evans Cycle doorway, but on passing, realize it's a plastic bag caught on the steel frame.

My phone rings. I give Trey a pressed-on smile as I'm reaching inside my suit jacket. I sigh, seeing it's David.

"What?" Trey asks.

He'll insist we leak Brody's death to the press. I can't handle that pressure right now.

"Wrong number."

I put the phone away and snuggle in close.

"Are the rumors about you true?"

"You mean that I'm bisexual? I had fun with that."

"Did you do it for publicity? Did Luke Scream put you up to it?"

The streetlamp where we've stopped at blinks on. Trey's got her hands shoved in her coat pockets when I tease the liner open and take a peek, like I lost the flat keys in her blouse. She regards my mouth before continuing toward the hotel. I do this—push—when a normal person lets the situation evolve organically. I shove my way into things: predicaments, prickly public clashes, women I desire. Claudia says I don't always filter. She says I have loose boundaries. Once, during a session, she turned on the lights then put her round, fleshy face right up in mine. "This is you," she said. "You get in people's spaces. People don't like that."

I catch up as we're crossing Hartfield Road. The rain's stopped, but there's a heavy gray haze in the sky. I've released the umbrella's tension, secured the Velcro strap, and now swing it like a forehand drive.

Trey regards me through narrow eyes. "What are you doing?"

"Visualizing thrashing Becker tomorrow."

"You're weird."

Things are happening. There's a current passing between this lovely woman and me. I'm seeing possibilities, new frontiers. We've reached Broadway's throb and hustle. Autos swish by in a black shimmer. Tennis tourists slouch toward shops in the Nike Day-Glo of their favorite players.

"You like that people misconstrue you," Trey says. "You like that people wonder about your sexuality. You're also full of shit. You care what people think. You care what I think."

Claudia says the best thing about me is my want to be good.

"Do I now?"

"I'm not sleeping with you."

"Where is this hotel of yours?"

Trey points across the busy thoroughfare at a modern building with white neon letters running the facade vertically. The Player's Inn. Then she walks dumbly into the street.

She doesn't look left or right, and Broadway is a cluster-fuck of moving parts—black cabs and splotched headlamps and rubber tires hissing water. Brake lights glow. Horns sound their ugly call. Traffic comes to a halt so this beauty makes it safely to the other side.

"Are you crazy?" I yell after her.

Trey shrugs, a delicate form in a glow-in-the-dark raincoat. She disappears through the lobby doors.

I find her at the trendy bar a few minutes later, standing next to a couple of handsome youths in blazers and loose-fitted ties. She waves a Platinum American Express at the bartender.

"What was that about?"

"What was what about?" she says, tongue-in-cheek. "You thirsty?"

When Trey doesn't give up any more information, I sigh. "Club soda, splash of grenadine."

I survey the lounge. A DJ spins puckish Blur. Beautiful people chat on sprawling cushioned seats. There's an air of sophisticated in-authenticity. I hate posh bars. Let me throw you a morsel, gents. If you plan to score, and by score I mean sex with a woman, any woman, regardless of shape, color or creed, kill time in dim grimy pubs, hotels off the main drag. But swanky joints? No way.

My phone rings. This time I pick up. "You rang?"

"Tell me you got your thing in her."

"Aren't we funny."

"You're banging the shit out of her, right?"

"No, David. I'm on the phone with you."

"What's that noise?"

"It's music," I say in a tired voice.

"You took her to a club? Doesn't Wimbledon quarters mean anything?"

The drinks arrive. We toast cooly, flirtatiously, my club soda, her martini.

"We're having a nightcap."

"Nightcap, my throbbing penis. What did your mom want?"

"I'll explain it in the morning."

"I know he's dead. Let's get the information out. Control the feed. We can spin this."

I glance at Trey. She's not happy being ignored. "Stop pouting," I tell her.

She turns to the young men. "Where would a woman go around here if she was looking for a good time?"

"Hold on," I tell David, pressing the receiver against my chest.

"In the Village?" the taller of the two says, raising an eyebrow. His eyes find my face before addressing Trey again. "We're having a drink, is all, and not too keen on getting between you and your fella."

"He's not my fella."

"Good luck tomorrow, sir," the other says. "England's pulling for you."

Trey chugs her drink then starts walking away. "I'm so out of here."

"Will you wait a minute." I've hung up on David and reached for Trey's arm. Meantime the DJ's new selection has me nearly keeling over. "Holy shit. Do you hear that? It's The Fangs. Luke Scream's band."

Sid on GRID

Sid on GRID

Ain't it awful

Sid on GRID

The music has a lean throb, fast and clipped like a brawl.

"You expect me to believe that?" Trey nudges her hips closer. "Then what's he shouting?"

"Sid, as in Sid Vicious, and GRID, as in gay-related immune deficiency. Luke reimagined Sid's life, not dying from an overdose, but a long, slow process brought on by AIDS."

"So, he's Sid Vicious in the song?"

"Essentially, yeah."

"But that's not how he died. He killed himself."

It's a bummer about Sid

Dirty needle and the GRID

He didn't flame out, he slipped away

Just as well, Sid couldn't play

Do your part and walk away

Do your part and wear a sleeve

Don't end up like Sid on GRID

No drugs, no booze, no sex, no nothing

A Buddhist life, a beautiful resurrection

Trey sidles back up to the bar for a refill. I get lost in the music. Memories surface. Luke and me charging the stage at a Fugazi show, the all-nighters that ended at the ocean or his apartment in Hollywood, where we sat up listening to music until dawn.

Soon Trey's back.

"How did you become friends?"

"In LA, after Dad died. He turned me onto this whole new scene."

"Love at first sight?"

I smile into my glass in a sad way. Then I drink it clean.

"You know that call I took? My mom's husband died. Cancer."

"His death really affected you, huh?"

"Yeah, I guess it did."

"You want something stronger?"

"You mean like a martini? I fucking wish."

"I think I misjudged you." She sticks her finger out. "Your graphite boner."

"You didn't find that incredibly sexy?"

"Maybe if you were pointing your thing at me."

I search the room for something real, something I can hold onto. Something I can control.

"Let's go to your room. No bullshit. It's getting late."

"What about your girlfriend?"

I avert my gaze. "It's complicated. I sometimes don't fit into her life."

"I won't tell her, if that's what you're worried about."

A short elevator ride later, we're inside her room. Trey's in the bathroom, freshening up. I'm snooping around. What exactly am I looking for? Sexual apparatuses? Drugs? Fuck, I don't know. I'm curious, okay? Her room is ordered. Shoes all in a row. The dress she wore this afternoon hung with care. I'm disappointed. Not in me, but Trey. Why didn't she do the honorable thing and rebuff my advances? Why is she so eager to fuck me?

"Do you mind?" I've popped a complimentary chocolate in my mouth.

I picture her on the toilet, jeans bunched around her knees, tissue in hand. "Mind what?"

"May I eat a chocolate?"

I feel her smile through the wall. "Suit yourself."

"I like what you've done with the place."

I slip the second wafer on my tongue, feeling better, like the load's lighter in my head. But is sex what I need right now? The first step to a healthy, productive life is control. Claudia's always saying that. It's like Trey's hotel room. Everything in its right place. Obvious and established boundaries. Order.

Even if we do it—sex doesn't mean I'm in the clear. Tonight is about feeding a basic need. We do it, and then it's over, and hopefully I'm in a better place afterward. Either way, I pick up my clothes and the heap of baggage I carry inside, and leave. I go to my flat, swallow the valium, and hope the dark stuff doesn't materialize.

I'm at the window, eying the murky street for malcontents, when the bath door opens. Trey walks out, wrapped in a towel. We meet by the bed. She smells like toothpaste and cherry-scented lotion. We kiss. Then Trey reaches between my legs.

"Not so fast. I need to unload all this liquid first."

I'm so stiff I spray urine all over the toilet. So I pinch my member, wobble over to the walk-in shower in my fancy suit, and let go into the drain. Jesus, the predicaments I get myself in. I'll tell you one thing. I'm afraid to look behind me. What if Luke's there?

"You need a drink?" Trey calls out.

"You got bottled water?"

I'm at the mirror now. And no ghosts. Which is a relief. But I'm not thinking straight. Why do I feel like I'm letting down the dead? How inane is that? The dead don't talk. They don't harbor ill feelings. Ghosts don't wander the space between here and the afterlife. That's my lively imagination at work. That's bollocks. I should take a page from Dad's book and do the right thing—apologize for pushing my way in and go.

I look in the mirror again. And I don't like what I see. I see a guy who wants and wants. All I do is want. This is the plague of the twentieth-century male—we always get what we want. What does Trey Hamasaki really think of me? Because I am moving against the night. I am perpetuating myths, myths about the night. Packages I'll send in the mail—love letters, duty-free perfumes, mixed tapes I'll spend hours toiling over. International calls so I can hear her voice. Just so I know her longing equals or surpasses mine. Just so I can further feel how isolated I am. *Myths*.

And when we're together, I'll conflate us. They'll be no downtime, no boredom, no hesitation. With us, it will be go, go, go. Weekend getaways, late dinners, catching a premier. And fast to bed. We'll always be under the sheets. We'll do it in every room, in every orifice, in every position imaginable. We'll stock up on smut and lubricants. I'll tell her everything—my fears, my disappointments, my dreams. Out, out, out. I'll psychoanalyze her until she screams mercy. I'll speak so fast, and with such aplomb, she'll be exhilarated and dizzy at the same time. I'll press her hard. I'll bend her. I'll pump her with promises I can't keep. Because I want and want and want. Because I don't know what I want.

"Richard? Are you okay?"

What am I afraid of?

I exit the bath, completely naked. Experience has taught me to wow them when you can. The lights are off. Through the window the sky is phosphorous, the clouds packed like dirty snow. Trey's a silver mound under the covers. I throw my shoulders back then walk across the room like it's a fashion runway. Trey sits up on her elbows, her little rump sticking up in the air.

My hands rest on my hips for emphasis. "I think it's best if I go."

Trey eyes my blue-veined tumescence, then lifts the sheets. "Yeah, get that thing away from me."

In this delicate light, her body is like marble, her areola like impassive eyes. I climb in bed feeling nothing for her boyfriend. If he were doing his part, I wouldn't be here. In a way, it's like I've got no alternative, or the alternative—getting the hell gone—is a trapdoor ripping out from beneath me.

Our mouths catch, teeth slicing against teeth. My fingers find the warm glaze between her thighs. I say yes to pleasure. I say yes to pain. I say yes when inside a voice screams NO. For a second, I think of Heather. But she's the national anthem; she's a story for another day.

Meanwhile, Trey runs her hands over my body, frantically, searchingly, a bit enviously. I'm used to this behavior. Rarely are women my equals in the physical department. Comparisons are also made, my sculptured ass versus their soft-puttied men back home.

"I like being on top."

I look down at Trey in the ghosted light. Most times, I'd insist on being in charge. With all I've been through today, maybe it's easier to lie back and enjoy it. Besides, Trey could be my future traveling companion, the mother of my children. Why start off on the wrong foot?

"That's cool. I'm worn rather thin as it is. I hope I don't nod off."

She gives my penis a yank.

"Careful now."

Trey produces a condom she fits into place. Then she settles on my erection. Her face fills up like a glass of water. I won't bore you with the details other than to say her back arches when she comes. I don't let Trey catch her breath, either, but toss her in the soft pillows. Then the granite rock-star with serious veins goes to work. I warm up the hips with a couple quick bursts. Fifteen minutes in, my thrust-rate at a solid thirty-eight strokes a minute (I count for focus), I start pumping harder. A glance at her tits has a pre-ejaculation warning going off in my head. I picture Grandma Blanco and her pucker face and hairy mole. When that doesn't work, it's back to the old standby, thrust-count (a one and a two and a three and a pause, a four and a five and a six and a pause). I'm pumping away at a steady forty-seven clips a minute. Trey holds on like I'm a bucking bronco. At orgasm, I raise my leg in the air, for increased sperm flow, maximizing pleasure. Then I collapse like a spent thoroughbred, race over.

I slime off her, my heart thundering mad.

"Wow." Trey kicks off the covers. "You've really got your routine down."

"Once you've had Richard Blanco—sex as you know it is a changed sport."

"Why do men always ruin the moment by opening their mouth?" I start removing the condom when Trey pushes my hand away. "Let me." She wraps the latex umbrella in tissue from the nightstand. "Fancy move there, in the end."

"You like? I picked that up in Brussels."

"You make it sound like an STD, Richard."

Trey slips from the bed, Kleenex in hand. She walks into the bathroom, all perky Pilates ass and pointy shoulder blades. She doesn't shut the door. Her pee is a steady trickle, not like a man's fire-hose spray.

"Tell me about your boyfriend?" I say, propping a pillow under my head.

"Christopher? He's in corporate real estate, donates to various indigenous tribes, and plays handball three times a week."

"You know I can't get involved, right?" I hear the toilet flush. "What I mean is, your life's as complicated as mine is."

"Exactly."

I turn on the nightstand. "Can you bring out my clothes?"

Trey exits the bath, sans makeup, in a hotel robe and clunky geisha sandals. A cigarette dangles from her lips.

"Do you have to smoke?"

She dumps the suit on my lap. "Are we really having this conversation again?"

"I'm just tired."

Trey sits on the bed's edge, facing the wall mirror. "Then sleep here. It must be more comfortable than your place."

I swing my feet to the floor. "A sleepover? Do you know how important tomorrow is?" I slip on my underwear and socks, then grab my trousers. "You ever stay in a love hotel?" I've got one leg in the pants when Trey drops the cigarette in my water bottle. "Hey, I was drinking that."

"I don't find Japanese men attractive."

Trousers on, I start buttoning my shirt. "Really? Are they too short?"

"No, Richard," she says, slowly. "Japanese men just don't do it for me."

Trey pulls a jar of facial creme from her robe pocket. She applies moisturizer to her face and neck while looking in the mirror.

"We should have love hotels in America. Think about it. They're clean. They're affordable. They're discreet. Americans, we're like quick in, quick out, in cars, in public bath stalls, at 42,000 feet."

"Maybe we should start a business venture," she says.

"You think so?"

Trey just gives me a look.

Luke was like this—secure enough in himself that he didn't care what other people thought. "You remind me of him."

"*Whom*, Richard?"

"Luke Scream."

"The quasi-famous, flamboyantly-gay punk rocker who died before his time?"

"Why did you walk into the street like that?"

"Why haven't you left?"

And why haven't I? Would spending the night be so bad? Then I remember the ghost sighting. I pat my pockets thinking I brought the valium, then slump in the leather chair.

Trey climbs onto the bed. "What was he like?"

"Luke? Crazy. Fearless. There'd be assholes at shows beating the shit out of him. They threw condoms, bags of vomit. Once this kid shit on stage and two skinheads dragged Luke through it. I'm like 'why the fuck are you doing this?' Luke says, 'it's the chaos, the gay chaos. My music is about penetrating through the chaos.'"

"He was out there, huh? And I remind you of him?"

We laugh, me sinking into the plush chair, Trey wrapping herself in the comforter like it's a cocoon.

Hey, Kid? Eh? Get a move on, Blank.

The hotel phone rings, startling us with its metallic clink. We stare at it like we've uncovered a bomb underneath the bed.

"Don't go," Trey says, reaching for it.

"I don't want to be here when you talk to him." I grab my suit jacket but don't move to leave.

"Christopher?" she says, picking up the receiver. "Hey, buddy. It went fantastic. In fact, he's still here."

"What the fuck, Trey?" I whisper.

She smiles into the phone. "I'm messing with you. Hmm? He's interesting. Oh, I almost forgot. He got us seats in his box tomorrow."

I start for the door, clutching my suit coat.

"What was that, buddy?" Trey blows me a kiss. "No, I don't have a crush on him. This is nothing like Sven."

Instead of bolting for the elevator, I hang back in the corridor, leaning against her closed door, half-listening, half spaced out. I should never have gone up. Sex with the woman trying to sign me? Cheating on Heather the night Brody dies? I tell myself to remain calm. I keep reminding myself what my name is (Richard Blanco), what city I'm in (London, England), why I'm here (it's my freaking job). This is a motion picture soundtrack. This is morning bells tolling in my head. This is the hero having a much-needed jag. This is him charging down the hall. This is him exiting the elevator into a rocking-loud bar. This is him seeing YOU-KNOW-WHO lurking by the DJ booth. This is YOU-KNOW-WHO'S skeletal treefingers lighting up a fag. This is our hero pushing past the attractive, wasted youth on the street. This is him sprinting past two lovers pressed against the door of a buttoned-down shop. This is me finally slowing down at Gladstone Road. This is me staring at the house with the monster hedge. This is my heart thumping when a light goes out on the second floor. This is Luke Scream waltzing out the entrance in skinny leather pants. This is him slinking toward me, an almost glide.

"You live here?"

I'm a construct of your mind, you idiot.

This is that moment when I fully comprehend the night ahead. "I haven't forgiven you."

Luke wears thick eyeliner, black nail polish, his hair spiky. *For offing myself? You ungrateful bastard. I left you my car.*

"That car cost me $200 to have it towed to a junkyard."

Luke leers, all crowded teeth and glistening lips. *She's a Blank chick if there ever was one.*

"What do you want?"

He takes his time lighting a cigarette. *Recognition.*

"Don't we all?"

Something near 26 Gladstone gets Luke's attention. The terrier's start up with their high-pitched yelps. *Shut them cunts up or I will.*

Then Luke bleeds into the nothingness. He becomes the nothingness. Then I can't decipher anything at all.

INDEPENDENCE DAY, 7:04AM

WIMBLEDON VILLAGE

Then day two.

And don't let the quiet fool you. Or the brilliant cloudless day. There's been a disturbance, a crack in the sky. I felt it this morning, like I was being watched. No, things aren't moving as smoothly as I'd hoped. I'd put a call in to The Player's Inn. I thought I'd reintroduce myself, ask her how she slept, see if she missed me. Trey never picked up. Granted, it was early, a pink champagne dawn. Then I thought— Heather never minds if I wake her up. Her voice is like the seashore to my ears. But I couldn't. She'd intuit the adulterous shit I'd been before I said, "Hello, sexy dancer."

I dialed my therapist instead, and got the voice box. "I'm feeling rather odd, Claudia." I detected a tremor in my voice. "Can we talk before I go on?"

Nothing better to do, I tied up my running shoes and hit the pavement, Wimbledon Commons, mile in, mile out, nothing crazy, just break a sweat to clear the head. Loosening up did some good. But I wasn't sure I wanted to play anymore.

* * *

I shower, throw on a practice jersey, collect my equipment, then hoof it to Village Life, a breakfast place that caters to Americans. The sky is blue as blazes. It's glorious, like London in those fancy travel brochures. David's the only person in the back room, toothpick in his mouth, reading a folded newspaper.

"Look over the menu. I want to finish this article."

Every morning David scours over the pickings at Sutherlands, a newsstand on High Street. They sell a selection of newspapers and magazines, high fashion ones, niche sports, tasteful porn. I glance at the paper David's reading, *The Guardian*, then play a hunch.

"What's Janet Stipe saying?"

David rolls his eyes. "Nonsense. A fluff piece, really. By the way, you look like shit."

"You don't want to know."

If I could only tell David about the valium taking hold last night, how it gripped me like a friend I hadn't seen in years. It was like slipping under the radar of things. Like I was invisible to my own self. It was two in the morning. I thought, who needs sleep? It was one bloody set tomorrow. Soon the sedative shifted gears. I found myself listening to a musician Luke turned me onto, Elliot Smith. I wore headphones. The music dug deeper in. Elliot Smith's mournful tenor serenaded me like a trusted accomplice.

I'm a roman candle

My head is full of flames.

I slipped into a dream. Dad and me hitting the fuzzy yellow ball in this glinted world. He looked young and slim, in sparkly new attire, like that suit John Lennon wore on the cover of *Abbey Road*. The image morphed. What was bright and pleasant was now under-lit and sketchy. There was a jagged cliff, waves pummeling a shore far below. Luke was standing there, minding his own business. Then he pushed me, head over heels, into the dark void. I woke, screaming for air.

* * *

Back in Village Life, David's devouring a pastry. His gaze hasn't once skewed from the page.

"What's my girlfriend calling the article?"

"Stipe?" he says. "'Tennis' Mr. Enigma.'"

I give David a long look. Should I tell him I'm chickening out?

"Mr. Enigma? I like that. It makes me sound like the international playboy I am."

"I'm sorry about Brody." David finally peers from over the newspaper. "Just so you know, it was your Mother's idea we get the media involved. Now all of London will cheer."

He starts closing the newspaper when I snatch it from his hands.

"You know that shit fucks with your head."

"Why can't I read it?"

David holds his hand out. "I'm serious, Richard."

Our waitress, the frumpy Kate, walks over wearing her ridiculous barmaid outfit. "What'll it be, Mr. B?"

"Double espresso."

"Double espresso? Where do you think you are, posh Kensington?"

David, seeing me distracted, attempts a no-look lunge, but I'm too fast.

"Coffee, Kate."

She peers at us over her writing pad. "And to eat, luv?" Kate has squishy old woman cleavage, a hefty sack. In my hellion days, if properly lubricated, I'd probably have bagged her. "Mr. O?"

"Get him the usual."

"Rumble, tumble, toast?"

I scan the menu. "Make it the Full English."

"Can you give us a second?" David waits for Kate to move off. "You don't want to play, do you?"

"Why would you say that?"

"Because I know you," he says. "When's the last time you ate a breakfast like that?"

"I'm worried about Mom."

"What about your sponsor obligations? What about your responsibility to yourself?"

Kate returns. "You decided, Mr. B?"

"Full English."

David regards me a long time after Kate puts my order in. "You know why you're not more successful? You spend your energy on everything but what champions should."

"Can I tell you a secret? I think I'm into her."

"China Girl? You thought Paulina was the one. Before that, it was that Olympic rower. Then I thought Marta might save you. You messed that up, too. Then, you meet sweet, lovely Heather."

"Trey and I have much in common."

David puts his hands flat on the table and leans in. "How do you know that? Because you fucked her? Look, Richard, you're a big boy. If you want to act like a pussy on the Fourth of July, what can I do? But don't read the Stipe article. If you want to read something, read this." He flips through the newspapers then pulls out *The Observer*. "There's a review of a thousand-page novel that takes place at a tennis academy in Boston. It's called *Infinite Jest*. And get this, the author is a strange bird like you. He wears a bandanna. You wanna know why? He thinks it keeps all the shit in his brain from making him crazy."

"I'm doing the right thing."

My agent pushes his chair back. "Like I said, that's your call. I'm taking a shit."

I watch David go.

And what does he know? He has no idea how much mental effort goes into playing this game. He has no idea my grief. Not playing is the honorable thing to do.

My steaming meal arrives. What's the Full English? It's like eating the entire farm in one sitting. Everything is heaped together like a torso blown in half. There's burnt toast, baked beans, eggs sunny-side up, tomato slices, mushrooms, kippers and gobs of meat.

I go at the food with everything I've got, lapping up the remains with the toast. Finished, I push the plate away. When I see David exit the restroom, I pick up the Stipe column and pretend-read.

"Is this smart, Richard?"

I read aloud in a prim, haughty English voice, "'*When journeyman Richard Blanco steps onto Centre Court to complete his quarterfinal match against Boris Becker today, he'll be thinking about his stepfather, movie producer Brody Simmons, who died last night in Los Angeles. Simmons, with his shock-tinged hair, hundred-watt smile, and dark sunglasses, was always a familiar sight in the Player's Box. He and Blanco co-produced an AIDS documentary last year, a big depar-*

ture from the campy extraterrestrial meets humongous-breasted bomb-shells in the zombiefests Simmons was known for.'"

David and his heft noisily sit. "Why are you doing this?"

"'I first met Blanco six years ago at Elaine's, in New York City, with his father, Fitzgerald Crutchley. Fitz, as everyone called him, was HIV positive. I arrived late to find the pair seated in back, next to George Plimpton and Jay McInerney. Father and son were both immersed in books, Gibbon's The Decline And Fall Of The Roman Empire *and* Portney's Complaint. *I bet you can guess who was reading Roth! Back then, Blanco wore a fisherman sweater and jeans tucked into L. L. Bean hunting boots. He could have been a Ralph Lauren model, a far cry from the dyed green hair and motorcycle jacket he took up a couple years later. Richard had his father's blue eyes, but his mother's spirit. Diane Blanco had been in the news recently, after being banned from professional events for storming the court during her son's match in Stowe, Vermont, to give a linesperson a profane talking to.'"*

"That mother of yours was always a pistol."

"'I found Fitz Crutchley very British. He suggested the veal chop then ordered for me. He liked the scarf I wore. He said his ex-wife would look divine in it. He said she was the only woman he ever loved. Blanco was less direct. He never answered questions straight on. For instance, I was curious if it was difficult concentrating during matches when girls screamed out his name.'"

David taps his fingers on the table. "We so like entertaining ourselves."

"'There was a naturalness between Fitz and Richard, a gentleness I rarely see between fathers and sons. Richard doted on his father. When Fitz shuddered from a cold draft, it was Richard who demanded Elaine turn up the heat.'"

I hadn't noticed an emotion creeping in until it's too late. I look over at David, a little teary-eyed.

"Hey, man, no worries."

After taking a deep breath, I continue seriously.

"'Despite his bawdy image and eccentricities, Blanco breathes life into the professional game. So many players today seem produced in Eastern European tennis factories or Nowhere, America. They're all polite

young men who run like antelopes. But they also seem like highly efficient cyborgs. Outside competition, what do these players stand for? What do they believe? Do they have opinions about tribal wars in Afghanistan or don't they want to be bothered? In a way, they're all blank.'"

"Blank. That's your nickname, isn't it?"

"'*This doesn't justify Blanco's X-rated Centre Court gesture yesterday, but it does help explain where he's coming from. Remember— he's the player who dressed in a pink tutu and matching leotard, first round, US Open, 1992, to protest paltry AIDS funding. This is also the player photographed the same year stumbling out of CBGB's with punk rocker Luke Scream five hours before his scheduled match against Juan Casals. Blanco played magnificently, winning in four sets. Afterwards, he told a surprised Pat Summerall he was still drunk.'*"

"Maybe your finest hour."

I cluck my tongue, pleased with myself. "'*Blanco offered this insight about his concentration lapses yesterday. 'I don't always have full control of my faculties. I'm like the Tourette's Syndrome of tennis players. I take things personally. Players know that. If I'm in the wrong frame of mind, I snap.' But who is Richard Blanco? Is he an entertainer? A clown? Is he a player worth respecting? At thirty-one, how many years does he have left? Barring a minor miracle, he'll never win a major.'*"

"Don't take stock in that shit. What does Stipe know."

"'*Now, his opponent, Boris Becker, I understand. He's all business. He knows distractions aren't healthy. Here's my prediction.'*"

"Why don't you give me that."

"'*Blanco goes down without a fight. Becker, being the gent that he is, once he's in control, will throw the old coot a bone or two. The final set score will be 6–2, Becker.'*" I stare across the table at David. "Throw the old coot a bone or two? Hey, bone this, Stipe. Here, you read the rest."

David extracts the newspaper from my hands. "That's enough punishment for one morning."

"No, this is therapeutic."

"How so?"

"Read, please."

David sighs then picks up where I left off. "*And Blanco? Savor the run. You've dazzled us, you've befuddled us, you've been good copy. You've turned the spotlight on the AIDS plight in America, and for that, we thank you. But your future in the pro ranks is bleak.*"

"Bleak? She really wrote bleak?"

"*Blanco's complicated. He's different. He might be crazy-mental. He's an enigma. Mr. Enigma.*"

"Well, she ties in the Mr. Enigma quite nicely with the heading, don't you think?"

Kate stops by our table. "Anything else, luv?"

"Please bring Mr. Enigma the check."

Kate gathers up the dirty plates, and leaves.

"They're just words, Richard."

"Mr. Enigma? I'll show her," I exclaim. "Why did you let me eat that shit?"

"So, you're playing now? Why don't you make up your mind?"

"I thought you'd be happy."

"I am. I just have to reprogram my mind, psychologically speaking. Don't worry. I'm with you, man. You rock."

INDEPENDENCE DAY, 9:46AM

THE ALL ENGLAND LAWN TENNIS & CROQUET CLUB

As restrooms go, the unseeded men's locker room isn't so bad. It could be worse. In London, a really foul shitter is called a bog. The restroom in *Trainspotting*—that was a bog. What we have inside the men's bathroom is uninspiring but clean. What I need is something to read. Nothing intellectual or taxing. See, we're at T-minus ten minutes. And Centre Court waits for no man. Then I spot the perfect confection on the counter—a worn, crinkly tabloid. *The Sun* is England's *National Inquirer*, but funnier, more infantile.

Some players crank Nirvana in the final countdown. Others knock out pushups or sprint in place. Still, others go all Zen and lotus pose. I like a quiet stall with my shorts around my ankles. Today, it's Page Three Girl and Public Enemy exploding from my Discman. This is my pre-match ritual—light reading, pumped up sounds, defecation evacuation. I come out the other side, popping like a firecracker.

Lighter, fitter, faster.

But I can't go. I ate an entire buffet for breakfast, but now I'm in a holding pattern.

Page Three Girl is a lovely tart with dirty-blonde split-ends and milk-white breasts that tumble to her naval. Her name is Charlene. She likes secondhand smoke, not going to university, and Elvis Costello's classical album.

Win or lose, at the match's conclusion, NBC's Bud Collins will want a word. What would be hilarious is rapping some Chuck D rant of my own. I think for a moment, then turn up the volume. Eyes closed, feeling the beat in my bones, I try out a few lines. *I'm an enigma, I prize the mad beaver, like a potent pain reliever. I'm into fancy clothes and kicked out... hoes, like the saying goes...*

Like what saying goes?

The phone's ringer goes off. I nearly fall off the bowl, fishing it out. I jerk off my headphones. "Claudia?"

"Is this a good time to talk?"

Weirdly, my therapist's voice is like crunchy fiber. For quite rapidly, I'm assaulted with earthquake-intense movement down below. Pain grips me so hard I brace against the stainless-steel stall. This ominous, subhuman moan spills out.

"Are you in the weight room?"

"I'm, um, I'm nearly there."

"You sound wounded, Richard."

"Oh, lordy me."

"Is lifting weights before the big game advisable?"

Then it's over, the steaming burger pinches free. Downstairs feels like something tore through me. "Wow. I mean, that was great. I've never felt better."

"I wouldn't be too cocky. Better to stay in the moment, enjoy the process, wipe all distractions from your mind."

"Funny, you say that."

"How's your mental state? On the phone, you mentioned feeling odd."

"I don't know how you do it, Claudia, but I feel five pounds lighter."

"Well, outstanding. Glad I could help. And see you in the semis! Oh, and Richard?"

"I know," I moan. "Don't think."

There's a soft rap on my metal cage. Under the door, I see monk strap-on leather beauties, double buckle. "Having a rather long go at it, are we then? In all seriousness, they're ready."

"Be with you in a minute, Miles."

* * *

How does it feel walking onto Centre Court to a packed house? The heart stirs. It's a tremendous honor. There's nothing quite like it for a tennis player. All that tradition, the shades of green so pleasing to the eye, the ghosts of the ones that came before you. But then habit takes over. You tighten your shoelaces. You cinch the bag over your shoulder. You channel your warrior self. Then you're escorted toward the tunnel. There's nothing like it, that walk.

Today, Miles walks over with a pleasant face on. "Need the arm, young man."

"What's this?" I watch him slip an armband up past my left hand.

"A little something for Brody," he says, securing the cloth around my biceps.

"But it's black."

Miles winks. "I think the members' will let the color scheme slide this one time."

Then, we're cleared.

Centre Court on the brightest of days. Everything outdoors like it was the day before, but now in vivid green Technicolor. The moment I feel the sunshine on my back, there's this intelligible roar. I raise an arm. The noise surges higher. "Bro-dy—Bro-dy—Bro-dy," the crowd chants. I search the sky, that blue emptiness.

* * *

Being down love-forty in the second game of a deciding set poses a unique set of quandaries. Errors are to be entirely avoided; nerves kept in check. This goes for temerity, too. A player facing three break points must think cautiously bold. In mountaineering, if there's a substantial gap on the ridge, the spirited climber studies the point of departure and where his foot will come down on the other side. Then he leaps. No second guessing. *He just goes*. This might mean serving up the middle even if that plays into your opponent's strength. What tennis comes down to is essentially this—is your service game more powerful than the brunt force of his return?

This bright morning bugs flit about. Laughter spills down the aisles like slinky toys. I'm amped up. The new shoes feel comfy nice. There's the hat. It's like a lightbulb on my head, white as snow, very doable with the money we're talking about. And the color is a dead ringer for Trey's sundress. Yes, a brand new day.

"Time. Fifth set. The score is 1–0, Mr. Becker. Mr. Blanco serves at love–40."

Only when the crowd quiets do I let the ball go into the azure sky. The toss is an extension of my arm, right of center, ten o'clock. As the ball reaches its full height, I fling my whole lot into the air—legs thrust toward blue, pelvic slides open, shoulders rotate up and around. The ball spins wildly away. The linesman signals good.

The thing about tension is it amplifies with each point won. So you do what you know: control where the eyes wander, gulp oxygen, bring time down. I resist eyeing my box and target the middle. The ball buffets off dry, caked dirt, and skids low. Becker flails like he's swinging a cricket bat. Then he barks German at his racquet, like it's the damn stick's fault. But winning the first two points means squat if you lose the next one, so I press on. At the line, straightening the strings, I decide to go into the body, right to left as the glare goes. Instincts tell you where to go. Becker can't get his sluggish feet out of the way.

"Deuce."

Okay then, all squared up, it's anyone's game now. But what's he thinking? What's he want? He wants it out wide. He expects heat. Maybe I'll surprise him—throw it at noon and a little over my head. I'll get my legs under the ball, really thump it with spin.

Here goes nothing—the uncoil. I feel a purity in the way the ball jumps off the strings. An auditory pop. Like I cracked the algorithm wide open.

Becker misses long.

The twitchiness from before slips into a relaxed tenacity, like my insides are a dog gnawing on a bone. I place the serve wide.

"Game Mr. Blanco. 1–1, fifth set. Balls change ends."

How's that for Mr. Enigma, Janet Stipe?

I can't resist peeking at my entourage. But it's Trey my eyes linger on. She brings a vogue missing since the Russian decamped to the Hollywood Hills. And Brody's seat? His is a bicycle at the scene of the accident, spray-painted white, with flowers heaped around the tires.

All players have idiosyncrasies. Between points, Carlos Sanchez studies his stringing pattern like a classical guitarist, Hewitt tugs the underwear bunched between his butt cheeks, and Becker opens and closes his mouth like a fish taking in oxygen. Especially when he's nerved up. Like now. His first attempt is a clunker that gets stuck in the net fabric. The closest ball-kid grabs at the suspended ball, but it won't budge. The fans eat this sort of thing up. Now the boy takes the ball with both hands. Finally, he dislodges it to applause. Becker throws his arms up like this beats all. Fittingly, his second serve finds the mesh. "Scheisse!" He berates his stick again. And they cheer. Get on the Brits' ugly side and watch out. Becker puts another ball into the lattice, dittos the second.

"Love–thirty."

We play another point and another miss by the German. He wanders the baseline now, inspecting balls, mumbling to himself, out of sorts. He kind of reminds me of me. Then his sorry ass double faults the game away.

"Mr. Blanco leads 2–1, fifth set."

In tennis, change comes quickly. Momentum steals across the fields faster than weather over London skies. With Becker coming undone, I rattle off three of the next four games. In thirty-seven minutes, I'm four points from winning. I am feeling it, not a tense nerve, all systems go. I'm so giddy keeping composed during the changeover proves problematic. I put my towel over my head, Centre Court a symphonic babel, and grin. Now's the time to practice relaxation techniques or read over my notes. Just don't think. About the hundreds of thousands tuned in, in homes and apartments across Europe, the Czech Republic, Slovenia, Christchurch, Tel Aviv and Cape Town. Across the wide swath of the South Atlantic, flying low over Uruguay's fractured coast, around the horn, picking up speed along the Andes, then Santiago, Costa Rica, Acapulco, the Baja peninsula, Southern California, Los Angeles. Home.

Try not to think.

About those bare-boned clubs in Budapest and outside Moscow where truly hungry players with nothing to lose huddle around 17" black-n-whites, the picture snowier than a Siberian winter. Try not to think. About what the BBC's John Barrett is saying about your chances or the helter-skelter atmosphere of a Clapham betting shop. Try not to think about those sports fanatics, men mostly, who watch televised sports for its esoteric rules, its mannerisms, its order and justice, its violence, its incontrovertible conclusiveness. Boy-men who love drama, any drama, as long as it isn't their own. Try not to think how boring and meaningless life would be without our sports, our sports columns, our sports ticker, our sports betting, our ESPN.

Try not to think.

About the first time you came here with Dad. To you—a teenager in size twelve shoes—Centre Court was the Grand Canyon. It was magnificent. What a trip that was—the blooming English countryside, a string quartet playing Schubert at Albert Hall, competing in the Wimbledon juniors for the first time. Did I really think of defaulting? On Independence Day?

"Time. Mr. Blanco leads 5–2, fifth set."

Centre Court is downright festive. Three-quarters of the spectators haven't taken their seats. They cheer the moment Becker and I rise from our chairs. Then, a young woman in a red, white and blue bikini, meant to represent the American flag, slips over a wall like a truant. She sprints for me, barefoot, with this twisted smile on her face. I look at Sverdes. Even Becker is curious about what this means. Security has hopped the tiny wall, but they won't catch her in time. She halts two feet from me, her breasts rising and falling with every sharp breath. The girl salutes me. I salute her back. Then she jumps into my arms. Her grip around my neck is viselike. "Oh, Richard," she says, her breath smelling like warm beer. "You're so adorable."

Guards sweep in. They pull her off me like she's sticky gum. Becker, near the far wall, hardly notices. He cranks his towel over his grip, really working it, like a PGA professional on the tee. His pal, a glum George Harrison, slumps in his seat. My team is reserved as if the jury's still out on this one. All this time the noise builds.

I retighten the armband then remove the hat to dry my forehead. There's this novelist with a peculiar headcover. I keep it all in check with my newly minted baseball cap.

The game begins on a sour note—this flinched volley, like I'm zapped with two-thousand volts of electricity. Could be the jitters. I never should have ordered that coffee for breakfast. Then three more get away.

"5–3, Mr. Blanco. Mr. Becker to serve."

So the German takes one back. Hey, even if Becker holds—*and why wouldn't he, Blank?*—I can still serve this match out.

"You got him thinking, Boris!"

"No wobblies, Blanco! Get your head straight."

Only after Becker bounces the ball does the noise depreciate to a diaphanous hum. Then he uncorks a 131 mile per hour zinger. Nerves tingle below like bad gas. What if I choke again? Becker's got my number, always has. It's like the Red Sox winning the Series—it's never going to happen. At 15–love, we trade careful groundstrokes when my pithy backhand catches the tape and falls onto Becker's side.

"15–all."

Tennis etiquette encourages a polite wave if luck plays in your favor. I've been on the losing end way too long for that. Rather, I dramatically fall to the ground, shimmy backward on the grass, like the knicker-clad, stringy-haired *Back in Black* Mr. Angus Young. I point at the armband, and the chorus picks up.

"Bro-dy—Bro-dy—Bro-dy."

In the time it takes to gather myself for the defining moment of my career, I see that Becker waits on the baseline. Then he does the strangest thing, considering I'm three points from victory. He smirks. I hop from left to right foot a couple of three times. What did that mean? Have I finally gotten to him? Is he throwing in the proverbial towel? Against my better judgement, I steal a glance at Trey. Sitting next to her is Luke. He cups a feel up her dress.

Jesus H. Not here. Not now, Luke.

There's no time to dawdle. For Becker's started his service routine.

He bounces the ball—once, twice, three times, four times (he's not real, he's not), five times, six times (Stipe's article, now that's real), seven times (last night, with Trey, real, too), eight times, nine times (Centre Court—REAL), ten times, eleven times (um, where's the toss?), twelve times (why hasn't he served?), thirteen times, fourteen times, fifteen times (come on you twit, let's go!), sixteen times, seventeen times, eighteen times, nineteen times (has Becker lost it?), twenty times, twenty-one times (why doesn't the Chair intervene?), twenty-two times, twenty-three times (what about the continuous-play rule?), twenty-four times (he should be warned), twenty-five times (a point should be taken away), twenty-six times (that's it, I'm pulling out). And I stand tall—all seventy-five gleaming inches—at the precise moment Becker throws up a very low toss. The problem is the 14,000-plus in attendance. They're fixated on Becker's underhand serve.

You heard correctly. *An underhand serve.*

Does anyone care that I stopped play? Does anyone care that I exist? Considering crowd reaction, I'd say the answer is an unequivocal no. People blink the way you do after a sudden turn of events (say your car spins wildly toward a great precipice only to stop inches from the edge). They look at each other and where the ball landed (it bounced three times in the box), like it's an elaborate hoax they've realized is on them.

"30–15," the Chair says.

Becker, being cheeky, puts a finger to his ear, like he can't hear them. The people are with him now. With one sneaky stunt, he's gathered them under his dark wing. And you don't want to know what I see. Try 14,000 Luke Screams' laughing like baboons with their shiny snouts, nearly human teeth, and silly red butts.

I find myself charging the net, a little out of control. "You're letting him get away with that?"

"The underhand serve is within the rules," the Chair replies.

"What about delay of game? I raised my hand." Sverdes remains unimpressed. "Ask the linesmen if you don't believe me."

The Chair summons the man—a spry Indian with a nervous gait. The conversation doesn't last long. "The call stands."

"You're joking, right? What was the guy looking at? My cute ass? Well, this beats all." I take my hat, my million-dollar dunce cap, and bash it against the net cord.

"Warning, Blanco. Equipment abuse."

"This hat? Equipment abuse? You're sad." And I storm off.

I'm so ramped up I've forgotten the score. Then it dawns on me—nothing's happened that wasn't expected. Well, the underhand serve was a surprise, but there's no need to panic, not yet. I get into return slouch, eying the German. The crowd is restless, there's tension in the cage. I'm ready for anything now—a long count, another underhand serve, Becker transforming into Luke and stage-diving the Royal Box.

The German taps the ball once on the grass. Then he serves—a laser wide. Did I say I was ready for anything?

"40–15."

You'd have thought Parliament passed a law providing complimentary fish and chips every Sunday to Brits age six to ninety-three. I mean the roar heard, this great cacophonous roar. The noise permeates my very being. It reaches down into the core of who I am. I feel it behind my eyeballs and in my scrotum. There's a scary thumping in my chest. I march straight up to Mr. Chair Umpire, gripping my racquet by the throat.

"He quick-served me!"

The decibel level is such that Sverdes has to bend over the armrest. "What was that?"

The clamor dies away in a swift swoop, all wanting to hear the exchange.

"He served before I was ready."

Sverdes finds me amusing. "He bounced the ball. He served the ball. That's how the game is played."

"Are you in on this, too? Is that what this is, you shithead Belgian? You want him in the semifinals, don't you, you prick-face motherfucker you?"

"Point penalty, Blanco. Game over."

"Jesus Christ. It's all about TV ratings. You want equipment abuse? How's this?"

I see the net post like that driver who cuts you off in traffic then gives YOU the finger. I let him have it, the post I mean, whacking it with my stick.

"I want order! I said order!"

Then, like yesterday, I can't see anything, nothing computes. I go blank. And when I come to, hardly any time has transpired. The ruckus is full throttle, Chair Sverdes' neck arteries bulge, and the score is still 5–3. Correction. The point penalty puts us at 5–4. My racquet, however, is no longer fit for play. The head's snapped at three and nine o'clock. Pieces of flower and dirt are stuck in the strings. It seems I took the heads off a box of hydrangeas.

I point a finger at Chair Umpire.

"I'm trying my ass off out here. There's no way I'm being up-staged by him or you. We either replay the point or I quit."

"5–4, fifth set. Changeover in progress."

"That was gamesmanship. You know it. For God's sake, he knows it. And the rest of the fucking world knows it."

"You're very close to a default, Mr. Blanco."

"I want to speak with the referee."

The Chair's earlobes turn a pinched red. No Umpire likes re-linquishing his power, but rules are rules. He snap-motions to where the important types stand around acting like superior species. Out of this blur of Windsor knots hurries a pear-shaped dweeb with thinning brown hair.

"What seems to be the trouble?" he asks in tidy British.

"Are you kidding me? You saw what happened. I want to replay the point."

He glances nervously up at Sverdes. "Sorry, sir. The point stands."

"Then I default."

The referee shoots an anxious glance at the members' area. Sir D. T. Hartley appears, a tall, mannered gent with cruel purple lips. Sir Hartley doesn't trot onto tennis' most hallowed ground—he walks, a hand tucked in his suit pocket.

"I've known you, gosh, since you were a lad, Richard. I don't think your father would approve of this behavior."

"Can we leave him out of this?"

"We can't have this at The All England Club."

"And dumb-ass over there—oh, now I see his halo."

Sir Hartley leans in closer. "You need to pull yourself together."

So we sit, me stewing like a pouty adolescent, Becker polishing off a banana.

"Is the little faggot going to cry?" some asshole yells.

I glare at the Umpire. "You're going to let that stand?"

"Ladies and gentlemen," Sverdes warns. "Patrons using inappropriate language will be asked to leave the Wimbledon grounds."

Time's called. I grab another stick, then walk to the baseline. There, I tilt the cap back. The sun beats down warm and soothing on my forehead. A pigeon darts off a perch, beating its wings. I lose the bird in the glare. We play on, but for me, the game is like a mad dream that continually loops. I'm not out, not yet, but everything's upside down.

Between points, I think about what the Greeks called melancholia. I think about the four humors, especially those associated with the moon, black bile and winter. I think about fate. I think about all you people watching, wherever you are. I know what you're thinking. How can I feel sorry for myself? I'm playing before a crowded house, on the fairest of days, against an all-time great. If that doesn't light a fire under my ass, what will?

This unexpected thing occurs.

The closer Becker comes to overtaking the lead, the more the applause grows for me. When I dig out a drop shot and send the ball around the net post, they rise in tandem. They chant my name. I look at my team. All I see is Brody's empty seat. Why do the people I love most in this world die?

"WE LOVE YOU, RICHARD," someone shouts.

Is this the career envisioned when Dad and I moved to Destafano Tennis Academy? I was to be world champion. Every boy across America was to have my poster hanging on his wall. Teenage girls were supposed to swoon. Ticker tape parades, confetti falling around, snapshots with movie starlets, a WOW bank account, Julian Schnabel originals, Bentleys and Ferraris, a cigarette boat... oh, what's the use.

How we spin things. All those practice sessions, the years spent fine-tuning an arsenal of shots. And for what? We're all useless inertia until a force propels us forward, backward, sideways. Dad would say, right or wrong, you act. You learn to live with your decisions, no matter how much they hurt.

Stop with the pity party, Blank.

Luke's right, you know.

I watch another ball zip past. Becker needs two more to reach the last four, with a shot at the final two, maybe even the Championship, if the gods show favor, his fourth overall. I do my best in helping him reach his goal.

"Love–40."

So, there it is. After two days, a rainout, all the theatrics, a pinched valium, the ghosts in me, Becker has match point. I sling a serve in tight. He steps around the ball then raps it in the corner. "Game, set and match, Mr. Becker. 2–6, 3–6, 7–5, 7–6, 7–5."

There it is.

I'd like to tell you I gave Becker a verbal ass-whooping afterward. I'd like to say I refused his hand. That I was booed all the way to the showers. Scoundrel Blanco lives up to his reputation, that sort of thing. But I'd be lying.

In fact, the spectators cheered as if we both won. I applauded them back. I even took off the armband and tossed it to screaming fans. You should have heard England, then.

Am I sad? What do you think? But part of me has already moved on.

I'm escorted inside. For the victor needs to sign autographs and politic the stadium court with goodwill. There, not ten feet away, holding a white microphone with the NBC logo, stands the bearded leprechaun himself, Bud Collins.

He's dressed flamboyantly; it's his trademark. Today he wears blue-and-white-checked polys, white slip-ons that match a thick rhinestoned belt, and a pink shirt.

"Richard."

"Bud."

"You had an impressive run, Wimbledon quarters, a nail-biter five-setter against a three-time champ in Boris Becker. So, what's next? An action-adventure role like *Escape Velocity 2*?"

"I think I'll stick with this tennis gig a while longer." I ham it up for the camera, twisting the hat sideways, this dope face on, like I'm the coolest white rapper in the world.

"Yo, Bud, it's been quite a week

Everyone counting me out like a freak

Then I go Wimby, final eight

Caught the Adidas and Bengay plate

Closed some doors, others still open

What's a man if he's not half broken?"

A beaming Collins shakes his head. "Always the entertainer, Richard. And it has been a good week, hasn't it? You always play well here. Your father grew up in Barnes, didn't he?"

"That he did, Bud."

"Does London feel like home?"

I give the heart a pat. "The Brits and I have a special relationship."

"You seem to be taking this eighteenth loss quite well. You're not disappointed? You had Becker on the ropes, but he got you again."

"You know, Bud, I'm not. And I'll tell you why. I had my chances out there. I was in the fight. That's what I'm taking from this outcome."

"And the squandered match point?"

"Yeah, it hurts. But it's not like I've never lost before."

"We saw a first out there—Becker's underhand serve. I was reminded of Michael Chang undoing Ivan the Terrible with a similar serve, French Open, 1989. Care to elaborate on how that went down?"

"I took it as a compliment. If he feels so threatened that he needs to serve underhand, then I'm doing my job."

"But you lost the point."

"Apparently, I'm Mr. Enigma."

"Ah, yes," Collins says. "You're referring to the Janet Stipe column this morning."

"Thanks, Janet," I say into the camera. "I guess Becker threw Mr. Enigma a few bones."

"Let's talk about that. You came out swinging like David against Goliath. Did Brody Simmons death affect your play at the end?"

"I thought about Brody the entire way. I tell you what—the crowd chanting his name, man, I appreciated that. But did Brody's death affect the outcome? I don't think so. I have trouble closing out big matches. I think too much. That's no secret anymore, thanks to Janet Stipe." This time I put my finger to my cranium then pretend-click a gun. "Mr. Enigma."

Collins then pivots toward his camera operator with a more wooden face. An assistant motions me forward, my cue to move along, that Becker awaits his turn with the nattily-dressed Collins. "And so the surprising run by journeyman American Richard Blanco comes to an end. What's next in store for the outspoken thirty-one-year old? Only time will tell. But here comes the winner, Boris Becker. It was a close one, Boris, but you prevailed. You have Blanco's number, don't you?"

"I am in his head."

I've pulled back around. I can't resist. "That's not technically accurate."

Bud cracks a smile. "So, the roosters circle."

"Who's in whose head? I'd wager you have two, maybe three voices in that skull of yours. The robotic German goes, 'Serve ball, Boris. Put ball through fence.' Your feminine side is like, 'Like, not to be a bother or anything, but I'm scared, and because I'm scared, I'm playing it safe. Underhand serve the sexy man over there. It's your only hope.'"

The mighty Becker rolls his tired eyes. "Next question?"

Just then, Miles slips in, a hand on my elbow, a paternal look in his old eyes. He steers me along the passage. "At times, you played like a god out there." His voice is low and measured. "Let the rest go."

"You seen Ms. Hamasaki?"

We've reached the entrance to the locker room. "There was plenty to take away from the weekend, Richard."

PART TWO

I stand on a small rise with Brody's youngest son, Remy. The service was nice enough, as funerals go. Remy, hunched over his Ducati, led the procession down Ventura Boulevard. I was moved a few times. Once, after the minister asked those attending to think of Brody at his best, three towering California Oaks stirred, like Brody was answering us. But it wasn't like Dad's funeral. I didn't barely keep it together. My soul didn't feel like it was raked across a lava bed. Today, if anything, I felt removed.

I pass the joint back to Remy. He tokes like a pro, tight-lipped, impressive lung capacity and smooth out-breath. My attention is on the sky. The color is disconcerting, burnt orange above the hills, metallic orange everywhere else. It's like Mars.

"You like the ravens they released? That was my idea," he says, handing me the cannabis cigarette again. Remy has inky stains under his eyes and a considerable paunch for a guy a year removed from USC. "No one knows how much Dad loved ravens."

The smoke feels like burnt fibers in my chest. I cough like an amateur. "I guess I'm out of practice."

Remy smiles for the first time all day. "That's the same shit Dad smoked. He was in heavy pain, man." Our gazes follow the road down the hillside where Brody's casket is hidden inside the dug hole. Fake turf surrounds the ditch so movie execs don't get their Jimmy Choo's soiled. Mom, wearing a provocative red dress, stands next to her best friend, Dawn Matthews. They talk with the minister, this bearded hippy wearing Wayfarers.

"Did you know ravens and crows aren't the same bird? So many people don't know that."

Remy's voice barely registers. Time passes like an ocean liner making steady progress across a topaz sea. "The sky reminds me of *Dune*. Did you read that book, Remy? It's good, but it's not *Do Androids Dream of Electric Sheep?* That novel inspired the greatest science-fiction film ever."

"*Terminator 2: Judgement Day?*"

"*Blade Runner*. Man, this pot is intense."

Remy whittles the joint down to pinch size, never once burning his lips. "Never saw it," he says, flicking the tab in the grass.

"Never saw what?"

"*Blade Runner,* you stoned fuck."

"Dude, tonight, or not tonight, that's not appropriate, but very soon, rent *Blade Runner*, turn down the lights in your movie theatre, and watch the director's cut."

"Director's cut?" Remy's eyes appear to breathe. "There some good sex in it?"

"Just see it."

"No need to get snippy."

I watch Mom hug Dawn. Then her friend makes her way toward the parked cars.

"How's your brother holding up?"

"You mean that Dad split everything fifty/fifty after your mom got her share? He'll be okay."

"It just occurred to me that nobody visits cemeteries. We visit a friend, but we *go* to a cemetery. Then we get the hell out. And why is that? Why do we run the first chance we get? Do we think the dead will leach into us like some industrial sludge?"

This grin erupts on Remy's face. "Dude, you're fucking enlightened. I love that right now."

Mom hears us laugh and points at the limousine.

"I gotta run. How do I look?"

"There's this joke, right?" he says. "One stoner says to another, 'Do I look high, man?' The other replies, 'Only when I open my eyes.'"

"See you later, Remy."

I don my Oliver Peoples then trudge down the hill, trance-like, my body akin to a marshmallow, to where Mom waits in her dress that leaves little to the imagination.

"You're high, aren't you?" she says the moment I walk up. "Did Remy put you up to this? He knows you're not supposed to partake."

I pull out my keys. "I'll see you at Brody's."

"I don't think you should drive."

"I'm fine, Mom."

I merge the BMW onto the 134, a blood orange smear out the windshield. Traffic is slow all the way to the 101 interchange. Antsy—probably the marijuana talking—I exit at Coldwater Canyon Drive, thinking I'll meander my way to Pacific Palisades. The KROQ DJ mentions three wildfires burning near Big Bear Mountain. Then he plays another cut off Beck's new album, *Odelay*. The song is the perfect anecdote for my buzz. Trippy, Dylanesque lyrics, a little *Pet Sounds* thrown in at the end. I crank the volume so high the road begins to vibrate. My head feels spongy, like helium. It takes all my concentration to keep the M5 between the lines. Eventually, I find my way onto Mulholland Drive. I know the road well, its long, slithery shape, the burnished hills and famous addresses. The Russian has a house around here. I thought she might crash the funeral. She liked Brody. And believe me, if the Russian showed, you'd know. She's a head taller than most. She's got that model's gaze. Her mouth is her best feature. Every time she smiles feels like being shot up with adrenaline.

Turning onto Sunset Boulevard, orange still eviscerates the sky. Luke loved the strip with its rock & roll past and fallen heroes. Sunset was our starting off point after he was diagnosed. He'd only go out after dark wearing a hooded jacket and these bleached jeans. He had this sour smell to him that had me cracking the window open. The M5's interior lit up like a runway, we'd cruise Los Angeles in an etch-a-sketch pattern. Some of my fondest memories were of us driving around the city, no plan, no agenda, letting the road be our guide.

I reach Brody's Mediterranean fortress twenty minutes later. The buzz has peeled back a bit. I hand valet the keys, then go to the bar where I'm poured a stiff vodka tonic. Brody was in moving pictures. Three of his highest grossing films were *Killer Zombies In The Valley*,

Return Of Killer Zombies In The Valley, and *Revenge Of Killer Zombies In The Valley*.

Guests walk the grounds. Ice sculptures carved into ravens drip translucent in the gauzy light. A mariachi band plays the theme from his zombies flicks, while Daisy Sunshine, the heroine from his trilogy, and some say Brody's mistress, is passed out on a lounge chair. No one is suspicious of the sky. People recognize me as the guy who failed to honor the man-of-the-hour. I sneak around back. There, I check my phone messages. Trey hasn't called. Last time we spoke she was outside the flat on Gladstone Road. David and I were waiting for airport transport when a sculpted calf emerged from a taxi.

"Tough one yesterday," she said.

I wanted to ask where she disappeared to after the match. Instead, I said, "You win some, you lose some."

"*That's so true,*" she said.

I wasn't clear what Trey meant. Was she talking about the match? Deals gone bad? Us?

"When can I see you again?"

Trey smiled, straightening my tie. This is it, I thought. She's blowing me off for Mr. Finance. She kissed me. "We'll have to see."

Soon David and I were cabbing it to Gatwick. Mom rang. She sounded loaded. She was telling me about her dream that night. Being hungover, I was hardly listening. "But when I woke up, he wasn't there," Mom said. "It was cold and empty. And that's when I knew my Brody was gone forever."

Things got worse on the flight home. It was David and me, First Class, row four. Dinner was served. David drank three scotches before we'd reached open water. When he fell into an apnea-fueled coma, I waved the flight attendant over.

"Heineken," I said.

Three beers later, somewhere over the Atlantic, I opened the *London Times* sports page. I'd purposely held off reading what'd been written, afraid of what I might find. My instincts were correct. For there on page one was this enormous snapshot of yours truly. The photograph took up half the page, shot from across the court, bird's eye view, wide lens. And the colors were tremendous. Imperial greens that gave way to paler jades that washed soft gray and stained white, a speck of red in the crowd like a drop of blood. I stood next to the net post, back toward the camera, in my tennis whites. Sir Hartley listened in. The fans in the background were like a Greek chorus. High above it all sat the heavy-lidded Sverdes.

It was how I looked that shamed me. I appeared enraged (the raised fist didn't help). I was the embodiment of the solitary man, captured in all his impervious captivity. There I was—and there was everyone else. The whole world. And me.

I sat there a moment, a last swig of hops in my cup, the airplane bouncing through flatulence-like air. We were screaming across the stratosphere at five hundred miles an hour. First Class was zonked out, oblivious. Way back in Coach, above air circulation clatter, a baby cried. I raised the window shade. The ocean was black like a city night was never black anymore. Movement off the wing caught my attention. I had to press my forehead against the thick cool plexiglass to see. Luke clung to the airplane's shuddering wing with a kamikaze headband tied around his head. He leveled his middle and forefinger at his pupils, then pointed them at me. I shut the shade and called the attendant over.

"Scotch, please. And keep them coming."

It was a long flight home.

* * *

My eyes latch onto the glittery sky knocking back the last of my vodka tonic. Then it's down the steps around back, past the infinity pool and tennis court, to the guesthouse where Remy lives. This is where Dad lived the last three months of his life. If there was a humane way to go, it was Brody's stronghold in Pacific Palisades. They had Dad's jazz records and books flown in. There was a twenty-four-hour staff on call. Brody and Mom made sure Dad was comfortable, especially at the end. The biggest obstacle after he died, what nearly sunk the plan before it had a chance to fly, was transporting a person, dead from a communicable disease, overseas. Apparently, the airlines worried the corpse might explode or leak mid-flight. It wasn't like an embalmed Dad was strapped down in Coach, but AIDS was a sensitive topic back then. Brody saved the day. He knew the CEO of the now-defunct West Coast Airways. After Brody put the man's son in his next horror flick, Dad was as good as gold, on his way home in a sealed casket, wearing his Sunday best.

Remy's room smells an amalgam of stale reefer and cologne. I refill my glass from his private stash, peruse the medicine cabinet, and then stare at his guitar collection, the shiny Ibanezes, Fenders, Gibsons and Les Pauls. Eventually, my eyes fall prey to the framed Pamela Anderson nudes from her various *Playboy* spreads. Remy's obsessed with P. A. Her initials are tattooed below his clavicle. He's attended her premiers. He's spent a summer at the beach watching her through high-powered binoculars during *Baywatch* shoots. He's even met Pam.

Remy was bouncing at a heavy metal bar on Lankershim when she and Tommy Lee showed up one night. He pretended to have a seizure on the sidewalk. The way Remy explained it, his acting chops were stellar. 911 was called. Tommy Lee took pictures with a disposable camera. And Pam held Remy in her arms and told him to hang in there, that help was on the way. Then Remy kissed her. Not full-on, not like they were rolling around naked in the surf, but with sweet tender lips, his on hers. Then he got up and brushed himself off. He apologized to Pam for any misunderstanding; then held out his hand to her hubby. Remy quit the bouncing gig that night.

I collapse on his waterbed, nearly toppling my drink, then wait for the lapping eddies to subside. How does he sleep on this contraption? This bed is like being tethered to the waves in a sea with no end. I dig my phone out. I should check in with Heather. No, she'll ask questions. She might suspect I'm under the influence. And I haven't used since the Russian dumped my ass. Instead, I dial Trey for like the sixth time in two days.

"Do you ever pick up? Just joking. Christ, what a day. But seriously, I need a woman's opinion. Is wearing a revealing dress at your husband's funeral considered bad taste? Anyway, if you're not in jail or dead, call me."

I top off my cocktail then step back under "Lucy In The Sky With Diamonds." Walking past the tennis court, I notice the clay's swept clean but the lines not, a detail that would never get past the Brodemeister. He loved his tennis like his bimbo's in distress in those campy horror flicks he produced. Speaking of bodacious blondes, Daisy Sunshine still snoozes by the swimming pool. A boy around thirteen pokes at her saline mounds with a twig while his friends egg him on.

"Guys, come on," I tell them. "Have a little respect, okay?"

In London, at Dad's funeral, this Dickens-worthy fog settled in. Lugubrious bells clanged, one after the other, slow and somber. The scene felt baroque, eerie, so English in tone. Here, the bar's in full swing. People mingle like it's a cocktail party. Remy talks with Dustin Hoffman. He's probably giving his ravens versus crows dissertation. Hoffman looks at me and swings an imaginary backhand. Then he taps the dial on his watch and spreads his fingers wide. Five minutes.

I spot Mom across the pool. She strides toward a waiter holding a tray of champagne flutes, picking one off as she goes. She drains the glass then pitches it in the pool. Then she turns in her lace dress. Mom's disappointed, not because she wasn't caught, but that her presence no longer receives the admiration it once drew. Our eyes meet.

"Can't I mourn my Brody with one teeny tiny drink?"

We've met by the cabana. "How many have you had?"

"One, I swear." Mom fluffs her dark hair then flashes a smile the way she does when she's lying. "Fine, two, if you're a stickler for detail. But that's it, no more for this girl." She notices my drink. "You need a pick me up, just ask."

"I don't do that anymore."

She sticks her finger in my cocktail, then gives it a suck. "Oh, that's right, Mr. Deadhead. You're in control."

"Do we have to do this here?"

Mom fidgets with the cross visible in the cranny between her surgically-altered breasts. She's done her eyes so many times her expression is slightly deranged, as if she's always hearing faint applause from some far-off stage.

"Oh, look. It's Anna Nicole Smith taking a nap."

"That's Daisy Sunshine."

"Who wears a miniskirt to a funeral?"

I could ask Mom about her dubious wardrobe choice but hold my tongue. She doesn't know about Brody and his favorite female lead.

Even Dawn Michaels, who's approaching fast, doesn't have the heart to tell her.

"You look good enough to eat, Richard." Dawn and I euro-kiss. A long time ago, she resembled Faye Dunaway. That was before the chin tucks and facelifts, the rhinoplasty. Now, Dawn can't even blink.

"Remy got Richard stoned," Mom says.

"It's no big deal."

Dawn attempts a smile, but her skin won't budge. "You're in pain, Richard. Anyone can see that. But anesthetizing your problems won't make them go away." She touches Mom's arm. "Diane? Samuel asked that I pass on a message. He said he's watching you."

Samuel is Mom's shrink.

"I haven't had a drink, have I dear?"

This is how it is with Mom and me. She's been in and out of several discrete and terribly expensive rehab clinics. "The only thing I've seen her drink this afternoon is Perrier."

Dawn's not so sure. "Your fealty is noted, but do I look like a dumb-ass?" Before I can respond, and it's near impossible reading a plastic surgery freak, another waxen creature approaches. She whispers in Dawn's ear.

"Nice catching up, Richard."

We watch the gossipers thread the crowd.

"What do you think of Dawn's lips? That look is so in right now."

"You are so much more beautiful than that."

Mom looks toward the pool, glimmering like Goldschlager in the afternoon light. Her mouth relaxes like the compliment stuck. I slurp my drink, eying the crowd.

She pulls a cigarette from her cleavage. "Do you have a light? That's right. The professional tennis player doesn't smoke *cigarettes*."

"I heard you came out okay with the lawyers."

"All the money in the world won't bring him back." She gazes up at me. "You don't know what it's like losing a spouse."

"I remember when Dad died."

"He wasn't everything you think he was. He was vain. He could be cruel. His expectations of me—why are we talking about your father?" Mom looks past me when her face brightens. "He's here."

Peter Bogdanovich stands over the appetizer table, holding a plate. He wears an ascot under his velour dinner jacket and these bizarre yellow-tinted glasses.

"How do I look?" She runs her tongue over her teeth. "Any lipstick showing?"

"You look great."

She hands me the unlit cigarette like I'm the paid help. "Wish me luck."

"Break a leg, Mom."

Before she heads over, Mom raises the dress's hem, as if she's wearing a gown and stepping out of a limousine while paparazzi shoot her, point-blank. "Peter," she calls out. "I'm so glad you came."

Dustin strolls over. His crooked smile gives him away.

"I'm not hitting with you, Hoffman. I got enough on my plate."

"But my game is in a real funk. And every time we hit I play as good as the tour guys." I give him an incredulous eye roll. "The lower tier, man. Not you. You're a fucking god."

Mom's laugh echoes across the swimming pool. "You hear about Bogdanovich's new film?"

Dustin looks over and sees Mom's arm draped over the director's shoulder.

"You fix my backhand, and I'll see what I can do. Noon, tomorrow, the Riviera Club, okay, smart-ass?"

"You want me to drive all the way over here?"

"What else are you going to do? Smoke more of Remy's pot?"

"Does the whole world know?"

"By the way, I cried when you lost."

"I'm touched, Dustin."

He thumps me in the chest. "I had money riding on you, you piece of shit."

* * *

I find Remy sitting lotus on the outer lawn. I hand him Mom's smoke. He brings it to his nose, sniffs.

"Dunhill. Not bad."

"You can tell a cigarette brand by its fragrance?" I say, stunned.

Remy sticks the cigarette behind his ear. "It's written on the label."

We both take in the sky again.

"I see you've added a few more Pammy posters."

"She's my girl."

"So, how's that working out?"

"I'm giving her three years to drop Tommy Lee. Or else."

"Hey, I'm taking off. Sorry about your old man. He will be missed."

"Call me if you need any more dope."

I'm walking the gravel path toward valet when I hear screaming. Daisy Sunshine appears, scrambling from behind the tall cypress trees. Boys chase her with squirt guns as big as uzis. Her breasts heave violently under her tiny dress. Way off, short of where the ocean spills out like a knocked over jar of magenta paint, two dark blips—birds—soar toward the flaming orb.

I get in my car and head into the sky.

I don't reach Manhattan Beach until dusk. Down Rosecrans I go, tired from changing time zones, from death, from dope and drink. The orange is breaking apart. The horizon is now flat and black, like a fat tire wrapped around the world. A minute later, I'm waiting at the intersection of Highland and Marine when a skinny young thing pads past in tiny running shorts. The Russian and I ran together. I loved that we had a shared activity. That we were more than a power couple the public saw at celebrity events wearing professional smiles and practiced poses.

In *An Errant Husband*, the Russian's breakout role, she plays a grade school art teacher opposite this womanizing Oxford professor played by none other than Christian Brothers. In the film there's a Leon Trotsky look about him, his hair cropped short and wearing wire-rimmed glasses. He's the Village's resplendent man-whore the Russian falls for not knowing his rakish past. In this romance-drama, she steals his heart.

There's a sex scene. Like all films of this ilk, the scene is carefully rendered. There's a roaring fire. Plush sheets obscure the Russian's bottom. Her long, tangled hair conceals her breasts. There's this moment when she removes Christian Brothers' glasses. The camera zooms in on his eyes so we know he's fallen for her. Then the Russian pulls her hair back into a bun. For ten seconds, the audience gets an eyeful of her naked body. Watching the woman I was in love with having sex, simulated or not, with a man I despised, on a screen two-stories high, in a theatre full of engrossed strangers, despite the tasteful Erik Satie employed as background noise, boy, that tore at my insides like nothing else.

I park in the garage, then sit there several long seconds. My energy concerns me. I feel lethargic, a bit off, like I should be worried about my mental wellbeing. Once in the kitchen, I flick on the cabinet lights. Did you know houses breathe, they creak, they have a smell? Mine, growing up in West LA, smelled of sunlight and freshly cut grass. Dad's place, like old leather. This boxy modern smells stale. Like an old rug in need of a good thrashing.

Piled high on the kitchen counter is mail, catalogs, and a couple month's worth of *Esquire* and *Spin*. My cleaning woman came yesterday. Bonita stocked the shelves with essentials. Evian, fresh fruit, cottage cheese and yogurts. I eat a few grapes then grab the Stolichnaya from the freezer.

The phone machine blinks. I reach over and hit play.

Beep. "David here. Call me, douchebag."

Beep. "As usual, darling, you left without saying goodbye." Mom's voice perks up. "I'm sure you're dying to know how it went with Peter. Don't be surprised if I'm cast in his next feature. I know what you're thinking. I miss Brody very much, but I must go on, Richard. I can't shrivel up and die. Oh, I thought we'd do brunch at the club, like old times. How's eleven sound?"

Beep. "Richard? Janet Stipe. That stunt you pulled with Bud Collins was great. Thanks for the PR. I'm in LA the next few days and was hoping we could meet up. I've got a proposition for you."

Beep. "Your humble agent, again. Where are you?"

Beep. "Claudia here. I'm worried. You haven't checked in. That's not like you. Hope all is well."

Beep. "It's me," Heather says. "I miss you. Call me. Please."

I'm tossing ice cubes in a glass when the phone rings. Could it be the Russian? Is she finally calling to offer condolences? I recognize the number and wince-grin. "Hi."

"I don't want you getting the wrong idea."

The vodka burns my throat. "About?"

"What happened in London."

My reflection in the window is slightly out of focus, double exposure weird. I dim the lights, not wanting to see my frayed image.

"Can I ask you something? Do you cheat on him often?"

Trey makes this taxing breath. "I'm not in a place, personally, professionally, emotionally, even logistically, to commit."

"That's a lot of adverbs in one sentence, Trey."

"How would it work? I live in New York."

"I'm flying into the city tomorrow."

"You are?"

Of course, this isn't true. Well, until it is. "I thought I mentioned it after I pulled out the other night. By the way, I'm still goosebumps from the romp in bed. You?"

"Are you really coming to New York?"

"Why don't we meet for dinner and discuss?"

"I'm on my way to Newport."

My mind, drained as it is, races forward, aligning dots, forming connections.

"Oh, yeah? My agent's trying to get me in Newport, last minute. So, what do you say? Dinner tomorrow?" When Trey's not forthcoming, I plunge on like a drunk navigating a tight spot in a bar. "You have to eat, right? We could do sushi, dim sum, burgers, whatever."

"I'm on the Upper West Side. And you? Where are you?"

I'm sucking rather loudly on an ice cube. "The Village."

"Now you're talking a few hours."

"A few hours to get Uptown? Maybe if I'm crawling on my hands and knees."

On and on it goes. Trying to arrange dinner with Trey Hamasaki is like making plane reservations with a ticketing agent who speaks Cantonese. She thinks screwing me is a conflict of interest. I focus on the near present, like securing the name of the Newport hotel she's staying. Then Trey says I'm too much to handle.

"You mean in the sack? Are you talking about that little leg move of mine?"

No sooner have I hung up that Luke's chomping in my ear. *What are you doing? She gave you an exit strategy, Blank. And what do you do? You dig your own grave?*

I walk from room to room, tumbler in hand, turning on lights. Did I mention I live in a glass house? It was the Russian's idea. She took everything after the breakup. The Saarinen dining table, the Ligne Roset section couch, my art collection. I thought if I was generous, if I didn't get upset, if I acted all adult, she'd come back. So I gave her her goddamn pick. And the Russian picked and picked. It's simpler, really, if I tell you what she left behind. The Le Corbusier chaise (I guess Christian Brothers is allergic to cowhide) and my Bang & Olufsen music system.

You're probably wondering what the Russian and I had in common other than jogging. Money, probably. And I like money. But being the next Bill Gates doesn't interest me like it did the Russian. She's an artist first, and a talented one at that, but she's also smitten with the almighty dollar. Why do you think she's with Christian Brothers? His family is only the third-largest oil producer in the UK. He's rolling in dough.

I'm heading upstairs for a steam when the phone rings again. Has Trey changed her mind? Might phone sex be on the menu tonight? Grinning, I check Caller I.D. Heather? This is just like her. She's got serious homing capabilities. Whenever I've done something I shouldn't, she's always on the line.

"Hey, hey, hey, hey."

"You sound in a good mood. How was the funeral?"

"Very interesting."

"He was a special guy, huh?"

"You should have seen Mom. She wore this dress. It was like something Sophia Loren would wear. Cleavage city, you know what I'm saying? And this was her husband's funeral. I was like, 'Really, Mom?'" I wait for Heather's reaction. She usually gets a kick out of Mom's Hollywood travails. Only she doesn't say anything. "You still there?"

"Are you drunk?"

I continue up the stairs, gripping the phone harder. "Why would you say that?"

To get to the steam, you must walk through the master suite. The bath is spacious—black marble, a steam/shower big enough to hold a slat-wood bench. I turn the switch on, avoiding the mirror, and then walk back into the bedroom. "Maybe I've had a few. I'm also looking on the bright side, Heather. Have you thought of that?" I throw my suit coat at the bed—miss. "Yes, Brody's dead. Yes, my mom's hurting. But maybe she needs a positive role model right now. If that's shocking, if that's too much to handle, well, I feel sorry for you."

"You don't sound like yourself."

I start back downstairs, noticing the glass empty. "I'm just exhausted."

"When are you coming home?"

"How many times have I told you—LA is home. Bradenton is a training hub."

"First, you're in a good mood. Now you want to fight."

I let out a frustrated sigh. "Can I call you tomorrow?"

I'm not proud hanging up. In fact, I'm punching her numbers into the handheld when the machine goes off like a beating heart. It's my agent.

"I want in Newport, David, a top seed. And a first-round bye."

"Okay, Mr. Big Britches."

"Just do it, okay?"

"Does this have anything to do with Ms. Hamasaki?"

"And get me a fat guarantee."

"You know what this sounds like? Spinning plates."

Back upstairs again. I check the steam's temperature. The phone rings as I swig from the bottle. This time I let it go through to voice mail. "Richard? Try not to be late tomorrow. I've got an appointment at one o'clock with my hair colorist. Night-night."

Hair highlights? Schmoozing at a funeral? How could Mom do that? This was the man who paid Dad's considerable medical bills. This was the man who stood up when asshole fans screamed out, *Where's your faggot Daddy, Blanco?* Where's Claudia when I need her? What time is it in Florida? She won't mind that it's late. Claudia adores me. While the call rings through, I sprawl out on the Le Corbusier. It feels more official that way.

"Hello?"

I definitely woke her up. "Claudia, it's me."

"Do you know what time it is?"

"Why give me your private number if you don't want me to use it?"

She yawns. "You tax me, Richard. You really do."

"Do you think I have trouble juggling things?"

An audible sigh comes over the line. "This couldn't wait until morning?"

"Please, Claudia."

"Everything in its right place. That's our motto."

Therapy is a game, like everything else. What we reveal, what remains hidden. I don't bring up talking ghosts, nor my new friend. Claudia would say Trey sounds like an impulse buy at Neiman Marcus. And spinning plates? Fuck, the madness of living. You know something else? I hate this chair. It's too comfortable. I'm convinced the Russian left it to spite me. So, every time I walk into the bedroom, I'd know she duped me. Everything about this house *is her.* I thought the day of closing was only the beginning. We wanted the same things. We'd eventually sell this place and buy up. We'd hedge money to earn money. We'd take chances when others played it safe. We'd risk it all.

You want to know why I didn't fight harder to win her back? Because I went into a depression. It was so bad Claudia sent an Academy coach to Los Angeles to bring me in. I remember the dude ringing the doorbell. I'd been indoors so long the light hurt my eyes. I'd grown a beard. The day we left for the airport I wore flip-flops with this buttery creme Versace suit the Russian insisted I buy. I was a freaking kook. By this point, I'd written her umpteen letters. How she'd broken me in two. How my life held little meaning anymore. I went on about Dad and AIDS and how unfair life was, how I didn't know how to go on living. Then I wrote *Christian Brothers? Really?*

Did you know the Russian also wanted her ears surgically altered? She thought they stuck out too far. Can you believe it—her ears? The Russian modeled swimsuits for *Sports Illustrated*. The Russian was *un-fucking-believable*. But her ears embarrassed her. That's what LA does to a person. This city makes you wish you lived in someone else's skin. Can I blame Mom for turning into the person she is? Or look at me. Look at my glass house. *Everything rots.* A voice jumps out like a mean dog on a short leash. I'm in the steam, sticky and naked, leaching toxins. Below my feet is the vodka bottle. Good old smelly Luke sits next to me on the bench. *Everything dies. So live, be present, do drugs. Screw anything you want. Screw a hole in a wall if it makes you happy.*

"I feel… sick."

The trembling apparition draws a heart in the foggy glass with its skeletal finger. Then the thing slashes a mark through it.

I pause a moment pushing down a sour taste of nausea. "Why are you here?"

I'm bored.

"You're bored?"

Yes, bored.

I nod off when my head snaps to. Luke still hovers like a dark gauzy rag.

"Aren't their other troubled souls you can bother?"

The ghost swivels its bulbous head. *Do you think being here is about me?*

The thing shows its silvery teeth.

And I scream. I scream like a boy who's lost his dog in a fire. The bile rises fast and hot, wanting a way out. I topple the bottle, exiting the sauna. Then I'm charging for the toilet, vomit in hand.

JULY 11, 1996, 3:34PM

NEWPORT CASINO, NEWPORT, RHODE ISLAND

Meathead is gargantuan. From where I stand—some seventy-five feet of latitudinal court space away—he looks more NBA forward than tennis player. My eyes move past him to the scattered spectators fanning themselves under the deadbeat sky. Above them, the international flags that circumnavigate the stadium hang like carcasses. Just before Meathead goes into his windup, my attention is diverted once again. This time it's the tunnel entrance where Trey stands wearing a thousand-yard stare.

The Serb slams another serve home.

"Hey, I wasn't ready."

"30–15." Even the umpire, this Hitchcockian bodhisattva in Sergio Tacchini, sounds bored.

God, I hate my opponent. I hate how huge he is. I hate his unimaginative play. I hate his sheared haircut and how his shorts ride up his butt. I hate how I can hit every shot in the canon, yet today I'm lucky to hold serve. The problem with players like Meathead is they can eke out a comfortable living owning one world-class shot. The guy can't even properly roll over his backhand. We haven't had a single proper rally, well, unless you count the warm-up. If tennis isn't careful, it's going to double-fault itself into a third-world sport. The networks will show taped, abbreviated versions on obscure cable channels at godawful hours with really awful camera angles.

Meathead clobbers another serve past.

"If history repeats, we should expect another ace."

The big man doesn't disappoint.

"Game, Drabomonovic. He wins the first set 6–3."

We sit, the knucklehead and me.

Today's program has Meathead at twenty-three years of age, provenance Belgrade, Serbia, world ranking #227. I, on the other hand, have a projected #28 ranking and am seeded #2. Meathead played the qualies then won a tightly contested three-setter yesterday. That same morning the Newport tournament people wrote me a big fat check for twenty-five big ones. Just for walking on stadium court and putting on a show. That's sort of how this match feels—like a show. And the Newport Casino is a tremendous place. I wish this tournament mattered more. Thirteen grass courts, a storied clubhouse, the International Tennis Hall of Fame. Did you know the first US Lawn Tennis Championships were held here in 1881? It's the one tournament other than the US Open where being American feels special.

Desperate, I gulp a Coca-Cola then knock out a few kanga-roos—knee-chest bumps—to get the juices flowing. It's a miracle I'm playing tennis after what happened in New York. I'd flown to JFK the morning after I got off the phone with Trey, bloody hang-over and all. I thought we'd start up where we left off in London, you know, a quiet dinner in SoHo, a roll in the hay, no crisis, no apparitions slipping through walls. I was staying at Dad's apartment on Bleecker Street. I figured if there was a place that explained who I was, that spoke to me like it had Dad, it was the third-floor walk-up in Greenwich Village. In preparation, I'd spent the afternoon scrubbing floors and bleaching bathrooms. I alphabetized Dad's albums. I'd even arranged his bookshelves on the color spectrum. At this point, Trey hadn't returned my calls. Mom called twice, as had Dustin Hoffman. Neither was pleased with me blowing them off. Even Janet Stipe left a message. Believe it or not, but she was interested in writing the story of my life. I had a good laugh after hearing that. If there was a person I should have spoken with, it was Claudia. She was afraid I'd had a relapse. Which meant she wanted me nearby. If I refused, she'd speak with Coach. I know—breach of confidentiality—but that was how things went at the Academy. The last thing I needed was my privileges rescinded. I figured I better call Claudia's office, control the feed, as David says. Joanne had picked up. She was from Baton Rouge and an employee since the early years.

"Is the big lady around?"

"Richard?" she said in her southern drawl. "When do we get the pleasure of seeing your acquaintance in person?"

"It depends on how Newport goes."

"You can say that again, sugar."

"How's the Academy?"

"Your blonde friend came in the other day. She made a stink."

I was dusting the oil painting over the firebox of the young man at the public bath, nude but for a towel draped over his arm, when I froze.

"She said Dr. Grobert was filling your head with nonsense."

"Did Coach find out?"

"You can bet your life he did. The Academy doesn't like a live wire running around, even if she's pretty as a peach and Richard Blanco's main squeeze."

What was Heather thinking? Her daughter was on full scholarship, thanks to me. And she was overstepping my authority?

"Hold on," Joanne said. "I'll patch you through."

"Richard?" Claudia said, coming onto the call.

"I met a woman." Now, why did I say that?

"We've been down this road before."

"Why can't you be happy for me?"

"A couple years ago, you met Marta. It wasn't long before you'd spent a considerable portion of your earnings on that house in California."

"This is nothing like that."

"You thought she was sleeping with Jeff Bridges."

"Christian Brothers. And she was sleeping with him."

"My point is, Marta may not have been everything you thought she was."

"I'm being more careful."

"What about Heather? Where does she fit into all this?"

"I heard she came to see you."

"She did."

"And?"

"And she was upset. She conveyed her feelings. Look, this behavior—womanizing, acting like a brat during competition—you know it hurts you. Maturity is your biggest challenge. Until you figure that out, you're going to struggle."

"This woman might be the one. How do I know this? Because I can feel it in my bones, Claudia. She reminds me of the Russian. Except that she's not the Russian, if you know what I mean. And even if you don't approve, I don't care. I really don't..." I'd lost my train of thought. "What were we talking about?"

"You're manic, Richard. I hear it in your voice."

"I'm in love, Claudia. You hear love in my voice."

I stuck my head out the living room window and started belting out "The Love Boat" theme at the New Yorkers passing on the sidewalk below.

"Richard?" Claudia yelled into the receiver.

"Yes?"

"Please listen carefully to me," she said slowly. "You have that Xanax prescription, right?"

"I'm fine."

"I think it's best that you come to Florida. Remember what happened last time?"

I thought about the Trey phone call I was 110 percent sure I'd get. "If I take the Xanax, and it settles me down, are you okay with me playing Newport?"

Claudia didn't say anything at first. "Will you promise you'll start taking it?"

I sighed theatrically. "*I promise.*"

"And if you're not feeling yourself, you'll come to Florida?"

"Deal."

* * *

Back on Stadium Snooze-fest, it's the start of the second set. I spin a backhand high over the net. It lands close to Meathead's baseline. There's a delayed call.

"Out!"

"What do you mean, out? That ball was on the line." I'm half speaking to the linesman, half to the Chair.

The Chair's myriad chins spill down his chest like a mudslide. "The call stands."

I look at my opponent for help. "How'd you see it?" Surely, low-ranked Meathead will set things straight. He shrugs and shuffles his large feet. "Fine. Whatever. So much for honor and sportsmanship and goodwill."

I give the back-judge a heartless glare, then throw in a high-percentage kicker that Meathead wallops. You could say he shoves the ball down my esophagus like a toilet plunger.

"Love–thirty."

"THIS SUCKS."

"My shot I think very good," Meathead says to the crowd.

I motion the immense animal to the net. His eyes are crude-oil black. "You know you're winning, right? And you want to verbally joust with me? I can play that game, friend."

"You forget score." Meathead's English is slow and halting.

"What you fail to understand is you play like a barbarian. Like you learned the game at boot camp. Your problem is you lack nuance. Your game lacks verve."

"Stupid American."

The Chair shifts in his seat. His flesh squeezes through the chair's slats like gelatinous goo. "Let's cool it, okay, gentlemen?"

I follow with two authoritative serves Meathead swats in the net. This is more like it. This is how the #2 seed dissects a guy two-hundred-some digits back. This type of play gets me inside Trey Hamasaki's silky panties tonight. Then I double-fault. Jesus, what's wrong with me?

This isn't how I imagined the day unfolding. In fact, I woke up quite energetic, this after my episode two nights ago. I thought I'd win easily. Afterward, in the media tent, I'd talk to the emotions pouring through me in my five-set thriller with Becker. I'd answer questions about my next opponent, the Irishmen, Doyle. I'd sign autographs; ham it up in photo ops. On my way to the showers, I'd tell it to Trey straight: London was great, but I can't be a gigolo my entire life.

At advantage out, I gamble and toss in a change-up, a soft tumbler. Meathead goes off his feet, swinging for the fence. His shot sails the court, the backdrop, the first ten rows of seats. A murmur moves through the seats that sounds like rustled papers. Me, I toss up an imaginary ball and pretend to whack it out of the park. This perks up the spectators for the first time all day. Meathead walks up, wagging a finger. Out of his mouth comes this tangled gibberish.

Exasperated, I look at the Chair. "You hear that? That's disgraceful, is what it is. I can't even repeat it, sir."

The Chair drops his gaze. "I didn't know you spoke Serbian, Mr. Blanco."

"He swore, your eminence."

"The score is deuce."

"You might warn him, sir."

"I'll keep that in mind."

Meathead hasn't left his spot at the service-T. "Blanco say terrible things."

"Now, that's funny coming from you."

"It is truth."

"Truth? You want the truth? You suck, dude."

The Chair Umpire runs his fingers over his shiny dome. "That's enough."

Okay, that comment isn't exactly true. *Meathead's not that bad.*

I take the long way back. A Japanese photographer shoots me with a long lens Pentax. You see, I'm big in Japan. Play continues. I start to find my tempo. There is a rhythm to this mad game; otherwise, it would be random and pointless, two men in silly tight shorts, a yellow ball tied to an invisible string, the jarring spurts of energy, the lulls in between. Trey hollers words like *focus* and *dig in, man*, and finally, finally, I start playing better. I get my first break of the day when a Serb passing shot soars long. Then Meathead does the unthinkable. He brings his Yonex Super RQ 1000 down on his thigh. The stick snaps in half like it's a pencil. Then he bonks himself on the head. Now blood runs down Meathead's forehead and onto his shirt. I grab my towel and hurdle the net.

"Put pressure on the wound."

"This nothing," he says, taking my towel. "I got bullet hole in stomach. You want to see?"

"Maybe later."

Meantime, help is called. Band-aids are put in place. The trainer takes Meathead through several cognitive tests—balancing on one leg, spelling his name backwards, walking foot over foot along the tramline. I lay down on the grass in the fetal position and suck my thumb. Meathead is finally cleared to continue. And we play two, *two*, stupendous points, the last an incredible sprint has Meathead laying himself out horizontal for my passing shot. And his band-aids fall off. He goes through the same routine with the trainer. This time gauze is wrapped around his head. Now Meathead is an ogre in a crooked tiara.

"What?" he says, seeing my grin. "I look stupid?"

Meathead finally feels the enormity of the situation and starts spraying balls like a cracked garden hose. At one point, I knock off ten points in a row. I win the second, then take the first three games of set three when Meathead breaks a string. No big deal, right? Every serious tennis player carries at least three identical sticks, all perfectly balanced, all precisely tensioned. Not Meathead. He brought only the two, the first splintered and in pieces by his chair.

"You can use one of mine."

Meathead is grateful. He gives me a pat on the back, then accepts the stick like a gift from a sitting president. I finish him off in no time.

"Game, set, match, Mr. Blanco. 3–6, 6–2, 6–0."

We meet at the net. "You really should get that cut looked at."

"See?" He lifts his shirt then sticks a finger in this dark hairy hole along his ribcage. "This from bullet. This hurt."

"Blech," I say. "Hey, I'm sorry for saying you sucked before."

"I understand part of game. Here, hold this." Meathead hands me back the racquet he borrowed then starts unwinding the tape around his head. "Say, you want we play doubles? I am in draw if I find partner."

Oh, why not. Meathead seems harmless enough. And hey, it could be worse. He could be plotting my demise. Like chopping me into travel-size pieces, flying my remains to Belgrade, where I'd be fed to starving cousins.

"Okay."

"We practice tomorrow?"

"How's ten?" I glance toward the tunnel, where Trey awaits.

"Ten good."

I leave my new doubles partner to applause then enter the tunnel. Trey leans against the wall in a smart-looking business suit tight in bust and hip. She claps slowly, like she's not too impressed.

"Sorry about New York," she says.

I shrug it off.

"Dinner tonight?"

"On one condition," I say, running my eyes down her outfit.

"Oh?" she says.

"Sign me."

Trey smiles then saunters off without me. "Good one, Blanco."

I blow off my post-match duties (press conference, an interview with a local TV station) and hop on the Vespa I rented for the week.

My thermo racquet bag is hung over my shoulders like a backpack. I spin down Ocean Avenue not ten minutes since I deconstructed the Serb. Warm, comatose sea air stings my eyes. The sun is a low burst of energy. Everything I pass—the Colonial Revivals on ludicrously wide streets, the geometrically-shaped hedges—are painted sepia. Life feels surreal.

I motor past Cliff Walk, the Bellevue Avenue of a far more gilded age, along the rocky coast, and when I circle back into town, traffic is motionless. I bypass a summertime jam and run the champagne scooter up a sidewalk, past a French pastry shop, laughing the whole way.

I have an enormous desire to flee. Run red traffic lights, punch it down flat straightaways, gun it over cobblestone alleys at a gyrating fifty miles an hour with the hopes of maiming one of the multifarious New England prepsters strolling the streets. I think crazy, outlandish thoughts… driving the Vespa over a high cliff, stealing a case of Evian from 7-Eleven, streaking through the historic district, asking Heather for her hand in marriage. Then my mind shifts gears, and I'm defaulting tomorrow's quarterfinal and disappearing somewhere in the Caribbean where pellucid water and warm trade winds flow, Trey Hamasaki at my side. We'll sleep naked and we won't have tan lines and our backs will be dark and strong. We'll be frugal and listen to reggae and snorkel reefs and run along the beach to stay trim and make love in the afternoon when the light cascading through the windows is delicate and ripe, a feast for the eyes. I want to spin past things. I don't want to blink. To swallow the world in a single blurred pass. Yes.

"Excuse me, but are you okay?"

I blink awake in a rupture of late afternoon sunlight. There's a man with an adolescent boy standing on the sidewalk.

"Oh, you mean the scooter. I can move it."

The kid tugs on his dad's hand. "He's one of the tennis players."

I look down genially at the boy. It might be nice having a couple rug-rats one day. I remember the tickets in my bag. They give players a few gratis in the early rounds. "You interested in seeing a little action?" I've already pulled off my thermo and unzipped the side pocket. I hand the dad two tickets. "They're good all week. Check it out."

"Wow. Thanks. You look familiar. Who are you, exactly?"

"Richard Blanco."

"Are you playing this afternoon?"

"I got lucky today." I turn the key over and throttle the Vespa. "But tomorrow's another day. So long."

I bump down the curb then shoot up the street. Soon, I lose interest in riding around. Valet parks the scooter around back. Not long after, I'm stalking the hotel corridor, keycard in hand. I throw my stuff on the floor then lie down. I must drift off because the hotel phone rings, waking me. "Hello?"

It's the Serb. He confirms tomorrow's practice time. "We go out tonight. Dinner, dance club. You and me. I pay."

"Are we playing a tournament or discoing the night away?"

"We need bonding to be effective team."

"What time is it?"

"7:14. I stop by in one hour. Goodbye." And the Serb clicks off the line.

I thought it might be Heather. She forgives easy. She doesn't hold grudges. And I can be a real shit sometimes. I dial her apartment, but no one answers. Frustrated, I hang up.

Several hours later, the Serb and I are standing in a Byzantine-influenced ex-library converted into a dance club called Glitter Life. On both sides of the crown-domed entry, two stairwells rise to a parapet where a loutish bouncer stands erect, searching for terrorists and ugly people. Deeply rhythmic, heavy bass music throbs. It sounds like the heartbeat from a giant beast. The Serb wears a clean shirt, ironed jeans with fancy stitched pockets, and a square bandage on his head wound. He also carries a man purse. Before clubbing, he'd bought dinner at a corner pub. I ordered a grilled chicken sandwich, side salad and Perrier. I thought I'd better set a good example and abstain. I also got the feeling the Serb wasn't flush with cash.

"Thirty dollars cover," the bouncer says. "Each."

The Serb almost swallows his tongue.

"Let me get this."

"No, no. I pay. I want to do this, Richard."

Once inside, the Serb goes to buy us beers. The club is jammed tight with drunk townies, girls down from Boston for the weekend, and two-thirds of the Hall of Fame Tennis Championships men's draw. Trey even strolls past. I catch her by the wrist and pull her in close.

"What are you doing here?" I yell in her ear.

She throws her arms around my neck. "Looking to get laid."

"You've had a few."

She turns to the guy next to her, an Italian kid with jelled curls and wearing a super tight sweater. "You wanna dance?"

He looks Trey up and down, too stupid to notice me. Then he smiles at his entourage. "Fuck yeah."

"Aren't we a little old for games?" I shout after her.

Soon, the Serb returns. We toast our Michelob Golden Lights, then lean over the rail, watching the action. He bumps my shoulder, eying Trey. "That your chick?"

"She can do whatever the fuck she pleases," I tell him. "And no one says chick anymore."

"They do on *Miami Vice*."

"That was so ten years ago, man. We say woman or lady friend, if they're older."

"Like your lady friend out there?"

"Are you a comedian or tennis player?"

Every straight guy inside Glitter Life walks past Trey with his tongue hanging out. Even my Irish opponent saunters by, impressed. What am I doing? Glitter Life is a joke. Drinks flow. If you listen carefully, the conversation has a vomit stench. The thump, thump, thump is a broken record of sobs. Nothing stops the big beats. They are relentless, like serial killers, like natural selection. Glitter Life reeks of cheap cologne and gauche. Me? I'm $45,000 richer. I play Doyle next, and this is grass, grass is impeccable, grass is clean, Doyle can't hurt me on grass.

"She good dancer."

"That she is."

"Very sexy. You mind if I..."

"If you what?"

"You know." The Serb lowers his head then rubs his dark hair back to front in a shy, charming way.

"No, you may not. Look, rookie. Rule#1—no women. You don't look. You don't touch. Women cloud our judgment. They make us weak. A player starting out can't afford to be careless."

He smacks my arm. "That woman got you good, huh?"

"We should go. We got a big day tomorrow."

I'm back in my room twenty minutes later. I scrub my face and clean the teeth. Then I scroll channels. Nothing interesting on TV, so I boot up my Mac Powerbook thinking Heather might have left a message on AOL. I listen while the phone screeches and clicks and clicks and screeches. Then a man's chipper voice says, "Welcome. You've got mail."

I click on my Inbox.

> You left me high and dry. Why didn't you save
> me?

I touch the device's keyboard, then start typing.

> You mean it didn't work out with Rocky Balboa?
>
> I saw you scootering around today. Why
> didn't you ask me for a ride?
>
> With the outfit you were wearing, you'd have put
> me in quite a tizzy.
>
> ....you busy?
>
> Can't.
>
> Why?
>
> I want to win this tournament.
>
> Hmm. I'm bummed. But I like a man who
> knows what he wants. Ciao.

I close my laptop, sighing.

Two nights ago in Manhattan, when it was clear Trey wasn't dropping by Greenwich Village to see yours truly, I'd gone out for a bite to eat. After Claudia's caveat, I stayed clear of Washington Square, thinking crowds and possible episodes weren't a good match. It was summer in the vertical city. Tourists roamed the streets, carrying shopping bags, looking exhausted in the face. The winds were high and warm. And I hadn't taken the Xanax because I didn't like Claudia telling me what to do.

I was walking the Avenue of the Americas, where the streets were wide and you got a sense of scale against the backdrop of skyscrapers. I turned down a leafy side street in the West Village. It was the sort of place Harry and Sally from the film with the similar name might have settled down. Or maybe Heather and me. A few blocks later, I sat down at a sidewalk table of some bistro. Interestingly, my waitress was Asian. I reeled off pickled vegetables, steamed rice, and grilled pork seasoned in sesame oil, then handed her the menu. The sky was bloodshot. Twilight was settling over the city.

"Busy?" Her name tag said Naomi.

"The usual," she said. "Hot washcloth?"

"Okay, Naomi."

Why was I interested in Asian women all of a sudden? Just so you know—I've had all kinds. But I always come back to motherly figures. Freud says we're wired for our mothers. That was Heather and the Russian before her.

Another staff person set my food on the table. I brought the bowl to my mouth and shoveled the sticky rice in. Naomi came around and asked how my meal was.

"You smell neat."

"Neat?" she said, giving me an entertaining look.

"I bet you bathe daily."

"I try to, yeah."

"On average, I bathe thrice, daily."

"I guess you're neat, too."

"It's because of my job. I play pro tennis." I pointed at the scar on my forehead as if the tiny red mark were proof of my professional status. "See this? Carcinoma."

"That's scary. You're what, thirty-five?"

"Thirty-five? I'm thirty-one, sister." I stopped. "Ah, I get it. You're pulling my leg."

What if I took this girl back to the place where Dad first styled his hair in a feathery Rod Stewart plume? Where he took men in, as lovers and friends. Where he finally lived the life of a dignified gay man in America. I could tell Naomi how I sometimes walked into the apartment, and all I did was think about him, his crusty old slippers, his silver comb, that old lounger he read in. Or the times I thought change was in the air. Either sell the six-unit building for a considerable profit or gut the top floor and start over. Then the memories would come back, tears would fill my eyes, and I couldn't fathom changing one goddamn thing.

My phone rang.

Remember what I said about Heather and telepathy? Well, guess what?

"Hey, I heard you paid Claudia a visit."

"She doesn't get you."

I picked through the vegetables until I snagged an orange pepper. "In some circles I'm called Mr. Enigma."

"Do I embarrass you?" Heather said.

Finished, I pushed the bowl away. I got Naomi's attention by scribbling a pretend pen in the air. "Why would you say that?"

"Then why don't we go somewhere together?"

Naomi walked over with the bill. I watched her go with my Mastercard, her hips bucking up and down like a mama giraffe. "What were you thinking? Vegas?"

"I want to plan a trip, Richard. Someplace like Alaska. I want to see humpback whales and the ice fields."

"What ice fields? I see you in a bathing suit, Heather. I'll go out on a limb and say the entire male species feels the same way." I felt like a jerk, sounding so superior, so smug. The thing was, we'd have a fantastic go at it, sightseeing the world.

"You're not being very nice."

Here came Naomi. I signed the check, a 25 percent tip. It was awkward being on the phone. "Just a second." I clamped a palm over the mouthpiece. "Nice talking with you, Naomi."

"Maybe see you around."

We made meaningful eye contact. Then I started for 7th Avenue and its worn down facades, the Twin Towers looking blanched and lonely in the evening sky. I glanced at the receipt. Naomi wrote her phone number and the time she was off. I shook my head, grinning.

"What were we talking about?"

"You know what? Fuck you, Richard. And don't even think about coming around when you get back in town." Heather severed the line.

This took me by surprise. It really shook me. I was a block from Naomi and her neat smell when I started crying uncontrollably.

I made a beeline for Bleecker Street, formulating a plan as I went. Once inside Dad's place, I'd lock the front door, draw a bath, turn down the lights, and put on soothing music, something like ambient Brian Eno. Then I'd pray the pill was enough to keep me on the level. I was at an intersection, waiting for the light to change. I still held the crumpled receipt. Another idea came to me. Maybe Naomi was the answer like Trey had been in London. Then I thought—was this what Claudia meant about me acting more grownup? I had another serious moment, fighting back sobs. I got out my phone and left word with Heather that I was sorry, that lately it felt like I was living in another person's skin, that I'd work harder at being a better boyfriend. I was crossing onto Houston Street when Dad stepped off the opposite curb dressed like it was 1976. I'm talking bold polyester shirt, high-rise slacks and platform shoes. He was humming "The Love Boat" theme.

Well done, son, he said, strolling past.

Why did I do that? Why did I need a phantom dressed like John Travolta in *Saturday Night Fever* to congratulate me on being sort of, kind of good?

JULY 12, 1996, 9:07AM

COBBLESTONE STREET, NEWPORT

So, quarters today, semis tomorrow, final on Sunday afternoon. It's been a long time since I thought I could win a professional tournament. Some players never look ahead when it comes to the draw. They think it's bad luck. Others stand over the names like a cartographer mapping roads for a new world. They make educated guesses, top to bottom. What player has the easiest road to the final, where the upsets lie, if there's a Cinderella lurking in the shadows.

I fall into the first category. I want to know who I play next. And that's where I stop. Otherwise, well, you know, the head starts yammering away.

I take the machine in. And I could walk. It's only six blocks. But why not? Riding the Vespa is like dating beautiful women. Not everyone has one, and most people stop whatever they're doing when you race past. Security has me park the scooter along the towering indoor center wall. I enter the player's lounge, looking for the Serb. Standing by the entrance is my journalist friend.

"If it isn't Janet Stipes."

"*Stipe*," she says, enunciating the P. "Like the lead singer in R.E.M."

"Michael and I go way back. He and Luke Scream were pals."

Stipe is mid-forties and a little on the plump side. Her hair is done up in a severe vanilla-almond bob.

"You've a compelling story, Richard. Playboy, gay Dad, sensitive athlete in a sports world chockfull of testosterone and homophobia."

"How did you know I was playing Newport?"

"Your agent told me."

"Did he now?"

"Have you thought about my book proposal?"

"I have… Stipes."

She smiles at my little dig. "And?"

I look past her, into the lobby din, at my tennis brethren. The brooding Slavs and handsome Spaniards, my loud, brash American peers, the contemplative Japanese. I look at these young men, and this wave of nostalgia does a number on my insides. It wasn't that long ago that I was wet behind the ears like them. And look at me now—the reigning old-timer, at least in this year's Hall of Fame Championships. Soon this whole fantastic draining way of life will be over.

I spy the Serb. "If you're interested," I tell Stipe. "I'm playing doubles after the Doyle match."

"With whom?"

"A guy named Drabomambo something or other."

"You're incorrigible, Richard."

Directly behind Stipe is an easel advertising the US Open in late August, featuring pictorials of the game's biggest stars. "Do you have a felt-tip pen?" She looks in her bag. "Excellent. Now, don't move." I reach past Stipe's dangling earring and give Boris Becker a black eye and handlebar mustache.

Stipe gazes at my artwork. "Still up to your old tricks?"

"See you around."

I slip past her then wander by the food digs. I'm intrigued with Stipe's offer. Who wouldn't be? But come on, me the focus of a book? I'm nil and fifty-three in major championships, sports fans. I may be interesting as characters go, but who wants to read about my neurosis or failed relationships? No, that sounds more like a scabrous novel.

Spotting me, the Serb rises from his chair like an Army recruit. The wound's been sutured closed. He unzips his warmup jacket. "You like?" He wears my exact outfit, even the socks match. "We look like team, no?"

"Or dorks." The Serb isn't sure what I mean. "I'm kidding, man. We better go. We only have the court for an hour."

A golf cart buzzes us over to the practice courts. I sit in the passenger seat, the Serb squats in back, holding the bags. We talk doubles strategy—crosscourt returns, exploiting the court's middle, energetic net play. Soon the driver skids to a stop. Another company man opens the gate, still another holds back the teenybopper crowd. McEnroe and his brother Patrick are putting their gear away when we step onto the grass. John, retired several years now, still hits with the guys when he's in town broadcasting. Patrick is seeded fifth. He's done alright for himself, considering his famous older sibling.

"Hey, Blank." Johnny Mac extends his hand. "I thought you had Becker beat."

I introduce the Serb.

"It is my extreme pleasure to meet you, Mr. McEnroe."

Patrick chuckles. "Another worshipper, big brother."

McEnroe looks the Serb over. "Relax, man. We're all professionals here."

The brothers start for the gate where teenagers lean over the fence, holding baseball caps, programs, anything to sign.

The Serb stares at his hand. "I meet John McEnroe? It is unbelievable."

"Lesson #2—everyone's shit stinks. You can't put the best players on a pedestal."

I look the Serb over with his mismatched sticks and worn sneakers. I was lucky my rookie year. The Academy was backing me. I had sound coaching and a team I traveled with.

"Last night, the carte blanche treatment was classy. But be more careful with your money. In Japan, it costs $300 to wash your clothes. A month in Europe will put you back $5,000, easy. The Reebok look is cool, but you know what's more important than clothes? Racquets, good string. And shoes. You're nothing without good shoes. What size are you anyway? Extra large?" The Serb stares at the ground, embarrassed. I dig in my bag then throw him shirts still in plastic wrap, tennis shorts, socks, a few sets of string.

"You don't need these?"

"Reebok's always sending me stuff."

The Serb stares at me a long time. "You fortunate man, Blanco."

"You think so?"

His expression dims. Then he shakes his head. "Another joke. We hit. One hour, remember?"

There is something about playing points without keeping score. How it frees the mind. How it dislodges the realized self, allowing me to roam elsewhere, to a place where I don't know my name. Nothing touches me between the lines. Here, in practice, I feel safe. The points are flawless, almost effortless in execution. There is little wasted energy; miscues rare. You hear the thump of the ball. You feel your beating heart. We play well-orchestrated rallies for maximum cardiovascular activity.

This particular drill is designed for the net player's benefit. Anchored deep in the deuce corner, I send balls this way and that. The Serb's feet never stop moving.

"Tell me when you've had enough."

The Serb's mouth is terse. "F-U-U-C-K Y-O-U-U-U."

"I'm trained in CPR."

He finds his stroke. The cut in his backhand volley is heavier. But now the grunting is more pronounced. The big guy labors. This is when the wheels fall off the cart.

Sure enough, the Serb drops his racquet, his chest heaving for air.

I feel Dad's presence sometimes. Like now. Like he's standing behind me while the Serb moves me along the baseline. Or I'll be on an overseas flight with a blanket up to my chin, and I'll open my eyes convinced he's sleeping in the berth next to me. I'll think—Dad's alive! Then reality sinks in. He's dead. I'll never see him again. I'll never hear his voice. And it hurts. It gets me every time.

Soon we gather up our equipment, the hour up. We're walking off the court when I see David in the bleachers.

"Let's sign a few programs."

The Serb points a thumb at his face. "Who me?"

The kids think the Serb is Alberto Berasategui. They won't let the Berasategui similarity go. I tell him the Spanish player is 5'8" and maybe a buck fifty, whereas the Serb is 6'4" and a two-dollar bill plus change. They're still dubious. So the Serb pulls up his shirt and flashes his bullet hole. "Berasategui not have this." The kids go spooked and give the Serb a little more space. We sign everything thrust in our faces, then exit the gate. There's a moment before we reach David and the golf cart, call it limbo-land, when the Serb and I move among the crowd, both of us a head taller than most. His face is lit up like a Christmas tree.

"Fun, huh?"

"Fantastic."

David meets us in the sectioned-off area by the golf carts. We man-hug.

"It's good to see you, David. But why are you here?"

"I'm here to support my #1 client." He gives the Serb a once over. "So, who's this?"

"My doubles partner." They shake, paw to paw. I look at the Serb. "You hungry?"

"I could eat entire cat right now."

"David, feed the boy."

"What about you?"

"I need to call my woman."

"He's like this," David tells the Serb. "Richard is a revolving door of T&A."

"What this mean, T&A?"

David sets his hand on the Serb's shoulder. "Tits and ass. You've got a lot to learn, kid. If there's one thing I tell my players, it's be smart with your money."

"Listen to him," I say.

My agent and the Serb walk toward the waiting cart.

"If you're thinking about buying a Lamborghini, and trust me, you'll think that one day, I say sleep on it. Or call me. A tour player doesn't rake in dough forever. You got representation yet? Stay away from IMG or Proserve, total sleazeballs. Here's my card. I'm available for my clients eight days a week. Isn't that right, Richard?"

They pile into the cart, Tweedledum and Tweedledee. The Serb's tennis shoes hang over the rear wheel hub. He waves as the driver speeds away.

I find a spot away from the crowds then put the call through. Heather's not happy with me. I almost tell her about my incident in New York, but pride or shame takes hold, and I can't.

"I don't want to lose you, Heather. Will you accept my apology?"

"I don't know." Her voice is testy. "I'm questioning everything about us."

And she hangs up.

* * *

I do a peculiar thing against Doyle. I cruise through him fast, losing only a single game. It's strange, this focus of mine, like a continuation from practice. The ball's the size of a planet; the court feels colossal. It's like I can't miss even if I tried. And the noise in my head? Gone. Same thing happens in the semifinals. Against Bopara, I'm all business. My deft play carries over on the doubles court, too. The Serb and I thrash the Aussies, Forsyth and Stewart, then we win a thriller over Banai and Akram. On match point, I tell the Serb to serve at Banai's gonads.

"Gonads?" the Serb says.

"His testicles, his nuts, *his balls*, man. I'll go."

"You poach?"

"Keep it down. Those guys read lips."

Packed crowds watch us. Heather's comment is like something I carry, a scar or memory from a past life. Trey becomes a face in the crowd. She follows me everywhere. She even finagles herself inside the press tent after the match.

"You're all business out there," one journalist comments. "You're not even sitting on changeovers."

"I feel like a rookie. No pressure at all."

Janet Stipe raises her pencil. "I don't know if I've seen a player make every first serve for an entire set."

My eyes find the Asian woman in back.

"What I mean is," Stipe adds. "You're not interacting with the crowd. You're so focused."

"I'm not questioning anything. I'm playing well, into the finals. But it's not like I'm holding up the winner's trophy."

Stipe gives me a thoughtful gaze. "Not yet."

Our doubles run ends against the Jensen brothers. The Serb is sporadic with ill-timed double faults and sprayed returns. Hey, I'm okay with his play. As partners go, we jelled. The Serb also Bo Jackson'd another stick. When Luke, the ambidextrous brother, saw the broken racquet, he jumped into Murphy's arms, mock-alarmed. This sound went off in my head. What if the Serb and I played doubles full-time? This could be the start of something new.

Later, in the locker room, we relax, sneakers off, feet up.

"Your temper fails you."

The Serb is stretched out on the bench opposite, sipping a beer. "This I now see."

"When you get pissed, you miss by a football field. I don't get your racquet breaking, either."

"I do not think. I do."

I lean forward, elbows on my knees, and give the Serb a close evaluation. "What if we take this to another level? Can you picture McEnroe and Lendl playing together? Talk about entertainment."

"If they not kill each other."

"That's my point. We put on a show. You miss an easy shot and I fire a ball at you. I purposely nail you in the head with my serve. It would be hilarious. Breaking the stick will be your signature move."

"I no more racquets."

"Talk to David about that." I stare past the Serb, lost in thought. "This could be another career for me."

"Us, you mean."

"Are you hearing me? Lesson #3. Be resourceful."

"I don't understand."

"Why pay for a room if you don't have to? Every tournament has women hanging around with flats of their own. Most will do your laundry."

"Be careful with money, yes?"

"No, man. Try to get laid."

"I thought women no good."

I smile. "Lesson #4. The best players have the shortest memories. Actually, I think Sampras said that. The point is we're all stealing."

"Stealing okay?"

"No, stealing isn't okay. Stealing is never okay. Is anything getting through to you?"

The Serb rubs his head. "I have headache from these lessons."

"Last thing is your name. It's not catchy. What if you changed it to Drabo Drabomonovic."

"Change name?"

"Drabo Drabomonovic sounds like Batman's arch-villain."

Fireworks go off in the Serb's eyes. "We wear robes? And masks?"

"Capes and masks? Let's not get carried away," I say. "So, what do you think?"

The Serb polishes off his beer. "Just not tell my father. I named after him. More beer?"

I've hardly touched mine. "No, thanks."

I watch him walk to the cooler. His face turns reflective. "My game not good, not like yours. But one thousand two-hundred dollar for losing? Free Heineken? I learn big thing today. Very little difference between good and great player. This motivate me, no?"

"That's the smartest thing you've ever said... Drabo."

The Serb pulls out a beer from the icy water, then sticks the bottle's neck into his mouth, showing his teeth. He pops off the cap using his molars.

"I'm heading to the Academy after the finals. If I can pull some strings, you wanna join me?"

"I not have money for this."

"Let me see what I can do."

JULY 15, 1996, 11:14AM

DESTAFANO TENNIS ACADEMY.
TEMPERATURE AN INDIFFERENT 93 DEGREES FAHRENHEIT.

Court #21 is famous for a variety of reasons. Two-time German Open champ Carlota Gomez held closed practices here in the early 80s. Jim Courier once tagged a supervisor's family jewels during a game of Olympics. And early in my third year, a kid named Tanner Montana spray-painted TENNIS BITES MY OSCAR WEINER on court #21. Which, coincidentally, was the site of his famous meltdown against Catherine Vernhes, the French beauty who beat him in a challenge match 8–6. Before the words were acid-washed off the following dawn, Tanner Montana sat inside the fuselage of a 737 high over Houston, Texas, listening to his Walkman. That was how the Academy worked. A rule was broken, a few important phone calls made, and then, bright and early the next day, the glorious sound of multitudinous tennis balls being struck lacerated the balmy Floridian air.

On this halcyon morning, Billy Strathers stands next to a diminishing hopper of balls. Scattered happenstance around him are hundreds of gold orbs. Like Coach, BS is outfitted in Adidas. During Destafano Tennis Academy's early years, Coach wore FILA, so everyone wore FILA. Supremely talented players got piles of clothes, umpteen racquets, spools and spools of synthetic gut, Shoe Goo. The extent of our paraphernalia was such that we set up shop in my bedroom then sold off our surplus to fellow students to fund our nefarious nightly activities. Destafano's sponsor list, like America's growing debt, grew and grew. There wasn't a company he wouldn't endorse—Lobster ball machines, Roto-Rooter, even Tang.

BS throws a stratospheric lob in the air. The sky is fathomless, white. It covers the atmosphere like a king-sized sheet. We go way back, BS and me. He supervised group #1. Later, after I turned pro, he traveled as my hitting partner. I let the ball bounce then smash it away. You're probably wondering why I'm on court so soon after Newport. When does a guy like me recharge the batteries? That's a fair question. Professional athletes listen to their bodies. Our bodies talk to us. Mine's feeling pretty outstanding, all things considered.

BS sends another ball up. I thump it out of the air.

"Side to side, Billy." Destafano is positioned along the side fence, hands on his knees like a football coach. He's shirtless, even with the snotty cloud mass.

BS does as he's told and drives the ball deep into the corner. He seems older than I remember, softer around the tummy, less happy. I unleash a backhand at his bellybutton. He slaps it away with a flick of his wrist.

"Easy, son, easy."

BS jams the next ball behind me. I have to switch gears, hard-like. I run it down, no problem. I mean, I'm only thirty-one. My roller disappears in the sandblasted sky.

"Relax the face, son."

I'm going the other way now, full sprint mode. Out the corner of my eye, I catch Drabo toweling off between serves. We arrived a few hours ago. The entire student body greeted us in the commons. I spotted Heather's daughter goofing with her friends and made a mental note to seek her out. I didn't want her mom to know I was in town yet.

I miss.

"Drop the hands, son. There you go."

I played a stellar finals. It wasn't even close. Even my opponent, the Frenchmen Giroud, said kind words during the trophy ceremony. Yet, winning felt empty. Here, my first tournament victory in seven years. And I feel blue? Trey wasn't in the Player's Box. She wasn't standing in the wings with her credentials around her neck, either. She'd followed me around like a puppy for three days, but when I reached the finals, she went AWOL? I was holding the trophy up for the fans when I realized it wasn't Trey I was bothered with. It was that Heather wasn't there. I wanted to celebrate with her. What the fuck had I been thinking? Trey Hamasaki? Really? It wasn't until Drabo and I touched down in Sarasota that Trey reached out. She said she was flying in tomorrow night. I was supposed to find us a hotel.

BS has drawn me forward with a softly hit shot that bounces a few feet off the net. He moves me side to side, stab volley after stab volley. My sneaker soles burn warm. The lungs are beginning to sear.

"Focus, son. Come on now."

I thought Heather and I'd take it slow. For once, we wouldn't screw first, catch up later. We'd have lunch, maybe a walk on the beach. We'd talk ourselves back into each other's lives. But no—I had to complicate things.

BS sends a ball over my head. I retreat fast, the body beginning to fade. I throw one up high.

"That's it, son. That's the ticket."

We're into the final stretch now. BS opens up the court like he's peeling back my ribcage. The heart beeps out warning signs. *Danger. Danger. This is a test. This is only a test.* That's what this is, a freaking test. I guess reaching the Wimbledon quarterfinals and winning Newport doesn't mean anything around here.

I get to another drop shot the masochist sends over. There's no quit, not on court #21. Then Strathers sends one out of reach. "Where's your fight, son?" Coach growls. This is a test, this is only a test. Trey Hamasaki is going to fuck this up good. I don't know how, I don't know when, but she's going to ruin everything. BS hits another lob into the drab sky. *Call it, you motherfuckers.* I miss terribly. Another ball hangs aloft. Why did I come here?

"Enough."

I bend at the waist, sucking air. And practice is over.

Coach follows me to the net.

"Claudia wants to see you this afternoon." The skin around his eyes is scrunched up with irritation. Like pandering to an athlete's psychosis wasn't part of the job description when he thought up the idea of a tennis academy way back when.

I bring a water bottle to my mouth. "Can't Coach. I got plans."

His gaze momentarily finds Drabo, who's picking up balls with a hopper. "Look, I'm proud of you, son. I am. But Claudia's got me worried about your well-being."

Strathers has walked over. He stands next to Coach, in solidarity.

"Fine. I'll see her. But can you both quit looking at me like my head's spinning like a top?"

Drabo got the standard contract. For room and board, use of Academy facilities, coaching, et al., he promises to give the DTA a percentage of future earnings. For a player at his stage of development, it's a sweet deal. For starters, there's a familiar sense of place here, of community. Distractions are few. Pretty much everything a player needs is situated inside the Academy walls. It's not perfect. There's a nearly imperceptible stasis in the air that long-run can send an athlete down ruts and stale play. But in small doses, the Academy provides the energy, guidance and inspiration a player needs. Call it a pit-stop between events. Or maybe the DTA is simply a much-needed change of scenery from the constant demands of tour life. When you've trained at the Academy as long as I have, it's home. Plus, Heather is here. Tonight's the night I brave the waters over at The Golden Banana. Just how do I go about getting my woman to forgive me? Believe me when I say the plan is still a work in progress.

I'm on my way to the phone booths when I run into Cherokee on the main road. She's talking to an older boy. One glimpse of me and she has him shoo off.

"Who was that?"

"Christian."

"He's a little old, don't you think?"

"What can I help you with, Richard?"

Being a teenager, Cherokee is all legs, metal teeth, and blemishes on her chin.

"Don't tell your mom you saw me, okay? I want to surprise her."

"And if I don't?"

"Do you think she wants to hear about Christian?"

I apologize if my tone is a tad irked. But there's something unsettling about Cherokee Harper, for the male species, I mean. She's got this steady, earnest gaze that sort of unravels you in its pure honesty and intelligence. It's like at fourteen, she already sees through all the male crap we toss on the road of life, seeing what sticks—the half-truths, the come-ons, the bold lies.

"I watched the match." Cherokee self-consciously tugs at the bra under her spaghetti-strap top, not realizing doing so has males zooming in on the one thing she hoped they wouldn't look at.

"The final was on TV?"

"Have you always been this dense?"

"Oh, you mean Wimbledon."

"I felt bad for you."

"Aw, Cherokee. That's a really nice thing to say."

She gives me a peeved look. "For being a mental midget."

I sigh. "I need to make a call. In private."

Cherokee sulks across the street. Then, seeing security, she ducks down a path carved into the flora from years of players short-cutting it to the back courts. Some things never change around here. When I was a full-time student, we had underage drinking, pranks galore and fornication, especially on court #21. Those were the wild years. Then Destafano put in ten-foot perimeter walls and a gatehouse with spotlight capabilities. We were inundated with "Academy Life" meetings. There, supposed experts spoke on personal space, hygiene and good study habits. They talked at great length about sexually transmitted diseases. How STD's caused major limbs to fall off and rashes so severe you'd never show your face in public again. They read from the DTA handbook. Dating was okay, but no touching al-lowed, even something as innocuous as holding hands. The one ex-ception was school dances, when during slow songs, the male could press his hand in the small of his partner's back (though the couple was subjected to the ten-inch space rule). Destafano conceived the idea of public phone booths after receiving the Academy's inaugural phone bill in 1977.

Sunlight reflects off the phone booth's glass. They sit like sentries across from the main building, a sprawling one-story that houses the front office, pro shop and the biggest of the two cafeterias. I feed the phone several quarters, for the Motorola is worthless here, the grounds being a cellular dead zone.

I dial Trey's number with the door open, me half in, half out.

"Hey."

"I'm buying a swimsuit as we speak. It's mesh."

Sweat pours down my face. The door handle is hot to the touch. Be strong, I tell myself, show conviction. "I don't think you coming here—*mesh you say?*"

And on it goes, the sinking, the quicksand, my asphyxiation. Then Trey asks about O. Maxwell. He's the Academy's new darling. So this is what her coming down here is all about.

"Have you seen O's commercials?" she says. "He's really photogenic."

"The one where he saves the busload of children caught in gang warfare using only his stick?"

"My favorite is where he swims with Great Whites, scales Everest, then schools Kobe in his Nike Airs."

"A superstar in the making."

"That was brilliant."

I flick sweat off my eyebrow. "I still don't see why he's so special."

"Did you book the hotel yet? Something ocean side, with a spa. I want to be pampered, Richard."

I lean my slimy forehead against the glass, sigh.

"Your girlfriend won't know I'm town."

We fight, another minute or so.

"Don't worry, little boy. I'll see you at the airport."

Coach lured O. Maxwell from a rival competitor this spring. He's talented and all, but why is Trey so obvious? I should give up the ghost. Or almost everything. London can remain a secret. A stupid mistake. When I bring up Saiko Investments to Heather, it will be casual. *She's with a Japanese outfit. They want to sign me. David's working out the particulars.*

The pro shop door swings open. Out saunters the great one himself, testing the tension of two sticks he's had restrung. Born Orenthal Maxwell, no middle name, called O, it was easier, the name had a nice ring to it, something the dolts on ESPN never tired of repeating. We size each other up, the young lion and his grizzled old foe. I've maybe got an inch on him. But O. Maxwell is more chiseled, faster looking.

"How does it feel being back?" O's voice surprises me. He owns a nice timber, warm, non-threatening, midwestern neutral. This is the same guy who threatened a line judge's life?

"Complicated."

He's got sparkly carat diamonds in each ear and chunky Rastafarian growths sprouting on his head.

"Are you really from inner-city Minneapolis?" I ask.

"It's not Compton, dog. But Minneapolis has its share of pissed off brothers."

"I read that you grew up in Minnetonka."

"I graduated from Minnetonka High. Why?"

"Minnetonka Lake is nice. I dated a girl who grew up in Deephaven."

He smiles. "They call it Lake Minnetonka, dog."

Now, it's me who's beaming. "So, you did grow up in the burbs?"

O. Maxwell's eyes go wary and hard. "What's your point, dog?"

* * *

Later in the day, afternoon sessions, the climate a wet, slimy affair, the four touring pros, O. Maxwell, Jeffries, Costa and myself bang balls back and forth on courts #45 and #46. Billy Strathers rubs zinc-oxide on his nose. He's a sun protection fanatic. He even applies SPF-50 when we practice indoors. And Drabo? Where is he this sticky afternoon? My guess is he's waxing Coach's Corvette. See, Coach D breaks the new recruits in slowly.

O and I are camped out in the deuce corners. We top ball after ball, crosscourt. The drill is based on consistency, three-quarter pace, and feel. And O hums during points. At first, I thought he was being juvenile, but now I'm thinking it's purposeful. Like a meditation. And O hits a heavy ball. There's a high sound coming off his topspin, like a whistle. A two-hander of mine lands short. O drives a forehand deep and approaches the net mumbling like a Buddhist monk. I decide to show him who's the big man on campus and absolutely shred a passing shot up the line. His expression hardly changes. He picks up two balls then retreats to the baseline. We stroke six, seven shots when another ball has him snaking in. This one I flick over his head.

"Keep em' in play, Blank." BS follows O around like he's got an invisible leash around his neck. Like he's O's new bitch. "Hey, O," he says, finger-thumbing sunscreen in his ear grooves. "You think the Twins are in contention with Puckett gone? Glaucoma? Man, that's bad luck."

O's had an exceptional rookie run. He won Acapulco and reached the quarters at Indian Wells and Rome. *Tennis Magazine* stuck him on the May cover. *Is O. Maxwell tennis' anti-hero? Or the next Arthur Ashe?* He lassoed his biggest booty yet, a clothing deal with Nike. I say wait until next year. By year two, players aren't fooled by your serve. They've scouted your matches. They know where you go under pressure and what shot you favor in the clutch. And that polished gleam every tournament holds that first run-thru? Gone. You find out the tour is a grind. Airports, aches and pains, players keeping their distance, everybody fighting for the same pot of gold. I'm not saying the pay isn't incredible or the fringe benefits aren't sweet. I'm only saying year two is when the tour officially becomes a job.

Suddenly vexed, I aim at Strathers, who's so busy gushing over O. Maxwell, he doesn't see the shot coming. The ball deflects off his head. "What the hell, Blank? Daydreaming again?"

"Sorry. My grip slipped."

He turns back to O while rubbing his scalp. "You're sponsored by Hilton, right, O? Think you can score me a deal in Miami Beach? The wife needs a vacation. Do it up right, you know?"

Hey, O? Blow me.

An interesting thing happens when practice is called. The South African, Jeffries, sidles up covertly, a grin on his face. He asks if I met Heather at The Golden Banana. I arch an eyebrow at O. Maxwell for some reason. He frowns, shaking his head.

"You wanted to know," Jeffries says under his breath.

Ah, so that's it. Well, O's got good taste. And what's a guy to do? If a peer of mine was dating a *Playboy* playmate, I'd check out the goods, no doubt. But if I got worked up about every guy moved by Heather and her shapely hips, I'd be more messed up than I already am.

"Do you really want to know where we met, Jeffries? Here, at the Academy. Her daughter is in the program. Any other questions I can answer? Good. I'm late for psychoanalysis. Mr. Enigma, remember?"

It's half past four when I step into Claudia's office. Joanne is watering the plants on the windowsill overlooking the back lot.

"Hi, Joanne."

"Well, aren't you a sight for sore eyes."

"She ready for me?"

Without another word, Joanne sets her watering can on her desk, then walks over and opens the French doors that lead to Claudia's inner sanctum. Then she bangs the gong. Claudia's in place, sitting behind a silkscreen partition. This is part of the experience. Soon the blinds will close. I'll lie on tatami mats as blackness gobbles up the room.

I hear the blinds faint whir kicking in. Then, the light turns over. In seconds the darkness is complete. "Welcome back."

"What do you think of O. Maxwell?"

"O? Nice kid. He's a good fit," she says.

"Don't you think he's overrated? Those sleeveless shirts? What a showoff."

Claudia slurps from her drink. She's an iced tea fanatic. "The persona, as seen by Jung, is an important aspect of the warrior self. How one carries himself says much about how he feels."

"You wouldn't believe Strathers. 'Hey, O? Do you think I'm fat? Hey, O? I can't impregnate my wife. Wanna give it a try?'"

"Are you jealous?"

"Jealous of what? He's a rookie. Wait until he cools off, then we'll see the real O. Maxwell."

"Did something happen between you two?"

Why did I bring up O. Maxwell again? "Trey Hamasaki is very interested in meeting him."

"She mentioned that on the phone."

I crank my head toward Claudia's voice. "You talked with Trey?"

"She was curious about protocol—wanted to speak with players."

"My god. Isn't anything sacred anymore?"

"Tell me about her."

"You mean you didn't check her dossier before giving her clearance?"

"You're being ridiculous. Well?"

I face the ceiling again, sigh. "I don't know. I guess she's easy to look at. She's ambitious, probably to a fault. She's a risk-taker, definitely some risky behavior there. But yeah, we have fun together."

"What do you mean, risky behavior?"

Should I tell Claudia about the phone call she made to her boy-friend after we had sex? Or how her no-show routine for the finals was something the Russian might do.

"I can't figure her out. Something tells me I should stay away."

"This means you're no longer seeing Heather?"

"I can't believe you haven't asked how I'm feeling. In New York, you made it sound like I was looney farm material."

A significant silence enters the dark. Claudia takes a pull on her straw, sucking the glass dry.

"You do sound calmer. And you cleaned up in Newport. Your agent told Coach D it was the best you've played in years."

I grunt but offer up nothing else. I'm still perturbed about Trey calling the Academy without my knowing. Soon we're diagnos-ing my magical play, as Claudia coins it. Then, she changes gears. "When it comes to this Trey woman, it's a good idea to listen to that voice in your head. Usually, our collective unconscious is tuned in to our inner emotions. I'm recommending your psychotherapist reevaluate you."

"Dr. Goldberg?"

"He does a thorough job."

"He's not nice like you are, Claudia. And his breath stinks. We sit opposite each other, and his breath smells like dog poop."

She laughs. "If you're not convinced, take my copy of the *DSM*. Read through mania and mood disorders. See if it jogs your memory. Let's meet in two days." With her foot, Claudia taps the steel knob that controls the mechanical blinds. Light slowly fills the room. She doesn't look up from her writing pad when I pull the *Diagnostic and Statistical Manual of Mental Disorders* off her bookshelf, nor is Joanne at her desk when I exit, having left for the afternoon.

I feel relieved stepping outdoors with the phone-book-size tome under my arm. But what if I'm tumbling down the black monster, only it might be ten times worse? I don't want to be medicated. I can con-trol this imbalance myself. Through exercise. Through positive energy. Through diet and willpower. Maybe Drabo and I should play the sum-mer circuit in Europe while the world tunes into the Summer Olympics in Atlanta. I'll keep two steps ahead by staying as far from Trey Hamasaki as humanly possible. It's one thing screwing a woman from a couple thousand miles away. But rubbing it in Heather's face? She deserves better than that. That's what the old me does, the guy who always gets what he wants.

JULY 15, 1996, 8:51PM

THE GOLDEN BANANA, SARASOTA, FLORIDA

The neon sign in the parking lot shows a voluptuous woman pulling the skin off a banana twice her size. The humor is in the details—the phallic-shaped fruit, how the woman wraps her legs around the banana's girth like she's taking it for a ride, her butt crack showing above her bikini line. David calls while I'm sitting in the Academy Subaru.

"Yes?"

"You sound on edge."

I let out a sigh.

"How's China Girl?"

"She's coming for *four* days," I whine.

"Ha! I wish I had your problems. This should cheer you up. Janet Stipe is flying into Bradenton this weekend."

I check my hair in the rearview mirror. "I don't have time for this, David."

"She wants to observe, that's all. Oh, that's Drabo calling. Gotta run." My agent clicks off.

I toss the phone on the passenger seat then climb out of the car. Here goes nothing, I think.

The cover is a crisp Andrew Jackson the bouncer holds up to the light because he doesn't trust me. He doesn't trust anyone. His equally burly partner frisks me while Einstein recites the rules. The world and its rules. The zero tolerance/no touching decree gets three notable mentions. Having passed the first hurdle, I come upon another behemoth slumped on a stool. His chin rests on his clenched fist like Rodin's *The Thinker*. I brace myself thinking he'll remember me. But the bouncer doesn't look up.

Inside, I move down weary carpeted halls. I smell disinfectants. I hear bottles being knocked around in garbage drums. And far off the sounds of George Michael's "I Want Your Sex, Pts. 1 & 2" plays. I nearly chicken out. Then fate or something has me staring at a platinum blonde in a cowboy getup. She gives me a sexy wink. That's how life works, doesn't it? A maybe cute, definitely slutty girl flirts your way, and you're handing over the keys to the houseboat without batting an eye.

"What you drinking, handsome?"

Another rule. Customers must buy a drink upon entering the premises. "Corona."

"Twelve dollars." Cowgirl wears blue suede and tasseled silver buttons. Her cleavage ends somewhere near Cuba. "You here to see Bambi Bottoms? She's our guest of honor. She's been in 563 pornos and counting."

"Would I know her work?"

"She holds the record for simultaneous facial shots, if that's what you mean."

"I guess we're all remembered for something."

"Up close or booth?"

"Booth."

I follow Cowgirl into the main room, then up the stairs. The bar's fluorescents lend the club a faded out allure, like an old theatre when the lights go up. Again, my instinct says run. I can call on Heather to-morrow, proper-like, as Dad might say.

Cowgirl and I pass the bartender on the second floor. I smile, but he doesn't reciprocate. Last time I was here, there was an altercation. I'd been seeing Heather for two weeks. We were quite the lovestruck couple. We did it on every flat surface in her apartment. We did it in the waters off Siesta Key at five in the afternoon. Once, out on a morning run, I dragged Heather into a grove of slash pine and had my way with her. Our attraction was like a thirst you couldn't quench. But with it came this needy obsessiveness, this malevolent paranoia. I shoved a guy at St. Armands shopping area for staring at Heather's chest. The idea of her working The Golden Banana in a Victorian lace bustier made my stomach burn. On nights she punched in, I sat huddled in the dorm with the lights off. Being on the tennis court was equally dangerous. Anything could set me off—a close call, a sarcastic comment from my opponent. I felt capable of violent things. Fourteen days into our relationship, I began following Heather. I'd park outside the club watching the men come and go. When Heather's shift ended, I'd confront her like the damaged man I was. Then one day, I waltzed inside the club. I had to see for myself.

Management got wind that a tan guy with surfer hair had thrown some loser to the floor for palming a dancer's derriere. Bouncers swooped in SWAT-style. The bartender pointed at me like I was the asshole who broke the zero tolerance/no touching rule. Rodin pressed me into a wall. And a half-naked Heather, chest doused with pixie dust like a sprite in *Midsummer's Night Dream*, jumped on Rodin's back and punched him in the head. That was nine months ago. I haven't been back since.

My attention is drawn to the stage. Spotlights circle the darkness while fog rises from the floor. Then KISS's anthemic "Shout It Out Loud" starts up. Out charges this scary brunette with basketball-size breasts. She wears black satin boots and red lingerie. The MC informs the room this is the celebrity, Bambi Bottoms. Bottoms works the stage, snarling at the first-row drunks, exposing a giant hooter every so often and knocking her head back to the beat. More girls enter. They take positions along the stage's end, flicking their tongues like Gene Simmons.

I scan the crowd. No Heather sightings anywhere. This must be a sign. I was a real shit-wad last time we spoke. And, knowing Heather, she'll take one look at my sorry ass and know the cheater I am. Yep, it's best I push off. I start inching my way out of the booth. Only Candy blocks the way.

"Hey there, Tennis Boy. Need any favors?" Candy sucks on a red-striped lollipop. She scares me. She scares most men. Or she should.

"Nope. My life is fucked up enough."

"We're telling the truth tonight?" Candy wears a wig straight out of *Clockwork Orange*, sixties Vuarnets, and a translucent rain slicker with a dominatrix outfit underneath.

"You seen Heather?"

She tongues the lollipop suggestively. "Why would you want her when you can bite into Candy?"

"Food for thought."

"Later, Tennis Boy."

Heather hates Candy because Candy does things management turns a blind eye to. Heather refuses to prostitute herself any more than she already does. I believe her (for sanity's sake, you have to). Her new role in management has tempered my nerves. But that doesn't mean I like her working in a strip club. It doesn't stop my mind from going places it shouldn't. Five months back, I tried saving Heather from this place. I offered a stipend, nothing outrageous, but enough money to help in raising her daughter. It was weird how Heather took it. She looked sad, even disappointed. "It's a generous offer, Richard. But what you're proposing isn't much different than my arrangement at the club. Either way, I'm stuck."

Stuck? That word always got me. The point of helping was so Heather would be unstuck, free from degradation and the sickos that roam places like this. It meant Heather could pursue that dance studio she was always talking about.

I finally pick her out of the crowd. And my heart soar-sinks. Her hair is tied up in back, so only a few blonde strands hang over her face. She wears a white lace babydoll that looks lavender under the black lights. I watch her bend over a table of guys to introduce a couple girls. That's when she looks up at the second-floor balcony and sees me staring at her like a lovesick lunatic. Her features darken. I watch her climb the metal stairs with her frilled garter and white pumps. I'm panicked. Heather is my rock, my ground floor. Did I just squander the best thing going in my life?

"Why come here, of all places?"

The moment I see Heather up close, I realize how much I missed her. I can't believe I was going to fuck it up by sleeping with Trey Hamasaki.

"I'm sorry. For everything." I glance toward the entrance. Rodin has joined the barkeep. "Will you sit down. You're making them nervous."

"You were a real jerk on the phone."

"Please, Heather."

She reluctantly slides in. Then Heather does something unexpected. She climbs onto my lap, wraps her arms around my neck, and hugs me. Like a moron, I open my big mouth and tell her I missed her. This breaks the spell. Heather undoes her embrace, her body language wary again. Meantime, Cowgirl saddles up with her six-shooter. Heather gruffly orders champagne. Another rule—if a customer invites a dancer to join his party, its drinks galore. A new song, U2's "Even Better Than The Real Thing" begins. Onstage, an all-nude Ms. Bottoms lies supine. She whips her legs around like a praying mantis on speed. Over at the bar, the help chitchat like gossipy grandmothers. Closer, Heather smells like apricot-scented shampoo.

"I need you right now." My eyes are shiny for some reason. "Everything is so out of control."

Heather cups her hands over mine, her eyes two blue circles of concern. "How do you mean?" I tell her about my episode. "Claudia wants me to see Dr. Goldberg."

She kisses my hand. "I knew it. I could tell in your voice, Richard." We cuddle one, two minutes this time, Bono cooing about taking it higher, Bottoms sticking her namesake into the air, and Rodin cracking his neck, but otherwise contained.

Heather feels so nice in my arms. This strong sense of goodness comes over me. I want to tell her how I feel, *how I really feel*, that I love her, that I've loved her ever since I saw her beating Rodin's skull in my honor.

"I can't believe how lucky I am."

She gives me a squeeze. "I missed you, too."

"I want to tell you something I should have said a long time ago."

Hmm, interesting move at a strip joint, Blank.

"What I'm trying to say is—"

"Here we are, champagne for two."

Cowgirl pushes her way between us with a bottle of fake champagne and two plastic flutes. Downstairs, Bambi Bottoms picks dollar bills off the floor using only her vulva. We watch Cowgirl pop the cork (also plastic) then pour bubbly in each glass.

"Anything else?" she asks.

Heather's eyes are on mine. "Leave us, please."

I hand Heather her flute then pick up the other. We raise our glasses in the air.

"You were saying," Heather says.

"A toast to us. And the future."

You dog, you.

We do that thing where we sip bubbly while staring into each other's eyes.

"I want us to be a real couple. No more games, no more stupid fights. You mean more to me than you realize. The thing is... what I wanted to say is..."

Don't do it, Blank.

"Heather, I'm in love—"

"Yo, Heather." A lanky, inebriated man holding a cigarette sways on his feet in the aisle, blocking the bar view.

Heather, who's been leaning into my every word, sighs seeing the man. She sets her flute on the table. "Not now, Elliot."

"But you promised to stop by like an hour ago."

"Get lost, man," I tell him. "You know the rules."

"But, Heather..."

One glance, and I know everything about the guy. He's smaller than me. His shirt is thrift-shop worn. And he's infatuated with Heather; something strippers deal with all the time.

"Listen, pal. I'm not asking again. Either move on, or I break you in two."

"I'd listen to him, Elliot. My boyfriend has a temper."

Elliot cocks his head, hearing this. "Boyfriend? Man, you're one lucky dude."

I reach out into the aisle and nudge him a foot to the left so I can check back on my friends at the bar. So far, so good. In the old days I'd have dropped this guy with one punch. But violence isn't the answer tonight. I've stumbled into Heather's good graces again. I dig my wallet out. "Buy yourself a drink, dog."

So very generous of you, Blank.

Elliot stares at the ten-spot. "You're okay, dude."

"That was gentlemanly," Heather says, once Elliot bolts for the bar.

"I don't know what I was thinking, letting you work here."

"It's not your decision."

"I mean the way they look at you."

"It's not real, Richard."

"It is to them."

Heather takes hold of my hands again.

"You know something—you're amazing."

She inches closer. "Am I now?"

"And I'm an idiot."

Heather's completely in my line of vision. My eyes dart from her mouth to her cleavage and back to her mouth again. Then she places her hands on my legs. Very close to Johnson.

"Tell me how you're such an idiot?"

"Dance for me."

"A dance? For you?"

I swallow hard. I can't move. I'm that transfixed with Heather. She leans in and bite-sucks my lower lip while her hand disappears between my legs.

"Richard? Are you getting a hard-on?"

"One dance. Please, Heather?"

I settle against the booth, one leg tucked under my knee, an arm slung over the backrest. We hear the soft guitar picking and spacey loon call intro to "Burning Down The House." The song's tribal drums kick in. Heather lets down her hair, shakes her locks once, then fixes her cleavage just so. The entire time she's got her fuck eyes on me.

Cool babies, strange but not a stranger

I'm an ordinary guy

Burning down the house

Heather sits above me, her knees squeezing my thighs. I get another whiff of apricot then stare at her crotch, hovering inches from my groin. Heather arches her back and grinds her hips. Her face beautifully pained, she pulls at the hem of her skimpy outfit like it's 105 degrees.

Hold tight, wait 'til the parties over

Hold tight, we're in for nasty weather

There's got to be a way

Burning down the house

At 34, Heather works as hard as I do keeping fit. She's even got a black belt in taekwondo. Like now, when she scoots her booty around in a space no bigger than a Geo Metro backseat, Heather makes it look easy. She straddles my hips, looking over her bare shoulder with her fuck eyes. Then Heather bursts into laughter, so hard her ribs show through her skin.

"What?"

"You're so serious."

"Only because you're the most beautiful woman in the world."

Heather sits on my lap again, done with the role playing, and presses her face against mine. Rodin looks over and shakes his head like he's giving us a free pass.

Three hundred sixty-five degrees,

Burning down the house

Some things can sweep me off my feet

Burning down the house

Then everything in the club fades away. The Talking Heads float on. I only feel the dense rolling beats. I only see my Heather. "I love you," she says, stroking my hair. Before I can respond, Heather exits the booth. "I'll get my things."

I watch her until she disappears into the dressing room. How hard would it have been to reciprocate? I have this moment, counting out the tip money, when I stop. When I fully comprehend the complete shit I am. When I realize I always get what I want. And it shames me.

I walk to the stairwell. Down below in the pit, my tour buddies are surrounded by a harem. Candy's got her claws in Costa. This waif-thin girl rubs her tush over Jeffries' crotch. O. Maxwell towers over three girls in different stages of undress. He tosses dollar bills like he's throwing playing cards. Even Drabo is taking in the sights.

I sense Rodin standing next to me.

"Should I inform management that Heather is taking a few days off?"

"If I tell you something, will you swear you'll act on it? See that big kid down there, the one with the wad. He's underage."

"You mean O? He's great—a big, big tipper. He's welcome any-time." Rodin leans in, smelling of cheap cologne. "He's got a thing for your lady friend. Something tells me you already know that."

I hardly hear him, having started for the dressing room entrance. By this time tomorrow, I'll be in tongue deep, hiding in the shadows, up to my ears in the high life. Can you hear what I'm saying? Can you feel the hypocrisy in my every breath? In less than twenty-four hours, I'm going to cheat on Heather Harper. I know it. Everyone except my girlfriend knows it. And why? Because I have impulse control issues. Because even the holiest of men would never say no to Trey Hamasaki.

I'm fucked, aren't I?

JULY 16, 1996, 3:17PM

DESTAFANO TENNIS ACADEMY, COURT #7

Another day, another workout. This is what a professional does. We sweat, we toil, we tinker, nearly every day of the year. It's as deep a com-mitment as any serious endeavor. Though today makes a player think about throwing in the towel, what with the heat index as high as it is. Can you say Hades on a bad day? Steamy. A bleary-eyed sky. Not a lick of wind. I've soaked through four shirts. Jeffries drags on like a child eight hours into a day at Disney World. Drabo, working on the new backhand, broke a racquet out of frustration. Only O. Maxwell remains unfazed. He's a humming machine. He reaches balls no player has a right to, or wants to—not in this heat. Half the time he slides into the ball like the surface is clay, up on an ankle like a skateboarder skidding to a halt.

We break. No complaints there. No one talks, not even me joshing the guys about seeing them last night. No, we're focused on water, as in pouring it over our heads.

"Remember that day your father cracked an egg on court?" Strath-ers says, grinning at me.

The air is so lifeless and baked, I can only muster a vacuous smile.

"Did it cook?" O. Maxwell asks.

"Hell, yeah," Strathers says. "That kid from Missouri… what was his name, Blank?"

"Jim Masters."

"Masters asked for it done over-easy. Then he swallowed it down. Man, that was funny."

"How come we never have fun like that with you, Coach?" Jeffries asks.

Just like that Strathers' face takes on a scowl. "Okay, ladies, break's over. Thanks to your friend, Jeffries."

We stagger back on court. It's O. Maxwell and me again. It's always us two, sparring. At one point, he motions me to the net.

"Can I ask you something a little off-topic? How do you let your girlfriend dance at that club?"

"You got it all wrong. She's in Personnel."

"I mean, be a part of that place, what it stands for. What your girlfriend does for a living would kill me, man."

I want to tell O. Maxwell to mind his own fucking business. I also feel, if circumstances were different, that O and I could be good friends.

"I live in a perpetual state of denial."

He chuckles. "You're a better man than me."

Strathers shuts down practice minutes later. I walk over to where Drabo sits leaning against the fence with a towel over his head. I toe-kick his sneaker. He doesn't move.

"Drabo? Will you take the towel off your head?"

He slowly peels it off. His face is a feverish red. "New grip is stupid."

"Are you talking about your backhand? You have to learn the rules to break the rules. Everything a modern player takes for granted, the spins and stroke production, the movement, all that, was passed down. And so was that grip. I didn't pull it out of the air." His eyes shine a brilliant obsidian in the heat. "I'm not suggesting. I'm telling you. If you want to compete with the best, change the grip. Look, I'll show you."

I pull him off the asphalt. "Shake hands with the racquet. Eastern forehand, right?"

"Sampras forehand. Only player in top hundred not use semi-western."

"Correct. Now, place the first knuckle on top of the grip. Spread your fingers. You feel the leverage when you do that?"

Drabo nods with his jaw. He takes a few tentative cuts in the air. "Like this?"

"Loosen up, Frankenstein."

"No make me laugh."

"You ever hear of Bill Tilden? He took a year off to revamp his backhand. At the time, he was the second-best player in the world."

"A whole year?"

"He won nine majors with that new stroke."

"Fine. I try it."

"Don't try it. Learn it, make it part of your game."

Soon, we're climbing the stairs to our room. I'm thinking about my meeting with Claudia. I tried backing out. I didn't want to face her. See, I blew it. I spent the night at Heather's apartment. And it was nice, real nice. This morning Cherokee beat us out of bed to make choco-late-chip pancakes. It was as if I hadn't been gone at all.

* * *

I take a long, cold shower. And I'm still sweating on the stomp over to Claudia's office. The heat beats down hard. Everything I pass is flat and withered. It's like the earth died. Not long after, I'm laid out on the floor like the chalked outline of a corpse, the blinds ticking shut.

"How did it go with Heather?"

Last night after we showered? Or this morning before Cherokee woke up?

"Great. Just great."

"Great?"

"Well, she cried out. She was in some anguish."

"And then?"

And then we cuddled.

"Heather actually nodded off."

"She fell asleep after you broke up with her?"

"In my arms. Weird, huh? It was a nice way to end it."

"It sounds like you handled that well. You were there for Heather in her time of need."

"I do what I can."

"And now this businesswoman arrives."

I feel my spine stiffen.

"I'd like to role play."

"Role playing?" I groan. "Anything but that."

Ever since Claudia returned from a Carl Jung symposium in Santa Barbara, we've been pretending during sessions. Claudia plays the tennis brat to my saintly Chair Umpire. Or I'm the victim to her angry young man. Today's role is about men and commitment. As usual, Claudia takes the juiciest role—in this case, a brash misogynist—to my Virtuous Man. Her voice goes gruff explaining that "bedding women is what I do." I crack up, hearing her stupid man's voice.

"You think this is funny?" she wisecracks. "I should kick you where it hurts."

"I can't take you seriously."

"Your turn."

"I don't want to play."

"Richard," she warns.

Sighing, I tell Claudia that Virtuous Man believes bagging women is short-lived. That unless love is involved, sex is meaningless.

"*Meaningless*," she cries out. "Some of the best sex I've ever had involved a woman I'd met an hour before."

"Now you're talking."

"Play the role, Richard."

"Virtuous Man lives on a higher moral plane, abstinence being the best medicine."

"Ha! Where are you from, Choir Boy?"

"I quote Paul Simon. 'I am a rock.'"

"So Virtuous Man is alone?"

"Man is an island, Claudia."

"You really believe that?"

"Are we done yet? This game's giving me a headache." What's happening here? I thought Claudia was clever. She knows juggling several women at once is my specialty. Trey is temporary. Throw our relationship against a wall, it's not al dente pasta; it doesn't stick. "I need to say something, Claudia. I spent the night with Heather."

There's a weighted silence in the pitch dark.

"Are you telling me you slept with her?"

"We had sex, yes, but let me explain."

"Please tell me you asked her to marry you first. Please tell me you told this Trey woman where to stick it."

"Um, no, on both ends, but for the record, although I didn't tell Heather I loved her, I think she understands I do, from my actions, I mean."

"*You mean fucking her?*"

I've never heard Claudia get this riled up. "Is cursing necessary?"

"Heather's feelings are at stake. Her womanhood."

"What about my feelings? I thought my coming here was about me?"

The blinds suddenly click alive. Fractured sunlight pervades my little space on the floor. I squint up at Claudia. She and her lamb shoulder calves struggle out of her chair. "I'm tired of your bullshit. You and your goddamn libido. If you want to screw up the best thing that's ever happened to you, go right ahead. But leave me out of it."

"But Claudia? I fuck around all the time. It's no biggie."

"Grow up, Richard." And she storms out.

I haven't moved from the tatami. It's like I'm Velcroed to the floor. Claudia can't walk out on me, can she? Doesn't she know I'm barely hanging on? Stipe flies in this weekend. I'm feeling insecure about O. Maxwell. We need to talk through my anxiety, my cheating ways. And I believe the tour fellas see me as a potential role model. I'm drowning here, and she says get out?

JULY 16, 1996, 1800 HRS.

HIDING IN PLAIN SIGHT

The moment I punch the Academy hatchback into second, my mind shifts gears. I don't think. I don't have time to. Take Claudia marching out in a huff. What was that about? I know what I'm doing. Trey's not the delightful girl next door Mom (and Claudia it seems) wishes me to marry. This is a fling, a diversion, my new drug. Thing is, when she's around, my insides thunder like an airplane roaring down the runway. I want to please Trey. Take booking a room. I reserved a suite on the Sarasotan's penultimate floor. The club level with its happy-hour sushi, fresh lox, cheeses and artisan breads. Where a bartender whips up Bombay tonics, gratis. I've arranged his and her robes, a spa treatment. There's even a Louis Vuitton metallic lighter that set me back five hundred big ones. The thing is, I feel self-conscious around Trey Hamasaki. It's like my whole body has this itch, only circumstances won't allow for proper scratching. I know I'm driving myself bonkers, but like that itch, I can't stop the ceaseless chatter.

Ah, speaking of my little charge, here she comes now, pulling her luggage like it's an errant Pekinese with a turned-up snoot. I step around the car, already falling hard. She wears a creme-colored power suit and black heels. I hand her flowers and a box of Godiva chocolates.

Trey makes a gooey face. "You are so sweet. Let's get a drink. I need to unwind."

Once we're properly lubricated, we do a quickie for old time's sake, then settle into something slower, hotter, kinkier. We've turned off the central air and flung open the doors leading to the balcony. It feels like being marooned on a desert island. Post-coital, our bodies exude the bored, entitled attitude of our generation. We're sweat-slicked, heat-stroked, buzzed. Trey's telling me about the community college ballplayer she's watching pitch in the morning. I'm relieved the subject isn't O. Maxwell.

"He's a probable first-rounder. Get this, he's 6'6" and chubby, but it's baseball, right?" She flicks my gift on and off. "This lighter is so boss." Trey reaches for the nightstand where her travel humidor sits. She takes out a cigar and bites the tip off.

"Balcony, please."

"Is buying me off your way of controlling my habit? Wow, Richard. I'm impressed."

Trey rolls off the bed and walks for the balcony. The sky over her naked shoulder is burnt-red, the sun sneaking past her hip a yellow glare. She lights the cigar in the doorway before stepping into the sunlight. Then the exhibitionist bends suggestively over the rail, her little ass sticking up in the air. "There's a place five minutes from here," I tell her. "They'll tip you a hundred dollars for that move. Seriously. Put on a robe."

Trey waves at someone below. "Hi," she says. "*It is* a beautiful sunset. Sorry, I'm busy tonight."

I'm up fast like the protective boyfriend I'm not. By the time I grab my robe and step outdoors, Trey rests her back on the rail, very pleased with herself.

I peer over the ledge, fastening the belt. And Luke stares up at me. This has me spooked and sucking in air. But then his face melts into a shirtless old man with a saggy face and shoulder hair. I walk indoors, toss off the robe, then throw myself back on the bed.

"How does that school of yours work? Do I check-in under Blanco? Or do I sneak into your bedroom after dark?"

"I booked us here for three nights."

Toking on the cigar, Trey's not pleased. "How do I sign O. Maxwell if he's there, and I'm here?"

"No one I ever signed with had to move into my house."

Trey walks inside and rubs the cigar out in an ashtray. I tell her how weird the Academy can be, how they frown on fraternizing with the opposite sex, that even players' wives get the cold shoulder. Trey stands at the foot of the bed. A slant of light fires perfectly between her legs. I feel the blood stirring below. Trey notices my penis inching up like a mechanical crane.

"You should get a haircut."

"What's wrong with my hair?"

"David Lee Roth is a bit 1984, don't you think?"

"I mostly keep it in a ponytail."

"Need I say more?" Trey crawls between my legs, flicking the lighter on and off. "Don't pout. You're still cute as ever." She tosses the lighter on the floor then puts me in her mouth, giving the skin a little teeth.

I tense, staring at the ceiling.

I really don't like this woman.

* * *

The following day, another scorcher, after I told Heather I had the stomach flu and wouldn't be joining her and Cherokee at Longboat Key, after I blew off the afternoon drills, Trey and I find ourselves under a private cabana at the pink stucco Sarasotan that rises six stories above the white sand beaches of Siesta Key. Trey lies on her stomach in her beige bikini. She reads a *Wall Street Journal* that's folded in half underneath her chair. She's in a good mood. Her dialogue with the ballplayer went well. We've shared a plate of prawns dipped in honey chutney, plus several beers. Drink. Eat. Sex. This is our mantra.

Mom calls while Trey's refilling our water cups at the bar. She's not pleased with my leaving Los Angeles without an explanation.

"I won Newport. I thought you'd be proud of me."

"I didn't get the part."

I look past the pool, at the shimmering ocean. "Sorry, Mom."

"Sharon Stone got it. And she can't act."

"Then you didn't see *Basic Instinct*."

"Very funny."

"Can I ask you something, Mom? Do you think of me as a grown-up?"

"There was a time when your father and I were very worried. You were so aloof and doing drugs."

"You're not answering the question."

Mom laughs and asks if this is my sneaky way of telling her the stripper has a bun in the oven. I assure her, no, not in a million years. But then, after hanging up, I picture Heather with tumid tummy and achy mother's breasts. The image doesn't gag me. The opposite occurs. I feel warm and fuzzy imagining Heather carrying my seed.

Trey returns with our fruit-incensed waters. She lies on her belly again.

The sun at this late hour is a fiery iridescent ball smudged on the horizon. I watch a pudgy family trudge from the blazing surf in snorkel fins and baggy swim wear. The Russian was an expert diver. She dove without tanks. Sixty feet she'd plummet with a dagger tied to her thigh. As a child, her father had taught her to slow her heart rate and clear the lungs. On our travels, I'd watch from the boat as she disappeared into the bluest color on earth. Gone two minutes sometimes. When the Russian surfaced, she wouldn't hurl upward like a breached whale. She'd slip the surface, this delicate mist escaping her mouth. I loved her then, her coolness under pressure, her courage. I loved her so much I wanted to put her in a box.

"You snorkel?"

Trey grunts, then flips the newspaper over. "Run an ice cube down my back, would you?"

I finger an ice cube from my cup and plop it in my mouth. Rolling it around with my tongue, I eye Trey's backside. She's not fit like Heather. My Heather runs a seven-minute mile in dead summer heat. My Heather is nothing without her stretching, her contortions. Trey's more skin and bone. Despite the filthy smoking habit, she's spectacular. We're getting plenty of looks.

I drop the ice cube down Trey's bikini bottom. "Hey!" Her smile burns.

"Let's snorkel. It will be fun."

"Isn't it kind of late for that?"

"You mean because sharks feed this time of day?" I can tell I've alarmed her. "Come on. It'll be invigorating."

Off we go to the shack that provides equipment, the waif-like sports rep in mesh bikini and her hard-muscled beau. The ocean at sundown is a dense blue enigma, flat on the surface, peripatetic below. It's another world under the dark water. Sea creatures running amuck. Nothing to protect man from the deep. And the sharks I warned Trey about? Every year you hear about another reef shark attacking unsuspecting swimmers in these waters.

We float side by side. Visibility is good with the white sandy floor. We see starfish and sand dollars. A stingray skirts past. I point out a family of trumpetfish in the soupy blue. The current pushes them sideways and the long, oddly shaped fish right themselves like buoys. I watch them, dumbstruck. This thought comes to me. Trumpetfish are like me. They drift. They are easily swayed. They're unmoored. This feeling stays with me long after we've taken the elevator to the second-highest floor. There, we shower, put on robes, then devour sea scallops over squid-ink pasta and drink two bottles of Chardonnay. During lovemaking, my mind drifts back to the Russian and the time we rented a cottage in Carmel. One afternoon I found her in the sauna. She was laid out on the top bench naked and covered in sweat. Things between us were already tense. We were at that stage where the relationship could go either way. The Russian said she loved me. And I cracked inside. I went to her and showered her hair and forehead with kisses. I thought—she's the one, I've finally found a woman who gets me. I'd never felt more sure of anything in my life. A few weeks later, the Russian moved in with Christian Brothers. I never understood that. How could she fall out of love so fast?

* * *

I wait until I hear Trey's drunken snores to walk onto the balcony. At midnight, the bay is dark and incomprehensibly big. So much so I face the other way dialing Heather. She picks up on the first ring. When she asks how I'm feeling, I remember my little white lie about indigestion. She thinks Alaska is the place to go. Last night she dreamed she was swimming with whales. Then Heather laughs. And me, what do I do? I succumb to tears. I stare at the Gulf of Mexico, sniveling like a little boy.

"Richard? What's wrong?"

"I love you," I manage to say without sounding too pathetic.

We hang up soon after. I'm relieved I finally told Heather the truth. But I feel this heavy burden, too. Slipping under the bedsheets, I can't help thinking this is something I can't undo. That for all my looks and charm, for once, I won't be able to talk my way clean. Sometime later, I wake in an alcohol fog. At first, I'm not sure where I am. Then I see this thing on the balcony. I peer harder in the dark. It's Luke. He's this great heap in the chair, half man, half something else. Like a bird-man sitting on top of a skyscraper, poised over a city in ruins. Soon I tumble into another dream. Luke flapping great feathered wings, keeping a threat at bay. Him standing over the bed, his wings spread wide, Luke leaping from the balcony, then flying away.

* * *

We leave early, groggy-eyed, cotton-mouthed, no morning sex. Trey's shorts are so teeny half her ass hangs out the back end. When the valet driving the car around sees her, he nearly loses control. What's Trey trying to prove? She could wear baggy prison garb, no makeup, and not brush her hair for a year, and men would look her way. We'd fucking ogle.

Then, it's through the Academy gates, 8:12 a.m., all according to plan. I turn left on the main road, driving slow like the blue-hairs you see in town. The street is covered in shadow. Sleepy-eyed students walk toward the cafeteria, some still in pajamas. I'm about to park when I apply the brake. Heather's Jeep is pulled up. What is she doing here?

I do a hard U-turn, then gun the Subaru up the drive three times the speed limit. I even hit the horn when this poor girl fails to move quick enough.

Luke clucks his tongue. *Oh, the pickles you get yourself in, Blank.*

"Is everything okay?"

"I forgot to fill the tank," I say, once we've cleared the gatehouse. "Academy policy. They're real sticklers about the rules. You'll see."

"You're being weird."

7-Eleven is a short walk from the south retaining wall. When I was a junior player, my friends and I scaled the wall after curfew for late-night food runs. Here I am seventeen years later feeling as desperate and sure of myself as I did back then. I fill the tank, then buy Trey an umbrella to protect her from the brutal Floridian sun. Soon we're waving to the old security guy again. I creep the hatchback forward, even slower than before. Heather's car is still parked at the office doors.

"Unbelievable."

"What is?"

Tell her, Blank. Spill the fucking beans, man.

Just what would I say? Oh, by the way, you know my girlfriend? She's a hostess/personnel manager at an all-nude club in Sarasota. Isn't that a hoot?

Instead, I pull up the frontage road that ends at Claudia's office. We idle there, Trey checking her makeup in the passenger mirror, me racking my brain with what to do next.

I place an earnest hand on Trey's knee.

"Stay close. We're covering a lot of ground."

We mow over the property like locusts on a killing spree. We scour every inch of land no one ever visits. I take Trey over shortcuts only students and staff frequent, narrow footpaths, the ground shorn clean. At every open area, I put a nose to the wind, smelling for Faberge Organics Shampoo.

"Adult pool, adult jacuzzi, adult cafeteria. Any questions?"

"Do we have to go so fast? I'm in heels."

"There's just so much to see."

Trey puts her nose to the air, too. With her, it's like she's sniffing me out. "You lived here five straight years? As a teenager?"

"I went home for Christmas."

"Talk about arrested development."

The things I could tell Trey, if I wasn't looking over my shoulder every five seconds. Like the kid from Pittsburgh, Rick Reynolds. Jesus, he was something else. He did this thing... how do I put this without sounding sick myself? It was his penis. He was always pulling it out to show the guys. Girls were scared stiff. But us? What could we do? Beat the shit out of him every time he exposed himself? He'd have been dead in three days. Anyway, there's no time for stories. I'm thinking the absolute worst.

"You seem nervous."

"I told you. Coach doesn't like us bringing the opposite sex around."

I avoid her inquisitive eyes. The woman unnerves me. Sometimes she gives me this look. Her eyes don't hold back. They go dark with censure.

We've reached the breezeway that connects the main building and back offices. Through the thick hedge, I make out the Wrangler's black grill. Then, voices on the road, adult voices, his and her voices. Strathers is encouraging Heather to visit the Academy more often. He admits Cherokee is progressing, but thinks it would boost her confidence if Mom supported her more in person.

"It's important Cherokee learn on her own, Billy. In tennis, a player is all by herself out there."

She sounds like you, Blank. You must be proud.

Strathers appears from around the clipped bush with his raccoon suntan and mirrored Revo's hanging by a cord around his neck. He doesn't see us, so intent on doing the gentlemanly thing and letting Heather pass first.

"Have I shown you the cafeteria?" I've opened the side door and pulled Trey inside.

Right away, we smell hotcakes and lemony disinfectant from the dishwasher area. The moment we come into view—me and my practice clothes, Trey and her miniature shorts—the room shuts down like Chernobyl after the nuclear meltdown. Teen boys, scarfing down rubbery sausages, drop open their mouths like a loader on a backhoe. The three girls singing Whitney Houston *a cappella* stop on cue. I've put considerable distance between Trey and myself, you know, so no one gets the wrong idea. A quick scan tells me Cherokee isn't eating breakfast. Drabo waves us over from the pro's table. He sits with O. Maxwell and the others.

Trey motions toward the table with eager eyes. "Aren't you going to introduce me?"

I'm torn. On one end of this long room sits my peers with their covert glances and mischievous grins. And behind me probably stands my pissed off girlfriend. We walk over to the guys. Trey hands out business cards. The guys act nonchalant but also steal prolonged looks her way.

"I work for Saiko Investments. We're based in Tokyo and always looking for fresh, young faces. It's a big market over there."

The students have lost interest. They've gone back to their maple-flavored corn syrup, their trays of milk glasses, their Top 40 hits.

The only guy Trey extends her hand to is the Academy's latest protege. "Great year, O. My team is very impressed."

He nods like he gets propositioned by sponsor companies all day long. "I'll pass it on to my agent."

I peek over my shoulder toward the entrance. "We should go."

In no time, we've exited the cafeteria. I breathe easier back in the stilted humidity. Strathers comes around the corner, whistling a tune.

"Morning, Blank." He takes a sip from his coffee cup, appreciating every inch of Trey Hamasaki. "You must be the woman who called down for clearance."

"Trey Hamasaki. And you are?"

"Richard's old coach."

"The venerable Billy Strathers," I add.

"I'm not sure if that's a compliment or not," Strathers says, winking at Trey. "Richard was always the smartest guy in the room."

"It's a compliment, Strathers."

We watch him go, the ice queen and me, then start around the building. And I see the sunny-fresh Heather Harper, not fifty feet away, in white spandex, a skimpy workout top, and aerobics sneakers. She talks with Joanne. I steer Trey back the way we came.

The problem is Trey—she's seen Heather. It's written all over her face. "Who's that? The Academy's Hooters girl?"

I've broken a sweat. "That's not fair. You don't even know her."

"It sounds like you do."

"Well, I do. And she's a lovely human being with lots on her plate, including being a single parent. You have no right to judge her."

You tell her, Blank.

Just then, the Rubicon takes the corner. I see a flash of flaxen hair. Trey looks in the direction I'm peering. "You're on the run from her?"

* * *

I give myself up to the gods.

You have to under the pressures of being found out. For starters, Cherokee is six courts away. Then there's the powerfully built O. Maxwell across the net. A lesser player wilts, he comes undone. Not me. The gods are with me. They hold me aloft this morning. I go higher and higher.

We're playing a game called Ping-Pong. Between points, I glance at the flavor-of-the-week under her black parasol. Man, I'm hanging by a thread, down love and four to O. My life feels like a balloon that's ready to pop. And Heather's doing what? Plotting my assassination? Cursing her luck? Asking a travel agent about direct flights to Anchorage? I give myself up to the gods.

Janet Stipe shows up at 3–11 with a scarf around her neck. She brought company, a photographer with the audacity to walk on court and snap pictures like I'm something special. Before O and I started the game, I did the gentlemanly thing and encouraged him to serve first. He said, "Be my guest." So we were civil and spun a racquet for the choice to serve or not. Oh, we competitive guys and the mental games we play. I won the toss. Smiling, I deferred. O shook his dreadlocks. "Okay, old-timer. I'll serve." Thus, we began, him serving five, me serving five, Ping-Pong, get it? Then, at 5–14, Trey bounds down the bleachers, making a clatter everyone notices, and disappears somewhere in the Academy's folds. Not a minute later teenybopper Harper strolls past. I'm picking up a ball wedged under the fence when I stop. My gaze goes from Cherokee to where Stipe sits. Is she thinking what I'm thinking?

You mean the juggling plates theory, Blank?

O and I play two more points. I steal another look at Stipe. What's her angle? Seriously, why write a book about me? I've done nothing brilliant in this life. I can't even commit to a woman. If I were a god, would I be Hades? Ares? The eternal adolescent Hermes? Mr. Impulsive? Precisely.

"7–17," O calls out.

The next exchange has me following him to the net. His yin to my yang. There, we unleash a torrent of volleys so fast I lose count. The point ends with me tagging O in the chest. We cue up smiles for those watching. He is like me. Or, I was like him coming out of the gates— fast on the scene, a flair for the big shot, controversial.

O inspects the mark on his chest. And we laugh. Big, forced yuks for the cameraman. Practice finally over, I skulk around the property, thinking the worst. That any minute now, big-boned Heather will come charging onto campus and break Trey's chopstick legs in two.

I cover the property, twice. I check the office and Academy car. I even pop by the room. Sitting his sweaty ass on a towel is Drabo, tuned into CNN. He's a political science junkie. He seeks news on the homeland, Bosnia/Serbia relations, war crimes, war criminals, all things Eastern European. Drabo has let the atrocities go. He wants reparations; two states.

"You seen Trey?"

"No, I not see her. Everything okay?"

"If you do, tell her I'm at the car."

Another go-round the amusement park. I finally locate her. She and O. Maxwell stand under a white mangrove that grows offshoot to the laundry room overhang. Sweat marks stain the armpits of O's gray T-shirt. He holds a plastic hamper of clothes. Trey says something and

O's face lights up. They've yet to see me. The longer I watch, the more I think Trey sleeps with all her potential clients but never signs even one.

"Hi, Richard!"

Oh, Christ, Blank. Not Cherokee Harper, not now.

She's standing on the landing of Condo C when she waves excitedly, a tube sock fixed to her arm. I shoot a mortified look across the drive. Trey and O see me hiding in plain sight. O says something, and Trey squints harder in Cherokee's direction. The girl's coming on strong, down the stairwell, into the brittle noon light, her pigtails bouncing in the air like flailing legs. Cherokee screeches to a halt.

"Say hello to Richard, Mr. Sock Puppet. *Hello, Richard,*" she adds, using the ventriloquist's tic of talking between tight lips.

"I can't talk now."

"My friends and I are doing "Bohemian Rhapsody" in the talent show."

Already, Trey and O have parted ways, him prying the laundry door open using an elbow and foot, Trey's hips sashaying up the road.

"I said, beat it."

Cherokee notices my incisors showing. Her face plunges, all the color sucked clean.

"Is something wrong?"

"I said go."

Cherokee takes off, her face collapsing in tears, with her sock puppet and sneakers and bouncing hair. I feel a hurt I've never felt before. It's like getting the wind knocked out of you. How could I be so cruel?

Trey reaches me seconds later, her smile hard. "You're doing her mom?" I search where Cherokee slipped through the flora. "Wow, Richard. That's, well, that's really charming. And she's a stripper?"

"She's everything you're not."

"I bet she is."

I tromp toward the car.

"You're pouting again," Trey says, catching up.

I stop and look back where Cherokee vanished. "How could I be so mean?"

"She'll get over it. Kid's do."

* * *

Drink, eat, sex. Then, a reprieve. Or maybe a haircut is a truce. Oh, I don't know. I don't know anything anymore. Trey suggests Janet Stipe film the event. Stipe loves the idea. So down to the lobby I go. The hotel salon is a two-chair operation, Aveda on the shelf, Yanni playing in the background, not another guest in sight. My stylist's name is Gregory. He has frosted bangs and a pinky ring. He shampoos my hair while Stipe's guy gets it all on tape. I look exactly like I feel. Like an overpaid, under-appreciated player getting more attention than he deserves.

Gregory takes a chunk of hair between two fingers. He angles my sun-ravaged split-ends toward the camera then makes his first cut. And there goes nine inches. Gregory clips and giggles and snickers and snips. He's having a grand old time. His hands make speedy work. In no time at all, what took years to grow lies at my feet in damp clumps. I could cry.

"It's only hair," Stipe says.

But that's not altogether true. I went long because of Bjorn Borg. He was my man. He had rockstar hair, whipping passing shots, and an otherworldly presence. Dad thought my hair ridiculous. That was equally significant. Now I'm clean on the sides, tapered in back, a sideways part. I look, I don't know—adult or something.

Gregory spins my chair around. The cameraman gets it all on film.

"The hairdo brings out his eyes, don't you think?"

"You've such a handsome face, Richard. And now we can see it," Stipe says. "I was meaning to ask about your time at the Academy. Where did you and your father live?"

I see the apartment like it was yesterday. The art deco building off El Conquistador Parkway. The matted shag carpet path from the kitchen to the living room. His books. That oil of Paris street-life hanging in the living room.

"We moved off campus when we could afford to. Dad had an open door policy. Players and coaches were always stopping by. They talked with him about everything under the sun."

"What was he like?"

"Dad? He was a complete joy. And I'm not saying that because he was my father. He had this rolling energy. He was generous and ethical. A great guy."

Stipe stares at me. "You're emotional right now."

I wick a tear away.

"Do you miss him?"

"Of course I do. He taught me so much. Sometimes he talks with me. I do something I shouldn't, something unprintable, let's say, and Dad's voice is in my head like a dueling stereo. 'Have you thought about what you're doing, son? I mean, putting your little willy *in her?*'"

Everyone laughs at my British accent, even the camera guy.

We make plans to meet the following day before Stipe leaves for Los Angeles.

"And no cameras," I say. "Okay?"

* * *

Up I go, my fortress in the sky. Trey is so thrilled with the new me she buys me a summer suit in Sarasota's white-brick district. She talks the clothing shop owner into delivering the linen Canali to our room an hour later, tailored to fit. I watch her carry a Bible-thick fashion magazine into the bathroom. For twenty-seven minutes, she doesn't make a peep. The girl's backed up—full of toxins. It's all too much, everything I mean, the lifestyle, the alcohol, this woman. I go downstairs to call Heather. I miss her so much. Of equal importance is speaking to Cherokee before she confides in her mom. Neither Harper woman answers the phone. I leave a scattered message, promising a trip to Los Angeles, Santa Monica Pier, Universal Studios, In-N-Out Burger, that sort of thing. Then it's back upstairs.

"How much longer?"

Trey sits at the make-up counter. I watch her apply her warpaint. "Are you upset?"

"Is a contract en route? Should I let David know it's in the mail?"

* * *

At Nobu, the sushi chef waves a sharp knife and yells out, "*Irasshaimase!*" as we're escorted to our table. Trey orders for us in Japanese. Our waiter, a slim man with delicate features, says a curt *hai* to every question she poses. The food arrives on a lacquer tray. Seared ahi tuna salad, deep-fried soft shell crab, grilled salmon marinated in teriyaki, and sashimi sliced like fleshy bread.

Trey orders a coffee after dinner. "Steady my hands for later."

I assume she means more cavorting naked on the floor. "Nothing's left in the tank, Trey. Honest."

We don't talk riding the elevator up. We don't talk much, period. I leave the keycard on the table then hop on the bed. Trey showers. She's in there a long time. I'm watching ESPN when she comes out wearing the colorful raincoat she wore in London. Her bangs are combed down over her heavily made-up eyes.

"Going somewhere?"

Trey points the remote at the TV, turning it off. Then she pulls a leather satchel out from underneath the bed. She sets a candle, a silk handkerchief, condoms, shaving cream, and strands of rope on the bedside table.

"What's all this?"

Trey lights the candle with her Louis Vuitton. "Turn off the lamp."

"What's with the rope?"

"Lights, please."

I reach over and click it off. The room is now dark but for the wicked flame and the night streaming through the French doors. Trey unzips the raincoat and lets it fall to her feet. She wears a coral-red negligee with pushup wiring. In the semidarkness, Trey looks like a kinky doll. She turns on the clock-radio then scrolls until she hears a Todd Rundgren hit from the 70s.

"How do you feel about being restrained?"

It doesn't take long for Trey to strip me, bind the cloth over my eyes, and secure my wrists to the bed's corners. "What's she like?"

"My girlfriend?"

Trey yanks cruelly on the final ankle strap. "Don't go anywhere. I left an important item in the shower."

A woman's never tied me up before. Nor do I remember ever being blindfolded.

A dangerous subtext, eh? This being held against your will. A person could have their way with you, and what could you do?

I hear feet pad across thick carpet then sense Trey standing next to the bed. She waves what smells like tequila under my nose. "No, thanks."

"From here forward, nothing is negotiable."

"Well, if you insist." I've hardly gotten the words out when Trey practically empties half the bottle down my throat. "Jesus, Trey," I say, choking. She pours another load in. "What the fuck?"

The alcohol feels warm and fuzzy in my belly, the throat raw. Then I hear the shaving cream dispenser's unmistakable hiss. Next, something cold and wet coating my testicles.

"Don't be alarmed, but there's a single-edge razor inches from your hairy balls." Hearing razor and hairy balls in the same sentence has me flinching like a scared animal. Trey touches my upper thigh. Her hand is cold. "Relax, big boy. This will be over in a minute." I yank my wrists, then jerk my legs. "That's only making the knots tighter."

"This isn't funny. Untie me. Untie me fucking now."

Instead, everything in my body constricts. Why? Because Trey pushes a thumb under the testicle sac, tightening the skin.

"Steady, Richard." Trey scrapes upward. "Sharp blade. Nice."

"Jesus Christ." I'm gasping, arching my back, trying to buck the psycho off, all at the same time. "Take these goddamn straps off. Now."

You got to give it to her, Blank. The woman has man-sized balls.

Trey leans in close. "It could get real messy if you keep this up." Two swift turns of the blade, and I hear Trey swirl the razor in a glass of water. "First nutsack smooth as your girlfriend's bottom. "

A rush of tequila goes to my head. Between swipes, Trey sings along with the music, about taking for granted that I'm always there, about taking for granted that I just don't care. Then she sits on my thighs. And I sort of half chuckle. That wasn't so bad. Okay, my penis is limp and petrified, but otherwise, he's hanging in there. It's when Rundgren sings about coming around once in a while, especially if he needs a reason to smile, that I stiffen up again. For Trey has taken hold of my little bugger.

Be nice if she was stroking it with pleasure, huh Blank.

Rather, she's turning my cock side to side, the way a dentist checks your tongue for gingivitis.

"You're ratty down here. I'd recommend being real still during this part. I'd hate to... well, you understand."

"Is this about the contract? Or my girlfriend? I mean, that's *so over*." Again, I hear the shaving gel's drowning fizz. "Please, I beg you. Be careful. We're talking about my livelihood."

"Livelihood?"

"My manhood. I can't think with this blindfold on. Please take it off."

Trey pats my hip. "There's a reason why they cover a horse's eyes when it's scared. Here, have another drink of courage." Trey pries open my mouth then dumps more fiery liquid down the hatch.

"There's an artery there," I say, gulping for oxygen. "A big one. So please, please stop."

"Richard? You're trembling." Then her voice turns edgy. "Seriously? Don't move."

My mouth dries up like a saltine cracker.

"Hello, It's Me" is now John Lennon's equally cheery "(Just Like) Starting Over." Trey sets the blade on edge. This whimper creeps up my throat. The scraping noise is like an old dog scratching its mangy fur.

"This blade is like plowing through snow."

I sort of lose time. Soon, it's over. Trey wipes the area clean with a towel.

"Who was your favorite Beatle? I liked Ringo. I liked his name. He was the smirk in the back of the room. He kept the Beatles from being pretentious, don't you think?"

"Is there blood?"

"Just a little."

"Will you take this goddamn thing off."

Trey runs a hand between my legs. As much as I don't want to enjoy it, I do.

"Fucking untie me."

Trey has other plans. Like tickling. The more I plead with her to stop, the more she digs her fingers in. I flinch and laugh and beg her to quit. Soon my side throbs and tears stream down my face and as much as I want to stop laughing, I can't.

"Tell me you want it."

"Just get it over with."

"Is my sexy man going to cry again?"

After she's through pleasuring us, she pours more liquor inside me—lots more. Then I hear her taking pictures. "Honestly, Trey? Haven't you done enough damage tonight?"

You should kill her.

"I fucking should."

"You should what?" Trey says, pressing the Polaroid again.

Are you counting, Blank?

"Eight, so far."

You sure? I thought it was nine?

"You don't think I can count?"

"Who are you talking to?" Trey screams.

Then, I'm not tracking sounds. I think I hear Trey on the balcony, but she might be in the loo. Or maybe she's on the hotel phone. There's a new one on the radio. Mom loved this hit single when I was a kid. She'd crank the volume then prance around our West LA apartment singing about dark desert highways, pink champagne on ice, running for the door. I get frightened again. What will Trey do if I pass out? By the fucking way—where is she? I call out her name. Maybe I scream. Then she's sitting on the bed, stroking my hair. The last thing I see before passing out is Heather. Heather and her blue eyes.

JULY 19, 1996, 9:01AM

THE SARASOTAN, ROOM #505

I wake, temple pounding, and lift the head to have a look around. And it hits me—the mad queen is gone. Everything, her fancy creams and cosmetics, her cigars and constipation, are cleaned out. All that remains is a large shopping bag by the door, crammed with shoeboxes, plastic wrap, and empty liquor bottles.

Spread-eagled, shackled, parched, and needing to urinate, I take a moment to compose myself. Then I peer between my legs and breathe with relief. Johnson may look idiotic, but the dude's still down there slumbering away.

Out the balcony window the sky is the delicate blue of morning. The air-conditioner fan whirs. Otherwise, no sounds come from the plush-carpeted hall. My phone sits within arm's length on the bedside table, next to the hotel cordless and my beeper. If only I could reach them. There's something else on the stand. A Polaroid of my Johnson in all his naked glory.

"That fucking bitch."

Maybe thirty minutes go by. I nod off, woken by the bladder alarm. Maid racket in the hall has me straining toward the heavy, white-paneled door. I yell out, not too loud, but enough volume that the voices outside my room quiet. A woman, presumably a cleaning lady, asks what she can help me with. Good question. I can't just come out and say I'm naked and restrained, please help, I need to tinkle.

"I can't come to the door."

"Can't get off the toilet?"

"Yes. Please help."

The door clicks open. A young woman holding a keycard and a dollar bill of an undetermined amount peers in. I'm craning my neck to see her reaction. Her dishwater-blonde hair is pulled into a mess. When she sees my predicament, she casts her eyes on the floor.

"Hi. As you can see, I'm in a tight spot."

"Shirley," she yells out the door. "You got to see this."

"Did Walker put a dead mouse on the bed again?" The woman named Shirley appears. She's older by twenty years or so. When she sees me stranded on the bed, a smile creases her portly face. She's missing several teeth. "Oh, lordy. It's a gigolo, Roxy. And I thought I'd seen it all."

Both housekeepers haven't moved. Weird, the things we do when we're uncomfortable. The younger one fondles a stray hair, the other sticks a finger in the space between two molars like she's rubbing whiskey on a rotten tooth.

"I know how this looks. But can you help me out?"

The two go back and forth, talking up a storm. The fat one comments on my brawny build. She wonders aloud why my private area is groomed.

The younger one has turned as pink as the popular stucco buildings in southern Florida. She's got a strain of the religious in her, the way she keeps submitting to the carpet with her "amens" and "oh, holy lords." I interrupt by telling them I'll double whatever the tip money is. The younger one leans in conspiratorially and asks her friend if this is a setup.

"You mean he set a large bill on the knob, shut the door, took off his clothes, shaved himself down there, and then tied his self up so we'd walk in on him?"

Roxy glances at me. "I guess I see what you mean."

"How much did she leave?" I ask.

"A hundred-dollar bill."

"There goes our negotiating position," Shirley says, sighing.

"I'll triple it. Now, please untie me."

"Let's say we let him go," Roxy continues, a hand on her sternum. "How do we know he won't attack us?"

"If he gets an erection, girl, you wait five minutes, then you call Walker, you hear?"

"Excuse me, ladies? Will you at least cover me up while we discuss if I may or may not be a gigolo who wants to attack you?"

"He's right, you know," Roxy says, glancing at my private area. "We should cover his, you know…"

"His George Washington? Let me." Shirley bounds past and walks into the bathroom.

Without her friend in the room, Roxy takes a fluffy tool from her outfit's front bin and starts dusting the light switch.

"Look, this woman tied me up. She got me drunk. I'm not a bad guy." I give the younger one the politest smile I can. Shirley returns from the bath. "Good lord. You brought me a washcloth?"

The towel resting on my penis is the size of a postcard. It gets worse. For the women pull up chairs like they're about to give me last rites. They converse like before, in half whispers. Should we cover the boy-toy with a sheet? Is shaving one's privates a popular new trend? What would they be willing to part with if the role was switched, and they were the ones lying naked and exposed, and it was me lording over them? Roxy wants to call Walker. I gather he's in charge of the cleaning crew.

"That's a great idea."

This falls on deaf ears.

Shirley thinks this whole thing stinks of a hustler tryst gone wrong. She wants nothing to do with the dirty details, although she is curious what a young buck like me costs for an entire night.

I shoot the fat one a mean look. "I'm not a gigolo."

"Of course, you're not." Shirley rises from her chair. She inspects the knots more closely. "The dude knew what he was doing."

"A woman did this."

"How many women know how to tie a slip knot?"

"It sounds like you do."

"My father was a fisherman," Shirley says defensively.

"Please untie me. I'm begging you."

Poker face on, Shirley lifts the tiny towel and peeks below. After she re-situates the cloth, she gives my pecker a pat. "Sorry. I wanted to see if George was getting enough air."

"That's not cool, Shirley."

She looks at the clock radio. "We should be getting back, Roxy. I've got six rooms that need cleaning."

"What about him?"

"Yeah, what about me? You know something—wait until Walker hears how you're treating a paying guest."

"The gigolo's threatening us, Roxy."

"I have money of my own. Name your price."

Shirley and Roxy have more words. Well, Shirley does most of the talking. Finally, she walks over to the bed. "You walk onto the balcony, look out over the ocean, then stretch like you've just woken up." Shirley breaks eye contact. "Then you walk in, give us a wink, and that's it. Oh, and $300."

"Fine, whatever."

Shirley undoes my ankle straps. She's untying my left wrist when she goes scared in the face. "You're not going to be violent if we let you go, are you?"

"I promise." Free at last, I sit up then rub my tender wrists. "Unlike you, I'm a decent human being. I'll prance around if you want. But first, I'm going to pee."

"I can live with that."

"You two are sick, you know that?"

"This wasn't my idea," Roxy says, making the sign of the cross. "I could have just stared at you all day."

Shirley's face burns. "You're the most beautiful thing I've ever seen."

I walk into the bath, one hand holding the cloth over my genitals, the other covering my ass.

In the end, I put on a Chippendale's-inspired show. At one point, I toss the washcloth at Shirley. She brings the loin-rag up to her nose and inhales like it's the scent of her long lost love. Roxy lies on the bed and suggestively twists the sheets between her legs. Johnson even wakes from his slumber.

Does my story seem farfetched? Am I pulling your leg? Did I really strut about the room like a proud rooster, chest puffed out, my jewels bouncing around like rubber balls? Or did I throw the maids out while tossing bills in the hall like O. Maxwell did the other night at The Golden Banana?

* * *

Housekeeping gone, the suite takes on a bothersome silence. I glance at the clock-radio. Saturday drill ends in two hours. Then the Academy shuts down until Monday morning. That means Coach goes home to his girlfriend, Strathers takes his family to the mall, and Claudia does whatever she does when she's not pontificating on Carl Jung. And I need her right now.

But first, a violent bout on the toilet. Then, while the shower heats up, I call Room Service, order a bloody-rare burger and a Coca-Cola to soothe my upset stomach. Toweling off afterward, I get a better look at the damage—the teeth marks, bruises and razor burns. And I lose it. My face goes contorted and weepy like it did the first few months after Dad passed.

I put on my suit, throw the Polaroid in my duffle bag, then wolf down the burger in the elevator. Once I settle up the bill, I walk out the automatic doors. It's another day in paradise, meaning hot, hot, hot. The glare is unbearable. I hand the valet a tenner then dig in my bag for sunglasses. The moment I enter U.S. 41, I call Joanne. She puts me on hold. I can't let go of last night. What if Trey had cut my Johnson off? Sliced it with a hooked blade like a butcher does a hanging piece of salami. Trey with steady hand and black heart, a long, clean stroke. The image is enough to make me panic again. And how about those housekeepers? The fat one especially. If I simply suggested the things she did, I'd be handcuffed to a chair right now.

I drive through a couple intersections, and honestly, I don't know if the lights were green or not. I pass Long John Silvers, a Hooters that's always trying to employ Heather, Glauser Mercedes. Finally, Joanne comes back on the line.

"Is Claudia around? It's urgent."

"Urgent? Or urgent-urgent?"

"It depends. Probably the latter." Joanne pencils me in, an hour later. Sixty minutes? What if I was truly suicidal?

I dial up psycho-woman and get bumped into voice mail. "My lawyer says there's enough evidence to press charges. Either hand over the photo collection, or I go to the police. And don't think I didn't count how many you took." I clamp shut the Motorola and toss it on the passenger seat. Thirteen minutes later, I lumber up the stairs. Drabo left the television on. The station broadcasts one of my favorite films, *Fast Times At Ridgemont High*. I happen in on the infamous swimming pool/masturbation scene. The song playing when Phoebe Cates' Linda Barrett climbs out of the pool is The Cars "Moving In Stereo." The music is this bleary landscape of feedbacked guitar and spaced out synthesizer reminiscent of the late 70s New Wave sound. The narrator is having a breakdown. He's suicidal or insane. Or maybe he's just having a bad day. Meantime good old Brad Hamilton (an excellent Judge Reinhold) is in full-on dream fantasy. We're in another world, where mist falls, lush flowers hang in the background, and Linda yanks open her bikini in such gorgeous light you see water droplets fling off her top. In the past, I've always laughed when Linda barges in on Brad jerking off. Today, I let out this heart-rending sigh. Today the pool scene has me thinking about female objectivity and the male gaze. It has me wondering if I see women like Brad does—through that same distorted lens.

I step outdoors in my summer suit to clear the head.

Past the clay courts I go, where the property opens up. The sun beats down on the athletic fields, the morning shadows gone. I hear the knock of the ball, a whistle here, a yell of encouragement there, that cute, annoying squeak-grunt Monica Seles made *de rigueur*. Every court is occupied by junior players swatting ball after bloody ball. Oh, these tennis factories we've devised. All the obeisance and blind devotion. All those reckless dreams. Let me tell you, these institutions suck the life out of you. I was in Hamburg the last time Dad saw me play. He had flown into Zurich to participate in an experimental AIDS drug trial. He took the train over with his nurse. They sat Dad and his wheelchair in the front row with a wool blanket wrapped around his legs. I played Shirokov. And I was playing lights-out incredible. Shirokov's got maybe the best backhand on the planet. He hits a one-hander so far in front of his body it's in the next time-zone. There was one point where he'd sent a rocket up the line. But I'd read the shot all the way. That's what the zone means. Everything is magnified. Senses, colors, focus. Shirokov's backhand traveled through a shaft of sunlight. And it lit up Cezanne gold. It was like an orb. I nearly toppled over. I thought—there's so much beauty in the world if you open your eyes. And I looked at Dad and broke down.

* * *

"Then a maid walked in." I'm telling Claudia about my ordeal. We're in our places. We're acting out our roles. The therapist listening in the dark, her patient lying on the floor trying to find the words. The tension between us isn't gone, but it's knocked down. "Her friend, another housekeeper, came into the room. She was older. And she had a thing for me, Claudia." Onward I journey, down the dark hole at a throttled clip. I tell Claudia everything about the weekend, not chronologically, but as it comes to me, the overindulgence, the boredom, the perverted shit.

"You wouldn't believe Trey. And I thought I had problems."

"It's good to hear you joking about it."

"I look like a little boy down there."

"Don't make me laugh, Richard."

"I think if circumstances were different, the old one would have paid to have sex with me. And she was fat, Claudia, not fat-fat, but robust, thick around the waist, you know what I mean? Did you know I've never been with a fat woman?"

There's a pause on Claudia's part. "Is that so?"

"Or at least I don't remember. Maybe when I was drunk. Does it count if you don't remember?"

"What did the old fatty do next? Eat her way through the minibar? I bet that was hilarious."

There's a bite in Claudia's voice that has me smirking. The thing is, last night—what Trey did to me—feels like a violation of the strictest sense.

"Oh my god. I'm so sorry, Claudia. I didn't realize what I was saying. I don't have anything against big women."

"Are you saying I have a weight problem?"

"Of course not, no. This is me making a big ass of myself and asking forgiveness. Where were we? Oh, I know. Can I make another comment?"

"About fat women?"

"Funny, ha ha. No, I've learned something today. Be careful about the company you keep. Also, I told myself if I got out alive, and believe me, it was touch and go for a while, I said to myself, 'I'm committing to Heather. I mean really commit.'"

"I've heard this all before. To be honest, I'm skeptical."

"I'm telling you, I've changed. She could have nicked an artery. Where would I be then? In the fucking morgue, that's where."

"Are you going to tell Heather?"

"Yes, I am. Well, I don't think I'll mention that the sex was unbelievable."

"Was it?"

"Holy Christ. I'm getting an erection thinking about it. And that shames me, Claudia. It shames me to the core."

"I think it's time I stop treating you, Richard. I don't know when you're being straight or screwing around anymore."

"But I'm not ready to face life on my own."

"I checked in with Dr. Goldberg. He says he hasn't heard from you."

"It's on my to-do list."

The blinds thrum alive, turning the light over. "With Heather, I'd suggest skipping the part about being shaved. That's the sort of imagery that ruins relationships."

"You think?"

Claudia gathers her notepad and iced tea and starts to leave.

"Hey, Claudia? Sorry about the fat jokes."

I hear her talking to someone in the waiting room. Farewells are said, and then the door whooshes closed. I wait another minute before leaving. There, flipping through this month's *Tennis Week*, is my agent. David is dressed like the southern gentlemen he's not—smart navy blazer, pink oxford, khaki slacks. Leaning against the coffee table are five new racquets.

"What are you doing here?"

He points at the sticks. "Drabo's first endorsement deal."

"Babolat's going into the racquet business? Good luck with that."

"You remember your first deal?" he says. "Chiquita. Ten thousand dollars and a year's supply of bananas." David takes a moment to look me over. "Sharp suit. And you cut your hair. Whose idea was that? No, let me guess. How's that going anyway?"

"I don't want to talk about it."

"She faxed us an offer," David says.

"How bad is it?"

I can tell by David's expression that the deal isn't good.

"125K, one year, no extensions. There's a $25,000 bonus if you sign within twenty-four hours."

"Fuck her."

"You schtuped her five, six times. Think of it as payment for services rendered."

"Why does everyone think I'm a prostitute?"

"You okay? Are you stressing about the book?"

The book? Oh, shit, the Stipe interview is happening right now. "Refuse the bonus on the grounds that I almost died."

"Died?"

I start walking for the exit. "Well, nearly. I mean, it was a possibility." David eyes me like he knew the day would come when I'd gone completely mad. "You weren't there. The blade was—she could have really hurt me."

"Are you talking about your haircut? It looks great."

I push open the front door. "125K? I take it, she wins. And if I don't? *She still wins.*"

I exit into the stuffy, torrid air. I can't expect David to understand. What Trey did was psychological abuse. And now I've got to act normal with Janet Stipe? There's Heather, too. How will that turn out? Bad, I think. How can it not? If she knows I'm a cheat, her mind might already be made up. I'm seized by more anxiety. I need to keep my shit together. We're talking my A-game when it comes to Stipe. How I come across—self-confident or gun-shy or dazed and confused—will end up in the book. That's what a good writer does. She burrows under the surface, brings to light a player's true character, gives the reader disparate perspectives. Hey, I'm coming clean to Heather. I'm praying it saves us. But if Cherokee's already got to her, I'm doomed.

Stipe sits under an umbrella at the adult pool. At noon the water is a crisp-blue, the glare sharp. No one else lies poolside. "I thought the celebrity had forgotten."

The reporter wears a black one-piece, her cleavage tan and spongy. Her hair is wet and swept off her forehead. She's even brought me a watery lemonade.

"Sorry I'm late." I've hung my suit coat over the chair then plopped down.

"You're dressed up. Big night on the town?"

"It was something, alright."

Stipe finds my partying ways amusing. She sets a recorder on the table and hits play. "Shall we begin?" Next to the recording device is a barely nibbled turkey-avocado-on-sourdough. I'm ravished, even after the greasy hamburger this morning. Stipe sees me eyeing her food.

"Go on," she says. "Eat up." I smile like a kid embarrassed about his growing metabolism. That doesn't stop me from stuffing half the sandwich in my mouth. "You're a hungry boy."

I swallow the whole thing down with the luke-cold drink. "You don't follow athletes, do you? I keep forgetting Hollywood is your beat. Well, we can put away food."

"And where does it all go?"

Good question. Does she mean the food? Or is Stipe going for something deeper? Does she mean, where does the time go? Is it fleeting like the great poets suggest? Will I wake up twenty-five years from now and think—what a blur life was? Is that why we write books? To put down in words what it means to live at a particular moment in history? To slow down the toil of time?

I shove the other half in my mouth. "We burn what we need," I say, between chews. "We store the rest in a reserve tank left of the lower intestine. Frankly, the tank's uncomfortable, especially if you're dehydrated." Parched, I pour the rest of the lemonade down.

"And I'm supposed to believe that?"

"You should see the women eat. They pile the carbs a foot high. It's a sight to see. Say, are you drinking your lemonade?" Stipe watches me drain her glass, too.

It is plenty warm in Florida on a cloudless Saturday in mid-July, even in the shade. My linen slacks are damp at crotch and knee. My dress shirt sticks to the chair's back. I catch Stipe scrutinizing my hair.

"How does it feel, day two?"

"Like a swath of my life was hacked away." I glance at her ring finger, not remembering if Stipe is single or not. "Do you have a significant other?" Stipe's eyes come alive, the interview swinging in her direction like that. "So, you don't see him often?"

"It goes with the territory. You know all about balancing your personal and professional life, don't you? Being on the road can't make it easy. Is that what broke you and Marta up? The distance?"

Here we go. The dirt and sordid details. Sex is what sells at airport kiosks and grocery store checkout lines. "Marta dumped me for that really good looking actor with the stupid name. It hurt for a long time. But I'm over it. We weren't meant to be."

"How is your love life these days?"

A honeysuckle Heather appears in my head. I sort of bliss out. "It's fucked."

Stipe's not sure what to think. So she laughs. "But your expression—"

"I'm in love. I'm just not sure how she feels about me."

Meantime something sinister is happening in my crotch. I believe it's leaking and on fire. I want to shove my hand in my underwear and scratch like mad. But the tape recorder is on. The reporter is taking notes about my life. So I do my best to appear calm. Stipe probes further. She wants names. She wants rumor and innuendo. I push back, a stubbornness I learned from Mom. I'm protective of Heather in a way that's honorable and touching but also tiresome and defensive. What am I afraid of? Haven't I always worn my heart on my sleeve?

"I've done things, okay? Things I'm ashamed of."

Stipe waits, her eager eyes fixed on me. The nicked skin feels like it's eating itself raw.

"Where were we? Oh, yeah. Heather."

"Is she the Asian woman I saw at practice yesterday?"

"Why would you think that woman was with me?"

Stipe picks up on my hostility. "Who is she then?"

"Did I tell you I've only got a few minutes?"

The groin continues to fester. We skip around a bit. This is how these interviews go. They're messy and jumbled, much like the early games in a tennis match, neither player showing too much game, both hiding weaknesses best they can.

"What do you think about O. Maxwell?" she asks.

We discuss his growing popularity. Did you know O's being called the future of men's tennis? Neither did I. I begrudgingly acknowledge O's talent. I mention he's a good breather. By now, the midsection has gotten nasty. I'm wondering if lubricant is in order. Like Vaseline or liquid nitrogen. Then I wonder if Trey gave me a ghastly disease. Crabs or maybe lice. You can never be too sure with aggressive women like her. *Did you say lice?* Freak-show Luke whispers. *If she gave you lice, pea brain, those buggers would need hair to hold onto.*

"And I don't have any hair." Did I say the last part out loud?

Stipe looks up from her notes, baffled. "Are you still worried your fans won't embrace the new hairdo? You have nothing to worry about, Richard."

You know what I'd like more than anything right now? I'd like to hold the interview in the swimming pool. Waist deep would do. Cold, chlorinated water—that's what my wounds need. That would feel better than the zone.

Nothing better than the zone, Blank, not sex, not blowjobs, not blow. Not even falling in love.

"Are you okay? You seem jumpy."

"Would you excuse me?" In standing, I knock over the cheap plastic chair. I take off, a desperate run-trot, leap a bright-white chaise, then duck behind the pump filter privacy wall. There, I shove my hand down my fancy britches. The groin is smeared and snotty and icky-hot, but that doesn't stop me from digging my fingernails in. Soon, I'm seated, the pulse up, sweating like crazy, the groin momentarily quenched. "Whew. Is it hot or what?"

Stipe leans over the table. Her mottled breasts are pushed to the brink of the suit's wired support. She stares at me an uncomfortably long time. "Are you hiding something? For this to work, for the two of us to write the page-turner that sells briskly, we need to trust each other. You can't hold back."

Talk circles around to Dad. His impressive library. His fastidious style. The stuff he taught me. Stipe asks what it was like having a gay Dad.

"You mean the penis thing?"

Her focus sharpens. She leans in again, with her journalistic talons, her predatory ambitions. "The penis thing?"

"You want to know if I questioned my sexuality because Dad was gay?"

"Go on."

"I think we all question which way we lean at some point in life. For me, it was puberty. Mom had already told me he was gay. So eventually, you're in the shower with boys your age. You look around. You think, does the penis thing do for me what it did for Dad?"

Stipe swallows her saliva. "Well, did it?"

"I think my track record speaks for itself."

"What about Luke Scream? You two were inseparable. Were you lovers?"

"Are you talking about that kiss?"

"That's a good starting off point. How does it feel kissing a man?"

I stop what I'm doing—nonchalantly jamming a butter knife into my crotch—to stare quizzically at the journalist. Luke smelled musty. And like burnt tobacco. I felt his day-old whiskers. I realized a man's face is rough, like sandpaper. But what was it like?

"Look, Stipe, all of us, meaning you, me, the pool guy, we're all somewhere on that Kinsey sexual continuum. You want me to admit I'm bisexual. But I can't say that. I wish I could because I'm a great supporter of Dad, Luke Scream, and gay people everywhere. But I'm not gay. To answer your question about kissing Luke, it was pretty disgusting. I did it to support him. People need to back off about a person's sexuality. If Jamie likes Alexis, and Alexis is into Sally, and Sally's brother, Liam, loves Jamie, so be it. Who cares?" Stipe's mouth droops with disappointment. "Did I shatter your hopes for a bestselling tell-all?"

"A little."

"Do you want the truth or a bestseller?"

She fingers the recorder, then looks into my eyes. "Both."

"Well, I'm willing to provide the truth, but I can't promise the book will fly off the shelf."

She doesn't care about you, Blank. She said it before—bestseller.

I cross my legs and, with my hip muscles, attempt to squeeze the unpleasant sensation for good.

"Can we talk about AIDS?"

"AIDS kills. Ask Dad, ask Luke, ask the twenty-five million gay men who died from AIDS before our movie star president, Ronnie Reagan, publicly announced it was a real thing."

"We've seen heterosexuals getting AIDS. Magic Johnson in 1992, for instance." *She's clever, this one.* "You've lived a promiscuous life. Have you been tested?"

See. I told you. "What kind of question is that?"

"You're upset. But I'm not doing my job if I don't ask the tough questions."

"Look, I'm thirsty. I'm hot. And I'm hungover. So sorry if I sound bitter, but is this book about me? I'm not clear what your agenda is." Stipe wets her lips, waiting. "I don't think I like you anymore, Janet Stipe. Interview over." I push back my chair and stand. Then I slowly, theatrically, slip on the suit jacket, taking time to pull the shirtsleeves below the jacket's cuff. I huff a farewell, then run for the swimming pool and swan-dive for the bluest section in my Canali and Bruno Magli. I hang over the blue for what feels like five incredible seconds. This feels about as pure as anything this world of ours offers. Before breaking the water's surface, I bring my hands together, point my toes, then slip under the cool lid where I sink to the bottom. There, I let loose a howl so loud it seems to uncage something inside me. When I pop open my eyes, I see Luke, sitting lotus, hands closed over his heart, in prayer. His black hair moves like sea grass. He gives me a clownish grin.

It's not long before I'm tramping through the grounds, plowing over flowerbeds and small plants, waterlogged, the shoes squishing. I used to be sharp-witted. Nothing got by me. How did I not see what Stipe was really after?

I spy Heather's spark-plug of a daughter on court #21. She and her partner are at the net, volleying back and forth. I walk behind her court, lacing my fingers in the fence rings. "Keep the hands up," I call out. Cherokee wheels around, hearing my voice. She gives me a dirty look. "I'm sorry about yesterday. I was awful. Will you forgive me?" Pretty much every other junior has stopped play to listen in. Even Strathers, a couple courts down, starts over. "Did you tell your mom?"

Three balls flash in her fingers. One rises into the air, and *whack*, Cherokee fires a whipping forehand, off her hip, open stance, like all the kids are learning these days. The ball clangs into the fence three feet from my face. Then comes the other two. Whack. Whack.

"Nice grouping."

Cherokee kind of does that Steve Martin bit where he bends over, arms and legs contorted, and makes that constipated face. Like I make her cringe. Then she lets go a hyena-like scream that makes the one I made in the swimming pool seem like a baby's coo. Next comes her racquet. Cherokee slings it with all her strength. *Whip, whip, whip.* It sings through the air like a boomerang. The stick makes impact, dick-high, something I note with a nervous swallow, then falls with a clatter.

Strathers walks over. He tilts his hat off his forehead, then bends over and picks up the racquet.

"It might be best if you shoved off."

"Tell her I'm sorry." I lean my forehead against the fence, eyes closed.

"You look spiffy."

I open one eye. "I fell into the pool. By accident."

Off I go again, my shoes squeaky, the suit stuck to my limbs like shrink-wrap. This is how my brain works. What manics can't do is sit around until tempers cool. No, we're impulsive, we're flighty, logic escapes us. Like why didn't I go home and change if I was seeing Heather? Was it only last night when I was in bondage? I unlatch the side gate, pleasantly cool in my wet suit. Behind me a good ten feet is Luke, hands stuffed in his motorcycle jacket.

The senior compound next door is called Eden. Eden is manicured like Beverly Hills. Serious thought goes into hedge height and shrubbery shape, garden aesthetics, the placement of old fashioned street lamps. The air even smells like gardenias, year-round. I cross a blazing hot lot, every third car a shiny Cadillac. Men and women in spiffy leisurewear play shuffleboard, ancient all of them, and I think, why didn't I take the car? The keys are in my front pocket. For a ruthless sun pummels down. With it, the glands regulating body temperature kick in. I start sweating in all the wrong places—armpits, butthole, cranium, groin. But I will myself on, zombie-like, afraid that if I let my trauma overwhelm me, I'll completely lose it and do something insane, like run through sprinklers with my slacks around my ankles.

Soon Luke strides with me. *You don't have it so bad. At least you're not dead.* I chuckle, wiping sweat off my brow. We've passed from Garden of Eden into less-inspired fare, i.e., Heather's apartment complex. Smoker grills sit out front. Kiddie bikes lie in the street. Every unit is a verified box; each painted the identical prosaic brown. I walk up behind a maintenance shed and start manhandling my unit. *Cripes, Blank. Someone's going to call the cops.* "I can't help it." I pull my hand out of my trousers. Underneath my nails are blood and cruddy, flaked skin. *What if she wants to screw? How will you handle that?* "Heather and I are early morning or sometimes after dark, but never after midnight, unless she's working, then there's a fifty/fifty chance we have sex. But midday? Never."

I bet she's horny after the good time you showed her the other night. After you tricked her into that lap dance.

"Oh, fuck off."

I leave Luke in the dust, as the saying goes, hightailing down the street like three squad cars give chase. And if she's in the mood? Well, one look at my scrotum, and she'll think I've slipped a mental rung or two. What I need is a plan. I'm walking the backlot of weeds and spent bottle rockets, cursing the sky and my luck. What if I ask Heather to marry me?

Marrying her will definitely solve your problems, Blank. Why didn't I think of that?

"I can't tell her the truth," I say. "Can I?"

I slip between buildings, the grass scorched in places, careful for the dog poop, and onto Heather's cul-de-sac. A massive pickup truck blocks my view of her apartment. I have this moment, standing in the building's shade, where I get scared. Like I should slink back to what I know best—tour life, boinking groupies, being hounded by ghosts. No, I can't do that; that's what the old, twisted me would do.

Then I see her. Heather lies in the front yard, frying her dermis a fine bronze.

I rush forward, into the sunlight, then take refuge behind the monster truck's front end. The tire I hide behind is chest-high with these knuckled nubs that smell like burnt rubber. I peek around the truck's hood. Heather lies on her back, legs slightly open, reading a magazine. *She's not like the rest, is she?* Luke crouches over my shoulder. *For once, you miserable sack of shit, you care more about how she feels than your own pathetic feelings.* Is that true? Not even the Russian? I massage my groin against the truck's bumper. *Would you call that bikini French-cut? And the color? Holy white? Neon white? Blindingly white?* Again, I peer at Heather. *Has she put on weight? Doesn't it look like she's been pounding donuts during the late, late show?* I squint harder in Heather's direction. Her endomorphic shape is splendid, womanly soft in areas, hard everywhere else. But what if Luke's right? Heather is packing on pounds.

A shiny chopper tools past, all chrome pipes and bellicose exhaust. The driver, a heavyset dude with a shabby beard, gives Heather a cool salute. His gaze lasts a beat past normal. *You could take him, man.*

Pussies ride Harley Davidsons. I bet he stands at his front window and jerks off to your woman. You know something, you should give him a piece of your—

"I see you, Richard."

I duck down fast. "Oh shit, she saw us."

"Who are you talking to?" Heather yells.

Of course, scaredy-cat Luke has left the planet. I come out in the open, into the glazed sunshine, shading my eyes.

"Where's your sophisticated bitch?"

I stop short of the chaise a good seven feet. I feel Heather judging me with her eyes. Oh man, they bore through me like they can see my pruned pubes under my showy suit.

"I don't think I follow."

The once-over Heather gives me feels like an infringement on my soul. "Who does that bitch think she is? She has no right to clothe you or cut your hair. Unless you're in love with her."

"Honest to god, no. Heather? I love you. I always have."

"Then why did you fuck her?"

"I can explain."

"I'm waiting."

"It's... it's... this is new territory for me. I mean, it's just, I mean the thing is—"

"Were you this pathetic when she told you to cut your hair?"

"No. I mean—"

"Why, Richard?" Heather's eyes turn this moist, tender-blue. She goes from hostile to the verge of sobbing in seconds. And I get it. I've wounded Heather. She's in pain because of me.

"Oh, Heather. I'm so sorry."

"Why, goddamnit?"

"The money. I did it for us."

She slings her fashion magazine at my head. "You cheated on me *for me?*"

That was brilliant, Blank. Brilliant.

Heather's had enough. She starts folding the chaise's three parts together, her heavy breasts slicked with oil and sweat, the tummy roll noticeable.

"Heather? That's not what I meant. Can't we talk about this?"

She marches up the stoop, then slams the door home. The walls and windows shake like the whole building might come down. These cheap apartments. I should never have let Heather live here. It's no place to raise a teenager. I should have asked her to marry me a long time ago. Then I wouldn't be in this mess.

I wait about a minute before walking up to the door. Then I crack it open, enough to peer in. Heather's not in the family room or kitchen. I quietly pad down the hall. I find her in the bedroom, lying face down on the bed, crying. And I leave her be. Look, we've had our share of fights, okay? Right now, she wants to be left alone. Instead, I go into the kitchen. Well, first I wrap a quilt from the couch around my shoulders, having caught a chill in my dank suit. I drink three glasses of tap water. Then I lean against the Formica counter. Eventually, I end up staring at the laminated photographs magnetically stuck to the refrigerator door. Toddler Cherokee in a highchair with pink cake all over her face. Cherokee and Heather, both wearing Mickey Mouse ears, the day we went to Disney World. And Heather and me, same day, in our cockpit seats, safety bar lowered, waiting for a roller-coaster ride to begin. Orlando was so much fun. I spoiled the kid rotten. Whatever Cherokee wanted—cotton candy, sodas, a foot-long hotdog, $250 in the Disney gift shop. By evening I looked like one of those proud dads three steps behind the family, playing catch-up in the rear, his arms stuffed with Dumbos and Goofys and Eeyores. This rush of emotion hits me. Tears spill from my eyes. I realize I don't want to lose the Harper women. I can't think of anything worse, not thermonuclear annihilation, not financial ruin, not terminal disease, nothing.

I open the refrigerator door. It's practically empty. Oh, that's right, spirited, chisel-cheeked blondes live here. I smell the skim milk, try a bite of tuna salad, then grab a Budweiser and twist the cap off. I guzzle half the beer. I'll tell her it only happened once. She mustn't know about London or the scrotum shave. Having sorted that out, I finish off the Bud. Then I set the bowl of tuna on the counter and scavenge around the pantry for crackers.

How can you eat at a time like this?

"Let me handle this. Okay, Luke?"

Because you're doing so well on your own?

I find Heather sitting on the toilet, door open, tinkling.

"Get out."

Her suit bottoms are stretched thin at her kneecaps. I've yet to cross the threshold. It feels wrong with everything that's happened. I stand there, clutching the quilt about my neck like a fevered old man. Again, my eyes find Heather's tummy.

She's let herself go, Blank. You're gone a month, and she's dining on Ding-Dongs and Twinkies.

The weight gain bothers me. I can't believe it. The last thing on my mind aught to be Heather's body-fat percentage, but that's all I can think about.

"What are you looking at?"

You've done it now, Einstein.

"You were looking at my stomach."

I eschew eye contact. "No, I wasn't. I was daydreaming."

She steps out of her bottoms, then turns the shower on.

"Can I stand here while you shower? Please?"

Truth is, I'm waiting for a kick in the nose. Heather could if she wanted. In her taekwondo class, she knocked an apple off her instructor's head. But Heather seems more annoyed than angry. I watch her undo her bikini top and let it drop to the floor. She steps into the tub. Steam rises to the ceiling. The water hitting her shoulders makes a beautiful patter. It physically hurts being here. My stomach is knotted, my heart split in two. I'm three feet from a woman I've made love to enough times to know her, inside and out. And I can't hold her. I can only stand and watch.

The shower turns off. Heather dries off, pretending I don't exist. She wraps the towel around her chest, then she leans over the vanity giving the mirror her full attention.

"Do you remember when we first met? We couldn't keep our hands off each other," Heather says. "We fought, too. You were something else. I was screwing the clientele. I'd done things for money. You were convinced."

"I wasn't that bad," I say, in my wrapped cloak.

Dude, you were an embarrassment to yourself, your family, men in general.

Eyes closed, Heather sprays her face with a fine mist. "Maybe a month into our going out, I told you."

"That guy you slept with. You were twenty and being evicted, Cherokee was a toddler. It was a bad time for you."

Heather dabs a finger in silky lotion. After spot-touching her face, she massages the moisturizer in. "Did you know I was more ashamed of what you thought than I was for fucking some loser guy for money? And you were cool about it. I remember when that sunk in. I was like, 'wow, Richard loves me for who I am.'" Heather's voice breaks. Her eyes haven't left the mirror when she removes a tear with her finger. "So, you've fucked a woman. For our future, you say. I don't know how to respond. You own a million-dollar home. The New York apartment is probably worth three times that. So, we're both prostitutes now?" She discards two eyeliner sticks before finding one she likes. "Does that mean we deserve each other? Because that's pathetic. Does it mean we should break up? Because I don't know."

Heather pulls on the skin under her pupil, then rather aggressively colors the bottom eyelid black.

"Careful. I mean, don't gouge yourself."

Heather throws the pencil at the mirror. Her face collapses with grief.

"Heather? Can I hold you?" She doesn't say anything. She just grips the counter.

I go to her. I place my hands on her shoulders. Then I bury my head in her hair.

"Forgive me. Please. I'll never hurt you like that, ever again."

"Richard, I'm pregnant."

PART THREE

Time. Where does it go? Dad died, what, four years ago? Has it been that long? In a way, it feels like only the other day we were eating cucumber sandwiches and watching *Benny Hill* in the Village apartment. But it also feels like another life altogether. Was it only eighteen months ago, fresh off my breakup with Marta, that I said I'd never fall hard again?

I'm at Mom's compound in Southern California. I lie on a raft in the pool, nursing a beer. The temperature is perfect—low 80s, little to no breeze. I'm missing two toenails, my elbow is scabbed, and I own three festering blisters, battle scars, all of them. I flew in two nights ago. You'd be proud of me. I left it all out there, half a year's worth of life, I swear. Blood, a few guts, a partial excavation of my right lung—spilled over, spat up, choked out, you name it, my DNA is back on Louis Armstrong Stadium.

You know what's different after fifteen years on the circuit? Recovery. When I was younger, a good night's rest, and the next day I was ready to go. Now, the team goes into emergency recovery mode. I've got to rehydrate. I've got to stuff down essentials—protein, carbs and electrolytes. I need massage and stretching out. Even after all that—the next day I feel the hurt deep in my bones. Time—where did it go?

Dappled sunlight bounces off the water's surface. There's no sound in Pacific Palisades but birdsong and the far-off hum of a leaf blower. Minus a dozen gardeners and the housekeeping staff, I've got the complex all to myself. The girls left a couple hours ago, a shopping spree with Mom at Beverly Center. And my friend, Drabo? He took Brody's Bentley out for a spin.

"I see Los Angeles," he had said.

I didn't have the heart to tell him he could be gone for days.

I take another swallow of beer. Then, dropping the sunglasses a smidgeon, I peer into the pool's depth. He's still down there, Luke, I mean. Me above, him below. Now that's significant, don't you think? He hasn't surfaced since Dr. Goldberg and I started talking. Visiting my psychotherapist is one of my conditions. And Dr. Goldberg has grown wiser in old age. His newfound smarts astound me. Now, when Dr. Goldberg suggests a remedy, it usually works. He says nothing's wrong in the chemical department. "Visions aren't a bad thing," he says. "In some cultures, they're revered. Are you out of the woods? In time you'll only be looney three times a week, two if you watch your diet, exercise, and make love to your woman."

He means a clean life. Part of that includes erasing Trey Hamasaki from my mental landscape for good. But the mind has its own agenda, its own rules. I still have scary, heart-thumping dreams. I still wake from nightmares, turn the bedside lamp on, and peek under the sheets. The bitch even sent me a Polaroid. I was in Indianapolis when the hotel desk clerk handed me an envelope. Inside was yours truly, bound and in the buff, off my rocker from booze and horror. She was following me. I was sure of it. I searched her out in autograph lines, the faces in the crowd. Details from that night railroaded me at the strangest times. Inserting a hotel keycard into the door slot and there'd she be with her shiny razor and hard alcohol. I was checking behind hotel shower curtains and underneath beds. I even left the bathroom light on at night.

Dr. Goldberg wants me to look inward. Ask myself questions like why did I cheat? My life was speeding along nicely back in London— Wimbledon quarters, a lucrative shoe contract, a woman in Florida who adored me. Why risk that? Was it because I felt unworthy of happiness? Dr. Goldberg likes to narrow down my problems to cruxes. He looks for moments of transcendence. "That night in the hotel was the culmination of years of self-abasement and guilt. You've entered a new phase now. A man chooses which direction he walks. You're walking west, into the sunset, toward Heather."

It was also Indianapolis where I first heard about the conditions. Two weeks had elapsed since Heather told me she was pregnant.

Things between us were still unclear. The thought of being a dad had done a number on my head. In those initial moments in her bathroom, hearing the P word, to be honest, I thought, *oh no*. I saw my life unravel before my eyes. No more freedom. No more seducing women. No more me, I thought. But slowly, inexplicably, I got this dreamy smile on my face.

Heather grew concerned. "Are you okay? Should I call your therapist?"

I thought—me? A father? I guess my smile was contagious because soon Heather's face lit up. She brought me up to speed. Only that morning, her gynecologist confirmed that Heather was indeed with child. Conception happened in May.

"Remember? You flew in from LA? Cherokee slept at a friend's house?" I only sort of heard Heather. "We took a bath, lit candles. Richard? Are you okay?"

"I never thought of myself as a dad."

"Well, don't get too excited. We're not having it."

"We're not?"

"Why would we bring another baby into the world?"

"Because we love each other. Because we'd be good parents."

"You're missing a crucial point."

I threw the blanket off and took Heather's hands in mine. "What if this baby is a sign?"

"A sign?"

"That we're supposed to be together?"

"I don't know if I want that anymore."

"What if we didn't choose the baby," I said. "It chose us?"

Heather got that worried look again. "It's happening, isn't it? You're manic."

"Who says how life works. My gut tells me we're supposed to have the baby, that the universe has spoken."

Heather teared up. "You really think—" She couldn't finish the sentence.

We held each other then. Man, that hug was real, full of truth and tears, sorrow, heartfelt words. And smeary kisses. Yes, things heated up. Towels came undone. Erections sported in fine linen trousers. Then the night before came bursting through my awareness like a brutal home invasion.

"I can't do this."

I stood so abruptly I fell back into the sliding shower door, knocking it off line. Instincts had me throwing the blanket over me and my hard-on.

Heather got this harried look about her. Like she'd reached a breaking point. Like she'd had it up to her eyeballs in weird-ass manic boyfriends.

"It's not what you think," I said defensively.

"Then what is it?"

And if I'd told the truth? That I thought I'd been sexually assaulted? What if Heather was disappointed in me? Worse, that she didn't believe me?

By then, she'd put on her robe and was at the mirror brushing her hair with forceful yanks.

"Can I call you tomorrow?"

Heather kept at the angry brush strokes.

"What do you think of us getting married?" This got a monumental glare. "One day, I mean."

I left. And I felt like shit. I felt worse than shit. But I was relieved. What Trey had done was too fresh, too much an open wound. I was heading across the apartment cul-de-sac when I thought of that night in Stockholm. We'd been drinking. The woman invited me up to her flat. We were in the midst of it when something changed. *She changed.* She got stiff all over like she was bracing for a collision that only she could see. Then this lone tear squirted down her cheek. I believe I was the reason for her pain. I didn't know what to do. I mean, fuck, like I pulled out and asked in the quietest of terms if she was okay. But what had I done? Had I used my charm and celebrity to press my way into her? And that look she had—like she'd shut down inside herself, like she'd separated best she could from the physical act—that's what I did that night in the hotel.

* * *

And maybe Heather was correct. We shouldn't have the baby. How would I survive living under the same roof with two, possibly three women? Managing curfews, grades and cleanliness? I'm a control freak. I like a neat ship. And women can be complete tornadoes. Undies drying on shower rods, crusty makeup inlayed in counter seams, those bloody tampons stinking up the garbage pail. Was I ready for that reality? Maybe more importantly—was Heather prepared to handle my issues, my tendencies?

Mom's voice was whispering in my ear, too. I had called to check in. And I let slip that Heather was pregnant. "You mean that striptease artist?"

"She's in personnel, Mom."

She took a moment to slurp whatever she was drinking. "Tell me the details. And leave nothing out." So I explained the timeframe around conception. "Wasn't she on birth control?"

"Things happen."

"Is that what she told you?" Mom said. "Have you tested to see if it's yours?"

"The baby's mine."

"She wants your money, Richard. This is her way out."

Then, a week later, another US Open warmup in America's heartland, the pregnancy issue still unresolved, my betrayal like a pink elephant between us, Heather let me have it good. "WHO. ARE. YOU?" she screamed over the phone line. "You act nicely. You tell me you love me. You pretend nothing's wrong. But you slept with that woman. You're no better than those disgusting men at the club."

"Lump me in with those perverts? Gee, thanks, Heather."

"I'm not joking. What would you think if I picked up some frat boy? Or, O. I bet he knows how to please a woman."

"That is so not funny."

"See what it feels like? It hurts. It really hurts."

"And it's mine? I mean, I wouldn't ask but—"

"I can't believe you. Whose else would it be?"

There was a rage in her voice that scared me.

"You're not saying... we're not...?"

"Breaking up?" Heather sighed. "Maybe it does, maybe it doesn't. I got to go." And she hung up.

And something happened. Our argument broke the ice. No decision had been made, one way or the other, but we were friendlier. It was like we'd reached neutral ground, some plateau. And Heather wasn't drinking. She wasn't even working. "I can't think about that awful place in my current state." She also had this craving for artichokes. Tortellini salad with artichokes, artichoke dip, stuffed artichokes, artichoke burger, artichoke on a stick. I found this new development fascinating. We said goodbye one night when I immediately called her back.

"Are we doing this?"

"Do you mean having the baby?"

"The baby, marriage, the whole enchilada. Or should I say artichokes?"

And Heather screamed. She dropped the phone and screamed.

* * *

I speed dial Mom's staff on my phone. I tell Jorge I'm in dire need of more *cerveza*. Now, this is the life. Floating on a raft under a cerulean glare, drinking cold beer, Luke like sunken treasure off the Blanco coast, and the sun warming my face. To put it another way—this is nothing like Heather's conditions. When I first heard her demands, I admit being disappointed. I kept my cool but got off the phone quick enough. Straightaway, I dialed up Dr. Goldberg.

"All she wants is my fucking money."

"Do you really believe that?" he said. "Why do you care anyway? She's good to you. She's good *for you*. She won't screw around. And she's gorgeous. All Heather wants is assurances. Is that such a terrible thing? Put yourself in her shoes. All the shit you pulled? If Heather had cheated on you with some big-shot athlete, someone like Steve Young, you'd want to kill him. You'd be thinking about yourself, too."

And these conditions?

Heather wanted half of everything. Half my investments. Half my real estate properties. Half my future earnings. She wanted half my soul, people. You know what I said after I calmed down? "You're kill-ing me, Heather. But if that's what you want, then fine by me."

"Really?" Heather said, choking back a sob. "I'm only being this way because of the baby. You know that, right?"

I wasn't so sure about that, but I played along. I was getting mar-ried. I was a proud father-to-be.

"I love you, Richard Blanco."

"And I love you, Heather Harper."

Did I feel like I was being taken for a ride? Maybe a little. But isn't that the price sometimes? Dr. Goldberg says there's no such thing as happily ever after. "Marriage is tough. Smart couples understand money as a component in a much bigger machine. Forgiveness, re-spect, love—that's how to survive marriage. And good sex."

I know some of you are scratching your heads. Heather a gold digger? Say it isn't so. Let's just say I planted the love seed. That seed, our baby boy or girl (we've decided to learn the child's sex on the birth day) binds us forever. So, naturally, that would mean real estate holdings, earnings, investments, et al. Trust me, we'll be fine. What the conditions do is assuage Heather's fears. The woman's calm, she's rational, but she's also freaking out a bit. Los Angeles takes some get-ting used to. Everyone's an aspiring actor or writes screenplays in their spare time. Everyone wants to know what you're peddling, what your angle is, if you're on the make. Let me give you an example. First week we visit, Mom invited us to an industry party in the hills. Heather and I were talking to the director who'd taken over the Bogdanovich project when Bogdanovich lost interest. The man stood next to his bodyguard when he caressed Heather's arm. "Are you single?"

Heather smiled at me. "No, I'm taken."

"Hold him," he said to his bodyguard, meaning me. "Would you fuck me for the lead in my new movie? Because wow. I mean, I hav-en't seen a body attached to a face this stupendous since the invention of plastic surgery. Fuck, I'd give up a testicle to pop you. You're not a virgin, are you, honey?"

By now, I was having an out-of-body crisis. Not that I could do anything. I was double-nelsoned and drooling with rage. Heather looked like she'd traded one Satan's crib for another. "Why do you look so offended?" the asshole said. "You know, fuck it. And Blanco? My man here is going to let you go. But you won't touch me because Diane Blanco is playing the kooky grandma in my new film."

His man released me. I straightened my shirt and jacket. I ran my hands through my hair. The director and bodyguard started off. "And you do good by Mother," I shouted after them. "Shoot her in favorable light, okay? Treat her with respect."

* * *

Questions remain. Like, what if I'm a terrible husband? What if I cheat and lie like I'm so very capable of doing? Some guys aren't meant to be dads. What if I'm wired that way, too? Here's another what if. What if I'm babysitting and lose time and the kid drinks a vat of rat poison? You see my concern? Dr. Goldberg says this is proof I'm on the mend. I'm thinking outside myself. I'm worried about others.

I was visiting his Sarasota office a few days before I embarked for the US Open.

"Will that night eventually fade from memory?"

"What do you think?" Dr. Goldberg's question implied no, never, sorry.

"Did I lead her on? Am I to blame for what happened?"

"That woman assaulted you."

"But I came. And I think I enjoyed it."

"Just because you ejaculated doesn't mean it wasn't wrong on so many fronts. This isn't on you, Richard. You did nothing wrong. It was not your fault."

His office got unusually quiet. Dr. Goldberg handed me a box of Kleenex. He gave me all the time I needed to compose myself.

"I didn't like you when you first treated me."

"You've come a long way, Richard."

"So, it's okay if I'm honest?"

"We've got a special relationship. You can tell me anything."

"Has anyone ever told you your breath stinks?"

Dr. Goldberg looked like he wanted to kill me. His face slowly relaxed. "I love your candor, son."

"For a second, I thought you were going to cry, Dr. Goldberg."

"Find yourself another therapist, asshole."

"What?"

And he laughed. "Gotcha."

Funny guy, that Dr. Goldberg.

* * *

My thoughts are interrupted by Jorge. He walks down the concrete platform that surrounds the pool holding a tray with a single Corona on top. I start over on the floatie, not wanting to disturb the sleeping giant in the deep end.

"Good afternoon, Mr. Blanco." Jorge kicks his shoes off then starts down the steps on the shallow end.

"You don't need to swim out here."

"This no problem. I do this for lady of house all the time."

We meet in chest-high water. Jorge's nipples show through his white waiter shirt.

"Lime, sir?"

"Please."

He smiles then pinches a green wedge in the bottle's top. "Anything else, sir? Lunch, maybe?"

"No, I'm good. And thank you, Jorge. I'll let Mother know you're doing a fine job."

* * *

We should probably talk about the US Open. I was up against O. Maxwell, a tremendous seesaw battle, third-round action under the lights. Twice during the four-hour match O received treatment for cramps. My throwing arm seized up so bad it took two trainers—one stretching the arm wide, the other lathering the rotator cuff with ointment—so I could continue. But the heart of the match revolved around officiating. Then O. Maxwell refused to play on. Leading up to the stoppage, there'd been a few close calls, all scored in my favor, but hold the match hostage?

This was Louis Armstrong Stadium, the Great Satchmo's bowl, a smoked-out haze of floodlights, USA Network broadcasting live,

14,000-plus on hand, the winner taking on Todd Martin, round sixteen. Night matches at the US Open have a distinct buzz. Celebrities sit court-side pitching new projects. On hand are ex-mayor Dinkins and Donald Trump's ex-wife, Ivana, the excommunicated Salman Rushdie, those on-again, off-again thespians, the Baldwin brothers. USA Network's color analyst Michael Barkann interviews stars like Lenny Kravitz and Meryl Streep. Airplanes taking off from LaGuardia temporarily overwhelm the court with roaring static, drunks shout out, and people talk between points. This is tennis, American-style. Everything is big—the seating capacity, the TV audience, the food portions. And my heir apparent was making a stink on national television?

We'd started late. Two thunderstorms rolled through in the afternoon pushing the day session back a couple hours. Then, the night's marquee slot—Martina Hingis-Amy Frazier—went long. We didn't step onto stadium court until well past ten. My Player's Box was at seating capacity. I'd thrown Claudia and Stipe an olive branch. They sat next to Dr. Goldberg and his wife. Drabo was sandwiched between David and Mom. Heather sat in the corner wearing a smashing white sundress.

It was equally packed in O's camp. There was Costa, Jeffries and Strathers. Coach sat between Valerie and O's mother. I knew this going in. I'd called his hotel after taking out Nystrem nil, one and six. He told me flat out, "O's got me on retainer, son. The game waits for no one." And it doesn't. The world spins on, with or without you. That's why David was grooming Drabo. Realistically, how much time did I have left?

Minutes prior to O's protest, the Chair had taken a point for cursing. *What the fuck do you mean that motherfucking ball was fucking out?* The penalty coincided with set point. Handing me the pivotal third without a fight? I was thrilled. Who knew how much energy was still in the tank. The dogs hurt. My shoulder felt mangled and numb. And O. Maxwell gave me a gift like that? I could have kissed him. Instead, I ran to the nearest cameraman and cradled my arms like I was rocking a baby. The crowd went bonkers. They focused on Heather, their oohs and aahs like waves of love. Then who do I see in the good seats? Trey and her finance boyfriend, Christopher. He was at least fifty and stiff as his starched shirt and suspenders, Bond Street all the way. Trey had turned into a bloodsucking ghoul overnight. She wore her hair over her eyes, a black tunic and sunglasses. Even her lipstick was black. I momentarily panicked. But then my eyes found Heather again. She was radiant, like an exploding star.

So, there we were, O and me sitting on the changeover, him still infuriated about the point penalty. Time was called. Then, on the very next exchange, O. Maxwell hit a passing shot directly under the umpire's shoes. The ball was good. There was no question it bounced off the line. Only the linesperson motioned out. O couldn't believe it. I wondered if the fix was on.

"The call stands," the umpire Pritchards said.

"Oh, boy," I said to the spectators. "This should be entertaining."

That's when O. Maxwell stretched out in no man's land. And he wouldn't get up. He lay there like a god, defiant and powerful. It was a beautiful sight to behold.

Once it was clear O wasn't getting up anytime soon, I had my shoulder attended to. I even thought about calling in pizza delivery. At the eight-minute mark, a clear rule violation, I turned to the Chair.

"This is your lucky night, Pritchards. Two crazies and a live TV audience."

"Would you do something?"

Why would I intervene? I wanted to win. And why help O. Maxwell? Yes, as friends went, we had potential. But the truth was, they couldn't default him. The person who made the controversial call was a white, middle-aged woman. The audience inside Louis Armstrong was predominately white. There were black faces and brown faces, but they were scattered among many more pink fat faces, red drunk faces and sunburnt cheeky faces. Then there was the stadium's energy. Early in O's dissent, the left-leaning New Yorkers rose up and applauded. But now, eleven minutes in, they were restless. People filed toward the exits. They booed. Not that O. Maxwell noticed. He hadn't blinked, twitched or sighed. I envied him. What O was doing—jamming a pipe in the natural order of things so people paid attention—took real courage.

Then someone tossed a beer cup that almost hit O. Maxwell. Another exploded court-side. I got up from my chair and faced the onlookers.

"Let's cool it, okay? O and I will be playing soon. I mean, it's almost my bedtime."

By now, the Tournament Director stood over the recumbent O, his dissent at the fourteen-minute mark. He read appurtenant passages from the *Official Association of Tennis Professionals Rulebook.*

Coach D waved me over. "Go talk to him," he said. "He'll listen to you, son. It's the right thing to do."

"It won't do any good."

"All I ask is that you try."

On the way over, I stopped by my people, my box.

"How are you feeling?" I said, eyeing Heather. "Are you keeping hydrated? You need anything to eat? Like artichokes?"

Heather flushed beautifully. "You're doing the right thing, honey."

I walked to O's side of the court. The fans, seeing where I was heading, screamed approval. I lifted my arms, encouraging more noise. "You hear that?" O was a specimen, all traps, biceps and quads. If anyone could hold the US Open prisoner, it was my young friend. "When this thing is over, they'll probably name a candy bar after you."

He fixed his dark pupils on me. "I know what you're going to say."

"Coach thinks you're being an ass."

"He really said that?"

"In so many words."

"Did you see those calls? Egregious doesn't begin to describe the horror, man."

I chuckled. "Save the big words for the press conference." I looked toward the tunnel. The tournament people were like big fat worry lines. "You know you're forcing their hand."

"They're too scared to default me."

"I'm totally impressed. But what do you expect them to do? Rescind the point penalty?" O flicked his eyes at the heavens. Then he sat up.

Me? I cocked an ear toward the cheap seats. Then I crouched low and snuck a few steps to the left where I held a hand to my ear again. The stadium roared. You should have seen them streaming back into Louis Armstrong after that. It was like torching an anthill.

And all the court-side characters, the line gazers and ball chasers, the lords quarterbacking from above, took their places. The score was called. All went hushed only like a tennis match goes hushed. Blah, blah, blah, blah, blah. What? Do I sound chagrined? Because O. Maxwell didn't go quietly into the night. He didn't lay down his arms. He made another stink. This one came first game, fifth set, deuce #3. At this point, I was running on fumes. The Citizen Official Time Clock read 2:31 a.m. Louis Armstrong was maybe two-thirds full. And O had swatted a forehand dangerously close to the baseline. The call favored me. But for some reason, I circled the mark with my racquet then held my palm flat. See, the ball hit *inside* the line. It wasn't even close.

Chair Pritchards didn't know what to think.

"Are you saying what I think you're saying?"

I nodded.

"Overrule. Advantage Maxwell."

Do you see what I did? I unleashed the dragon. For once in my life, I did the right thing, and O. Maxwell repaid me by playing blinders. I didn't win another game. He even did that annoying thing with his breath. That ancient Tibetan humming.

* * *

Janet Stipe's *Los Angeles Times* headline was "Player Protest Brings US Open to Standstill for Eighteen Minutes." She talked about the five heart-pounding sets, how it was too bad the match ended so late, that more people didn't see the outcome. She called O. Maxwell a modern-day Muhammed Ali. She spoke to his courage, his refusal to quit under extraordinary circumstances, his superb play in what she saw as blatant and irrefutable racism. She called on tennis' governing bodies to establish a formal bipartisan commission to investigate racism and discriminatory hiring practices. In the next breath, she thought I should retire. Go out on the same court where I'd first championed gay rights in my pink tutu. Prove to my peers, critics and fans I was no longer tennis' bad boy. This was proof that men eventually grow up. I'd lost but held my head high. Was there a better way to honor my father?

Stipe described me like a hero. I didn't know how to take that. For starters, wasn't O. Maxwell the real hero in this story? But I got what Stipe meant. The world needed more people to stand up to injustice, no matter one's race or creed. Look, I'm a guy pretty good at his chosen profession. I'm a guy trying his best to be less of a fuck up. My universe hasn't changed. True, I'm playing for more than me now. But next month in Tokyo, I might punch an umpire in the face or dance Matilda with a ball-girl. I might be tempted to cheat on my fiancé. I can't predict what I'll do. But if I'm a hero, then we're in big, big trouble.

* * *

Can we talk about anxiety? Anxiety that parches mouths and causes early graves. I'm talking about my condition, not my conditions, my *condition*. My pared flute, my grazed whistle, my cropped prop. For Heather had to regard Johnson, eventually. It only made sense. We were newly engaged, with child—a celebration was in order.

Heather had flown to New York while I prepared for the US Open. We were staying at Dad's place. And it was fantastic. Carriage rides in the park, an engagement ring from Tiffany's, espresso at the Plaza with none other than Princess Diana eating breakfast with *The Times* folded over her lap.

"That's not her," Heather whispered, us two tables down from royalty.

"Yes, it is. We've met."

"Bullshit. Then say hi to her."

"I'm not going to disturb her. She's eating breakfast."

Heather loved Manhattan. She loved how we were a real couple. However, there was one more hurdle—seeing me in the buff. Four weeks in my undercarriage was military-cut stubble, a full house but without the robust sheen. I'd prolonged intimacy for as long as I could, feigning neurosis-triggered headaches or sneezing attacks. But then the moment arrived. And Johnson was a nervous little twit. Heather came into the bedroom in a lacy thing she'd picked up shopping on Fifth Avenue, attire that always perked up Johnson. And nothing, not even a faint stir. Alarmed, I turned her over, whipped off the sheet, yanked down my briefs, and prepared to enter my fiancé from the rear.

Heather whipped her mane back, then flashed her blue eyes. "What are you doing?"

"I've got this new technique I want to try out."

"You know this position reminds me of the club."

"Exactly." I slapped Heather's booty.

"Richard," she warned.

I pulled the sheet up, covering myself, while Heather rolled onto her back. She was quite a sight naked and drowning in pillows, with her brimming breasts and faint mama tummy. She ran a fingertip from her sternum to naval.

"This is the first time since we've been engaged. I want it to be special."

"It's been a while. I hope I don't disappoint you."

She sat up on her elbows, then hugged a pillow to her chest. "Disappoint me? What's gotten into you?"

I sighed at the ceiling. "You know how I cut my hair?"

"Is that what you're nervous about? It's cute. Didn't I tell you that?"

"That's not it, exactly."

"What, Richard?"

"Well, I, um, I cut the hair around Johnson, thinking it would look bigger. Stupid, huh? You want to see it?" I dropped the sheet.

Heather eyed my trimmed bush, frowning. "Interesting," she said.

In my panic, I stammered on like the liar in me is prone to do.

"Honestly, Richard? I don't want to know."

* * *

Voices drift down to the swimming pool. This is something I'm getting used to—sharing my space with others. Cherokee is asking her mom if she can swim before lunch and Drabo's retelling his Arnold Schwarzenegger sighting. I lean over the raft and peer into the water. Nothing stirs below.

Sometimes I have these moments. I think—what just happened? A month ago, I had seriously cool hair. My game was first-rate. I wasn't talking pre-nuptials. I wasn't taping paint chips to nursery walls. Now look at me. Testing breast pumps? Buying classical CDs guaranteed to turn our baby into a genius Einstein?

I think of Dad in situations like this. I see him sitting poolside, book in his lap, him bright as day. He'd have been proud of my run this summer, especially the way things ended in New York. Same goes with how I worked things out with Heather.

Time's a funny thing when we're young. We think of it in abundance. Like it's a bottomless well. Or we're caught in time's arrow. Which way does it point? Where does it send us? Sometimes life can feel like too much. Like it's coming at us from every which way. That's more reason to stop and smell the roses. Because it could be gone tomorrow.

"Swim with me. The water's fantastic."

Heather stands with Mom and Drabo on the far side of the pool. My doubles partner is talking a mile a minute—Schwarzenegger's shiny Hummer, the fat cigar he chomped, how the movie star was generous with his time. He told my friend America was still a place where dreams come true, that he was living proof. Mom walks over to the intercom and calls in lunch. She asks Cherokee, who's charging down the deck steps, coke or lemonade?

"Coke," Cherokee shouts.

"She'll have milk," Heather interrupts. "Or water."

Mom looks at me with a frown on her face. What does she expect me to do? Argue with the woman who's bringing my baby into the world?

My focus is on Heather. She looks across the pool to where I float, her hand touching her belly. Her eyes blaze blue.

ACKNOWLEDGEMENTS

This book was a long time coming. Try eighteen years, raising two kids, three family moves across state lines, and so many rewrites I've lost count.

I'd like to thank the following people:

My thesis professors, Mary Rockcastle and Mona Susan Power at Hamline University, for their patience and guidance in the early drafts.

Ian Graham Leask, for believing in this book. And me.

Calumet Editions, my publisher.

High Touch Consulting's Ann and Melissa, for their support and many talents.

Nick Bollettieri, for his profound influence on me and the writing of this book.

John Fanselow, for a brutally honest critique. You made me work harder, John.

My tennis aficionados, Jon Carlson, Erik Donley, Roger Gilbertson and Tony Zanoni.

Advice/guidance from Peter Leugers, Jim Pacala and Jason Paschall.

Tye Trondson, for her astute editorial comments.

Special thanks to Mark Dalzell, Kevin Hart, John Munson, Steve Shulla, and Scott Berler at The Vintage Club in Indian Wells.

My wife and family, for their incredible love and support.

ABOUT THE AUTHOR

Tom Trondson has taught tennis all over the world including the famed Nick Bollettieri Tennis Academy in Bradenton, Florida. A native of St. Paul, Minnesota, he holds graduate degrees from Gustavus Adolphus College and Hamline University's MFA program. He lives with his family in Minneapolis. *Moving in Stereo* is his first novel.

Made in the USA
Monee, IL
26 June 2021

72279561R10121